# THE DART OF PERSUASION

## A MATTHEW DIGGERSON MYSTERY

by

# D. G. Gillespie

For information, email Cozy Cat Press,
cozycatpress@aol.com
or visit our website at:
www.cozycatpress.com

**COZY CAT**
P R E S S

ISBN: 978-1-946063-80-9
Printed in the United States of America

10 9 8 7 6 5 4 3 2 1

To my brother and sisters, who have walked the same paths, known the same sounds and scents, trod the same stones, and who have helped a little brother along the way.

# Table of Contents

# Chapter One:  The Rhetorical Triangle

An argument can be broken into a single visual, the rhetorical triangle, each point representing part of the persuasion:  ethos (the arguer), pathos (the audience), and logos (the argument). Any statement, any gesture, affects at least one point on the triangle—as we shall see.

The room at the end of Ward C held an air of mystery, not only because few outsiders had ever ventured through the dark green door that told so little, displaying just a posted-on gold number 21, but also since its lone occupant had not uttered a word during his entire four-hundred and forty-five day stay. Rumor had it that the police had requested the private room, and further gossip relayed that armed guards had once been stationed *down there*. Of course, since few of the home's attendants stayed long at the low-paying job and since doctors rarely bothered to pass even the time of day with their underlings, new workers had to decide for themselves if the tales of gun-toting cops were true.

The man behind door number 21 did not seem particularly worthy of guarding. Fair haired, white to the point of death, he seemed small and almost weightless when an attendant rolled him over daily to prevent bed sores, but a coma will do that, will eat away at a human body, reducing it by a minute click each day, one bite at a time.

Ana Cepatos, the most recent aide hired at Breezy Seas, was accustomed to the droopy eyes and long breaths of the aged, coming from a tight-knit and large Columbian family, so the ghostliness of Ward C failed to rattle her in the least—except for the Crypt. That's what the other aides and even some of the nurses called the last room down the hallway, the one that faced her when she turned left or right and entered the ward, heard the beeps and moans and occasional calls of the 'patients' who were one stage, even one broken breath, away from transcending to another plain. *Room 21*. The door was always closed, always watching and beckoning as Ana made her way from room to room, doing the endless tasks required of nursing home aides, the jobs that few Americans could even imagine, let alone undertake.

*The Crypt*. The dark green immobility of the door challenged Ana's logical mind, introducing a crawling pathos.

"That's where they stack the bodies," another of the aides, Julio, said, his eyebrows raised and head nodding.

"It's true, Ana!" said Margrita, an older woman who liked a poke of fun, an escape. "It's a big refrigerator, the Crypt!"

"All the bodies are stacked up," added Julio, smiling his crooked grin. "Like sardines!"

"O-oh-o!" said Ana Cepatos, who was still quite young and who would always be quite gullible. "Oh" was her usual response to the world, a word that was more a sound, but Ana had a pleasing way of saying it, turning the letter or two into three syllables, the second one high, the first and third being the same flat note. Together, the three-syllable "Oh" made listeners smile and feel in control. The reaction was like a sunray landing on a sparrow, highlighting wonder and innocence and a complete lack of aggression.

"I once counted twenty-seven," continued Julio, eyebrows still up, chin pushed forward to hide his teeth, his hidden grin, eyes swiveling side to side as though he were offering a secret.

"O-oh-o!" said the young aide. Ana Louisa Maria Consueala Cepatos, that's what it said on her birth certificate, but in America everything was shortened, made practical, so this flowing ancestral designation became at Breezy Seas just three letters, two the same. Rarely did a soul call her Ana Louisa, as her mother always did, and sometimes the nurses used no name at all, just beckoned with fingers. *Come!* As though she were a dog.

"Don't let these two scare you, Ana," broke in the slightly rough sound of Nurse Addie as the chubby woman passed by the supply station, where the aides tended to cluster. "There are no bodies in Room 21, except, of course, the poor man who has been in a coma for so long, and he's no one to be afraid of, the poor soul."

"O-oh-o!" said Ana Louisa.

Nurse Addie turned to the two aides, both smiling rather sheepishly. "You two should be ashamed of yourselves, scaring Ana!"

"We are, Nurse Addie," said Julio, but everyone but Ana could see that he was still acting.

"Do not be afraid, Ana Cepatos," said Margrita, putting a rather big paw on the younger woman's shoulder. Margrita was the head aide, for she had been at Breezy Seas the longest, many years. In charge of training every new recruit, Margrita exuded the pride and understanding of age but also the playfulness of youth. Like Nurse Addie, Margrita could afford to lose a few pounds—fifty or more to be honest—so she jiggled noticeably when her youthful spirit broke out. Multiple chins danced now. Nurse Addie frowned.

"No fear, Ana *Cepatos*," agreed Julio, adding "They're just bodies anyway!"

"You two!" Nurse Addie declared, but everyone but Ana Louisa could tell that she was just pretending to be mad. A bit of goofing around was required in places like Breezy Seas, perhaps in all work places, a bit of fun and distraction to stave off the sadness and the madness, the sameness, the grind. Nurse Addie had worked at Breezy Seas since its beginning, over thirty years now. She had been young then, and thin. At home, when she felt like complaining to her equally chubby husband, she would often say, "I've given my whole life to that place!" True in a way.

"Don't you two have anything better to do?" That question, clearly a statement, one repeated everywhere people punched a clock, broke up the scene, the two older aides turning to the supply shelves to search for what they needed, but not before Julio grinned at Ana, who realized that Nurse Addie had not been chastising her, that she was not included in the "you two."

"They mean well," said Nurse Addie to the new aide, who definitely seemed a little vulnerable. "At least I think so," added the older woman, but Ana said nothing. Maybe she smiled quickly. Apparently, this new aide had nothing better to do than stand here, too.

"You haven't cleaned in room 21 yet, haven't been in there?" Ana Cepatos shook her head twice. "No time like the present then," decreed the older woman, one of her mantras, adding, "Let's take a look now, and I'll give you some instructions about our special room."

"O-oh-o!" said the young woman, who was Columbian in ancestry but American in fact, having been born on U.S. soil, unlike her mother, who had done the illegal bearing. The elder Cepatos had dodged government authorities for decades now, hiding in New England's migrant fields, also known as fish-processing plants, restaurants, and hotels/motels. Maria Cepatos had done a lot of cleaning in her life, from fishes to dishes.

They moved down the corridor, past the rooms where patients in varying degrees of slumber moaned or stayed silent. Nurse Addie glanced into each room, as was her habit. She stopped suddenly and turned back to the trailing aide. "Has Margrita showed you how to change the outflow bags?"

Ana shook her head again, but this time up and down, twice, just a little bobble. Oh, yes, Margrita had shown her about those bags, about the garbage bins and other smelly things, about the mopping, the wiping, and those bags.

Nurse Addie was satisfied with that, so she turned and continued her perusal down the hall, the dark green door getting larger with each step. Ana could read the '21' on it now, and suddenly the older woman was reaching toward the doorknob. She turned back again, though. "You really haven't been in this room yet? Margrita didn't tell you what to do in here?" The nurse shook her head and pursed her lips, the universal sign of judgment wrapped in disbelief. "Coma patients might not moan and complain, but they still need care. They need to be moved, monitored, and waste baskets fill up, Ana, even in here."

The young aide showed satisfactory agreement, so Nurse Addie turned back and pushed open the door, which wasn't locked, as Ana had expected it to be. *The Crypt*, she thought as the other woman moved into the darkness, and like a shadow Ana followed her, like a child in a department store, all eyes and trepidation. Inside, the darkness gave way to mere dimness, and Ana Louisa Cepatos whispered, "O-oh-o" because the room seemed to require peace, solemnity, like a library, and because the soft lighting was pleasing. When a metallic beep rang out, Ana actually jumped, thinking that the shape in the bed had cried out strangely. Like an exotic bird, a colorful Columbian macaw.

From the base of the bed, Nurse Addie was looking down at a man who didn't look at all alive, and for a moment, Ana found herself in church, gazing up at the cross and the man hanging from it. That's the feeling that she had now, one of great reverence.

"Like an angel," she whispered, and the older woman turned and stared at Ana Cepatos in astonishment since she had as of yet never heard her make a statement, or even just a phrase carrying an opinion. And Nurse Addie realized, too, that what the other woman said was true. The far-away man, whom she had always thought of as a *poor coma patient*, did indeed look like an angel.

"So young," said Ana.

"No," said Nurse Addie, still staring at the motionless man. "Not really young. Fifty years old or so. Of course, that's still 'young' to me, but old to you."

"But his skin, so clear," said Ana.

"That often happens around here. Even the really elderly patients, when they're at this last stage, just sleeping, their wrinkles often seem to disappear, get ironed out, and that makes the years fall away."

The machine behind the bed beeped again and then fell silent. For a full minute, at least, Aide Ana and Nurse Addie gazed in quiet reverie until the latter remembered the moving world outside room 21, but still she did not move. She, too, felt something not quite life-like in this room, and she pictured lighting a candle for her mother, for her memory, in that church room full of little candles.

"Like an angel," said Ana Cepatos again.

"Yes," responded Nurse Addie. "Like an angel. But he was actually a teacher, a college professor in fact."

Ana Louisa Cepatos grew to enjoy her time in room 21, the Crypt. Going there became a break of sorts, a darkened and peaceful spot, and she would often stand at the foot of the bed and gaze upon the poor coma patient, the angel, whom she began to think of as a sleeping prince.

Ana had a small mouth that formed a sort of bow, almost a pout, the type of expression that many western women much admired and sometimes even had surgically affixed to their faces. Yet Ana was no great beauty, she knew that. She had been called "Mug" by children, her peers, long ago it seemed. They had laughed and pointed and shrieked "mug, mug" at her. As a child, she had cried a river of tears over her face, but her mother had quieted her youngest child, had told her that "white women would pay a million American dollars for those lips." Ana had believed her, but she also had believed her chanting peers, taken their opinions with her like a battered old suitcase and carried them to this very day. *An ugly duckling*, Ana always concluded, and she dreamt often of swans.

*She* was back. The woman. An actual swan, a princess. *The Princess*, Ana Louisa named the woman, but maybe that was not true, maybe she was just his sister, for like him she was light haired and skinned. Light in bearing, too. The woman walked with sure steps down the long, straight corridor of Ward C, not hesitating before the dark door like Ana always did, always wondering what she would find inside, an illogical fear yet one that the young aide could not master. The woman was protected, though, by a golden aura that blossomed around her head like a spiritual crown, so perhaps that was why she could stroll right into the room and talk to the sleeping man. Nobody else talked to him, just this woman and Ana herself, Ana when she cleaned the wastebasket that was never full or the outflow bag that was never full either. Ana would tell the sleeping prince that he could wake up now, that the threat was over, that nobody was trying to kill him, that his head was healed. She knew this because she listened to the nurses and to old Doctor Sam, who hustled in and out of room 21 every couple of weeks, never visiting long but always giving the nurses, usually Nurse Addie, specific instructions that never seemed to change: roll the patient, keep the nutrients going, monitor the functions and eye movements. Doctor Sam was particularly interested in the eye movements, seemed satisfied to hear about them. "Good ting!" he would always announce in his funny accent. Of all the doctors she had seen, Ana liked Doctor Sam the most. Sometimes, he would even wink at her, but not in a bad way.

*The woman* had disappeared into room 21, and Ana made her slow, deliberate way down the hall, emptying baskets and cleaning messes. She had a cart that contained all she needed to keep the world clean, and she would leave it outside whatever door she entered. Soon she stood before door 21, yet she was reluctant to interrupt the princess. Many times, the golden woman had held a cell phone to the sleeping man's ear, and many times she had sat and read a book to him. "He wrote this book," the woman had once said to Ana, for this floating human was not like nearly all of the doctors and most of the nurses: this woman actually noticed the aide and communicated with her. That's partly why her aura was so big and golden, Ana knew, her mother's having taught her all about auras, how to spot and interpret them. The sleeping prince had a golden one, too, but his was held tighter to his head, like a heavy mist, a crown.

Ana cocked her head toward the closed door, the Crypt. She thought she heard *voices*. Voices plural, but then she realized that the other voice must be coming from the phone. Ana heard the woman laugh, but it was a short laugh. No long laughs ever erupted on Ward C, except for Julio's and sometimes Margrita's. Ana waited until she started to feel embarrassed standing and doing nothing, and then she crept into room 21. "Hello," said the seated woman, who was no longer on her cell phone. "He looks brighter today, doesn't he?" Ana came over to the base of the bed, to her spot, and looked down on the prince, who did look brighter.

"O-oh-o," she whispered, for the sleeping man for a moment had seemed about to rise, as though he had just been kissed, but probably it had just been a deeper breath.

"The nurses say that his rems have increased—his rapid eye movements. They're optimistic that he might wake up!"

In response, Ana smiled at the woman, who was beautiful and kind, yet who would take away the prince if and when he arose.

An hour or so later, the golden aura appeared and glided away down the hall. Nodding and smiling at Ana, the Princess passed by without looking to either side, like a bride heading for the altar. Later still, when Ana slipped into the Crypt, she heard the Prince's machine beep, as usual, but then three quick beeps erupted, startling Ana Louisa Maria Consueala Cepatos so that she looked quickly into the bed and froze in both thrill and horror. The eyes were open, green and gleaming, and the aura had risen too, hovering a foot above and around the yet unmoving head. A moonlit mist. Then the figure's white lips broke open, and then a word escaped, once, twice, three times. "Anna … Anna … Anna."

The young aide unfroze, crossed herself, and exited the room like a cat. For the dead man not only knew her name, but had called it.

# Chapter Two:  Ethos

This point on the rhetorical triangle represents the arguer's ethical qualities—his or her ethos. Aristotle reasoned that if an arguer displayed intelligence, goodwill, and morality, then "he" would be deemed credible, but any adjective could fit this rhetorical appeal: determined, objective, passionate, even friendly. And, of course the opposite could occur, too, the dark side of ethos, for an arguer could display negative qualities, such as ignorance, selfishness, narrow mindedness, etc. As politics reveal, the audience plays a prominent role with ethos, often deciding on what qualities are good and what are not.

Nurse Addie would not soon forget the sound of Ana Cepatos' running down the corridor of Ward C, the repeated "He's alive! He's alive!" Afterward, the older woman could never be sure if the younger one had been excited or terrified or most likely both. The aide had slid to a stop before her, and Ana's eyes had looked like silver dollars, so wide and shiny. "He's alive!" she declared again, and Nurse Addie certainly did not have to ask "Who?" Instead, stifling an impatient "He has always been alive, you silly girl," she hustled her big body down to room 21, which was wide open, and burst in to discover who knows what.

Her patient's eyes were blinking, his mouth moving as though trying to form and release words.

"You're safe," said Nurse Addie. "Have no fear, Professor Diggerson. You're healing, you're safe." She wasn't sure why she kept saying 'safe,' but it made sense considering the bullet wound to the awakened man's temple. "I'm Nurse Addie," she added.

To that introduction, the conscious patient made a noise, four notes: up, down, down, and back to the start. They reminded Nurse

Addie of her husband's trying to start their old lawnmower, which always refused to kick into life. The incoherent man made the same sound again, and Nurse Addie realized with surprise that the professor had giggled.

"Anna?" he said, and then "My dogs?" The words were all stretched out, played on a different speed.

"Your wife was here earlier," she responded, "but I don't know about any dogs."

"Simba and Snodo," the man whispered, and his eyes grew rounder with each blink, as though he wanted to see more. "Anna," he said again.

"Yes," said Nurse Addie. "Anna was here."

"My wife?" said the groggy man. "My dogs?" he repeated.

"Your dogs aren't here, Professor, but I'm sure they're fine. Everything's been taken care of."

The man made that noise again, a four-note giggle, which Nurse Addie couldn't understand. "My fingers," he said. "Look at my fingers." The latter word came out "fiiiiinnnnngggers."

"Yes, you've lost considerable weight, Professor. Now I'm going to call Doctor Sam. And your wife, too."

"My wife," she heard the man say as she exited the room, and hustling down the corridor, she thought she heard him repeat it.

Matthew Diggerson just breathed and stared from his fingers, which looked like pencils, to the ceiling. He counted six rows of ceiling panels, white, Styrofoam looking. The corner tile just behind his bed seemed stained. *Water*, he thought. He realized that he needed to hire two adjuncts, and he thought about a plan that had been forming in his dreams, something to do with having more papers in class, more graded papers and less versions per project. He could have paired projects, three of them, the second paper in each pair counting for more points. That would put more importance on class lessons, and students would be required to transfer what they learned from one paper onto the next. He wanted to get up and find paper to jot down these ideas, but his body wouldn't respond right. He felt so tired, so empty, as though he'd fallen from a great height or been run over by a steam roller. Peaceful, though. Except that his fingers looked like pencils. *My wife?* He thought again, for he had forgotten the word for a bit.

Nurse Addie returned, as though beamed into the room beside his bed. She looked grandmotherly, plump and caring. Digger tried to sit up.

"No, no, Professor Diggerson. Not yet. You need to go very slowly, and we need to see the doctor before you start moving about."

"Where am I?"

"Why, you're at Breezy Seas Rehabilitation Center."

"Why?"

"Why are you here? Well, maybe I should let the doctor explain, or the police."

"The police? No, please, you explain. What's going on? Did you say 'my wife'?"

"Yes, your wife, Anna. A beautiful woman, and very attentive. Despite her work, she has visited you every week, and she and I have talked many times."

"I'm in the past," Nurse Addie thought she heard the man say, followed clearly by "What year is it?"

She told him the year. After all, the question made sense from an awakened coma patient. To the conscious man, though, the year made no sense. Digger looked up at the ceiling, which offered no answers as to why he wasn't in the past, but the future. He said the year aloud, then returned to "Why am I here?"

The nurse looked down at him, seemed concerned, hesitant, and then she said, "You were shot, Professor Diggerson."

That word, 'shot,' had the same effect on Digger as the year had, and he spent a few seconds wiggling his appendages, which felt alternately as light as sticks and as heavy as logs. Had he fallen into his book, into *Composition Murder*, and become Billy D Wilder, his protagonist and alter-ego? He giggled.

"I don't feel any wound," he finally said. "Where was I shot, and by whom?"

Again, Nurse Addie hesitated, but then she touched her own left temple and said "here." Digger lifted a heavy hand to his own right temple, and Nurse Addie reached over and redirected it to the other side. "Right here," she said, and Digger could feel a rough spot. "It's all healed up now," the woman said.

Time made no sense at all. "Who shot me?" said Digger after a pause.

"You don't know? Well, then nobody knows, Professor Diggerson. I know that the police were hoping that you knew. That female cop has dropped by occasionally and called, too. What *do* you remember?"

"I don't remember anything, at least not about being shot or by whom, or why. Who would want to shoot me? Not Paul Smith, right? Paul is in jail."

"I know that name," said Nurse Addie, looking pensive. "He killed a couple people at your school, years ago, a decade ago."

"He's in jail. At least, I think he is. Did you say that you've talked to Anna, that my *wife* has been visiting?"

"Yes, she has. What's the last thing you remember?"

Digger paused. "I need to hire a couple part-timers, and I'm waiting for a print copy of my book."

"You're a writer, too?"

"Well, I wrote a murder mystery, so I suppose you can call me a writer. It's about a writing teacher turned sleuth. It's called *Composition Murder*." Then he giggled again. "I just giggled," he announced.

"Yes, I heard."

"I've never giggled like that before."

"You got shot in the head, Professor Diggerson, and you've been in a coma for a long time. Who knows what changes you will encounter?"

"I don't like change," said Digger, but then he giggled. "There it goes again. Can getting shot in the head make a person giggle? And did you say 'coma'?"

"From the evidence I've seen, I'd say 'yes' and 'yes,'" said

Nurse Addie, smiling, the words or maybe the woman's attitude setting off another giggle—four notes: the second rising and then falling back.

"There I go again! Is it an annoying sound?"

"No, no, it's quite pleasant, not annoying."

"Will it wear off? Do you go back to normal after a coma? Will I start to remember the last, what, year?"

"I imagine so, Professor Diggerson, but the doctor will know more. Given time, you will no doubt get back to normal."

Time had been taken; now it had to be given. Wouldn't that mean more time taken? Digger had too many questions in his head.

"What about my dogs? Where are Simba and Snodo?"

"I don't know anything about that, but don't worry about them now. When Anna comes back, maybe she can find out. Maybe she took them."

"Maybe Anna took them?" Digger repeated to himself, but that didn't sound right. "The person who shot me," he said, "did he kill my dogs? Did he shoot them?"

"Stay calm, Professor. I'm sure that your dogs are safe. Nobody shot them. I remember the story on the news very well. Ocean View doesn't get stories like armed break-ins and shootings too often, and I don't remember any mention of dogs being shot. The news would have said so."

*Break ins?* He had been shot at home, so Simba and Snodo must have been there. Digger settled back, felt sleep enveloping him. *Anna was coming.* Anna was really coming! Anna!

"Anna's coming," he said, and Nurse Addie took it as a question.

"Yes, from the Cape. As I said, she has been here every weekend, reading to you, calling your mother on her phone and having her talk to you. Do you remember?"

"No, I don't remember. I don't remember her voice or my mother's. My mother lives far away, hours by car. She hasn't been here?"

"No. Anna told me that your mother wanted to come, but that

she could not find a driver. She has been very upset apparently."

"She's eighty-one years old," said Digger, who then giggled.

"Eighty-two now," corrected Nurse Addie, "maybe eighty-three."

"Oh, no!" said Digger.

Then a dark-haired, big-eyed head appeared halfway down the open door, momentarily confusing Digger again. He didn't recognize the young woman peeking into the room. "Hello," he said to the head.

Nurse Addie turned and then said, "Come in, Ana, and meet our sleeping beauty. As you said, he is definitely 'alive.'"

But all Digger heard was "Anna," and for a second his heart plunged, for this woman was not his wife. Why would the nurse call this woman his wife? Anna was *not* coming!

"This isn't my wife," he said, and both women looked at him.

"Of course not," said the nurse at last. "This is Ana Cepatos, one of our hard-working aides. She's the one who let us all know, quite loudly, too, that you had woken up. Your wife's driving back from Cape Cod."

Digger's heart had seemed too big for his body, but it stopped pounding now. He hadn't *lost* Anna again. Had he actually found her? He had woken into a dream, and anything could happen in dreams.

"I'm just confused," he said. "My brain," he added but then didn't continue that thought. "Hello, Ana," he said instead.

"O-oh-o," said the aid, standing behind Nurse Addie. Digger giggled. "O-oh-o," said Ana Cepatos again, and again Digger giggled.

"Okay," cut in Nurse Addie. "While you two are making noises at each other, I need to get back to work. And you need to rest, Professor Diggerson, because more visitors are coming. Your wife, the doctor, and no doubt the police, who I need to call right now. I was supposed to call them when you, if you, woke up, and that day is gladly here. I'll be back."

She was gone, dragging out the young aide, young Ana, in her wake. Everyone seemed to move quickly in this dream. "Thank you," he said to the empty room, and again he looked up at the rectangular ceiling panels, six of them per row. Six down and six across. A nice balance. Except for that one discolored spot in the corner. What this room needed was a window, but what would he see? Snow, green leaves, a barren landscape, *sun*? He would see sun. *Anna was coming.*

He must have dozed off, for suddenly she was there, standing in the doorway, not peeking around it, all light and beauty and wonder, the most amazing moment of his life. "Anna!" said Matthew Diggerson, and then he said the name again, again, trying to stamp it into reality.

"Matt," responded the woman in the doorway, and she had tears running down her face, and then she was rushing to the bed, to him. And time disintegrated into lightness and being.

Nurse Addie had brought him soup, broth really, and Anna was spooning it into his fumbling mouth. Nothing seemed to work quite properly, and Digger didn't care one bit. He felt broth dribble down his chin yet again and let out that four-note giggle.

"Getting shot didn't take away your sense of humor," admonished his one-time wife, his one-and-only wife.

"I think it gave me one," he sputtered and then giggled again.

"You sound like a little engine that won't quite start but that keeps on trying to."

"My father had a lawnmower like that. I sound just like his lawnmower."

"Matt the Lawnmower Man."

"That's a book, by Stephen King, I think."

"What isn't?" said Anna.

"I'd like to read *The Shining* again," said Digger. "What a great book! Do you remember how those two little girls, the ghosts, scared you!"

"Me!" laughed Anna. "You were curled up next to me like a

kitten. Those two creepy twins, I think they're why I never wanted to have kids."

For a moment, silence settled, both humans' thinking about kids and not having kids.

"I have dogs," said Digger, and then he giggled.

"So I've heard," said Anna.

"Anna, I need to find out where they are, Simba and Snodo. Would you? Do you have time? I'm a little indisposed."

"Don't even think about getting up, buddy!" said Anna, making Digger think that his ex-wife could have been a mother after all. "Before you're 'disposed,' you're going to need a lot of physical therapy, a *lot*. You've been in a coma for many months, more than a year, Matt. You can't just get up and go find your dogs."

"More than a year," said Digger, "so where can they be? They must have been taken to the pound and adopted out."

"I'll find out, Matt. I'll go and ask our old neighbor, what's his name, the sort of nosy one next door?"

"You mean Graham? Nosy? Maybe so, and that's a great idea, Anna. He probably saw who took Simba and Snodo. If not, you— or I, for that matter—could call the pound or go down there. The Ocean View Animal Shelter, down by the docks. Do you remember?"

"Yes, Matt, I remember, and I'll go and find out about Simba and Snodo. Simba looks like a lion, right, and Snodo's all white?"

Digger smiled but didn't giggle. "Yes," he said. "Simba's like a female lion but with a little mane and very short legs, some corgi influence. And Snodo's like a white beagle with a mane, too. I didn't go looking for dogs with hairdos, though."

Anna laughed at that. "Dogs with hairdos," she repeated, getting up. "I'd better get going, though, Matt, because I do have to get back home, to the Cape."

*Home*, the Cape. What or who was she going back to? Digger feared asking that question. He didn't know if Anna had remarried, but he didn't think she had, knew she hadn't somehow. "Okay, Anna," he said, "but could you do one thing for me before you go?

Could you get me some paper and a pen? I need to write down some stuff, some teaching ideas. Apparently, they've been percolating as I slept."

She rummaged in her purse and magically came up with both items. "For grocery lists," she said, leaning down and kissing him on the forehead, then the nose, then briefly on his lips, which tingled. Color had returned to them. "I'll be back," she said. "I'll find Simba the lion and Snodo the white beagle." Then she smiled and left. In her wake, she seemed to drag away the light.

"Thank you," said Digger, again to an empty room. *Anna will be back*, he thought and then started writing notes on her little pad. His fingers felt clumsy, and just holding the pen and small book made him tired. Or maybe it was the thinking that brought exhaustion, or maybe he had lost energy when Anna left the room.

No, it wasn't that, for Anna was *back*. He knew that. No worries. He had been shot in the head and woken up giggling with no worries, with so much more than he had left—yet? *Yin and yang*, he thought, *darkness and light*. Why did both have to exist? *Balance*. Simba had brought a flame into his shadows, all those years ago, and Snodo had intensified the light, but now that the biggest blaze of all was back by his side—forever?—Digger could see neither of those canine lights. Dogs were simply 'put down' in this world. Often! Beautiful dogs, simply extinguished because humans couldn't be bothered with time or money to neuter their pets or take care of them, and for a moment Matthew Diggerson lay in bed so angry that he thought he could concentrate hard and move objects, hurl them into the windowless walls.

*No*, Simba and Snodo had *not* been put down. Life could *not* do that to a man, no way. Anna would return with good news, maybe with one or both dogs on a leash. Yet who would have saved them? His mother was too old and too far away anyway. Life had taken his father long ago and his only sibling long ago, too. What 'friends' would have stepped in? His colleagues? Lou Knightly, Lip Licker Lou. He might have helped, or maybe Eliot Gladstone, whom Anna had once called Professor Happy Rock. Diana Pell?

She seemed more like a cat person, like Patricia Pauley, the night-class teacher. Any of the adjuncts? Bill Jacobs? Digger had known him the longest, yet Bill didn't have a dog, did he? Would Digger even want Simba and Snodo to be with that grumpy man? Gwena Schmidt, the Grammar Nazi. She was long gone. Digger hadn't even heard from her in decades, it seemed. Time was elusive.

Maybe his vet, Sarah Palmer, had taken Simba and Snodo. She loved Simba, especially, and would never have let either dog be put down. Who but her would have euthanized them, anyway? Digger did not want to think of any dog-pound back rooms, any chambers. *No!* Although he had made few additions to Anna's notebook, the little pad and even the pen slowly dragged his thin hands into his lap, and Matthew Diggerson slept again.

This time, when he awakened, a man stood looking down at him, smiling. An older Indian man in a white coat. *The doctor,* thought Digger, and then "Anna? She's out looking for Simba and Snodo. Driving takes time." He and the doctor looked in silence at each other.

"Hello!" said the standing man suddenly and happily. "I am Doctor Sam. I am quite happy to see tat you are awake at last, and how are you feeling today?"

Digger giggled. He liked this man's Indian accent, the way the words seemed to float by themselves and sing, the missing letters in some, causing no comprehension problems. "Doctor Sam," he said, "I feel great one minute and exhausted the next, giddy and clear headed one minute and groggy the next."

"Ten you are normal," said a smiling Doctor Sam.

"Do you know anything about my dogs?" asked Digger, for his mind had gone back to Anna and her trek.

"About your dogs?" said Doctor Sam. "No, what should I know about tem?"

"Well," said Digger, "where are they, for instance? If they're okay."

"Hm? I do not know about your dogs and deir whereabouts and

state of being. I will ask Nurse Addie to look into dis."

"No," said Digger. "That's okay. My wife is looking into it, and she will be back." How good it felt to say 'my wife.'

"Dat is good," said Doctor Sam, who then did most of the talking, asking yes-and-no questions and noting responses on his clipboard. Digger asked about the giggling, though, and Doctor Sam said, "Dese tings happen," making Digger giggle again and then say "Sorry."

"No need to be sorry," said Doctor Sam. "You are a very good-natured gun-shot victim, my favorite kind." Doctor Sam asked about Digger's memory loss (apparently, about a year and three months of shadow land), about his level of pain (none in his head, just a few ripples elsewhere), about bed sores (none that he knew of), about his mobility (appendages working but everything was exhausting), about his appetite (none, really). The doctor talked about medications, such as anti-inflammatories and even steroids, about their fear of blood clots and pneumonia, about physical therapy and even other kinds (such as electrotherapy), about a gradually increasing diet (he had lost fifty pounds—*how could that be!*). "People tink dat when you need to put on weight you should eat just meat, lots of meat, but dat is not true. Balance, Professor Diggerson, everyting is balance."

"I was just thinking the same *ting*," said Digger, and then he giggled.

"Dat is good," smiled Doctor Sam, but then the smile left his face. "One more ting, ta bullet. It is still in your temple. We could not remove it. Doing so would have risked life and limb, too. You might have been paralyzed. We decided to leave it dare, in ta soft tissue, where it is secure."

From his pocket, Doctor Sam produced a hand mirror and angled it above Digger's head. "Oh," said the patient. "I can see a red spot, sort of puckish."

"Yes, puckish. Dat is all. The bullet is inside, embedded in tissue. It will not boder you dere." The doctor could not say his th's, which sometimes became d's and other times just t's, but

Digger had no trouble understanding the friendly, trustworthy man. Perhaps due to the doctor's calm bearing, the bullet nestled in Digger's head didn't really bother him. He kept thinking of Anna and his dogs. Could Anna actually find them? Would the cops have bothered to contact his veterinarian about two orphaned dogs? *Chips!* Digger should have had chips embedded in them. Safer than bullets, anyway, and more useful.

"Would the police take the time to help a person's dogs?" Digger asked, and the question seemed to stump the white-coated doctor.

"Yes," he said at last. "Ta police would help your dogs. Dey are very interested in you. Ta police have dropped by often and called often. Dey would have helped your dogs."

Digger thought of Detective Doyle. "They have? Was it a short cop?"

This question made Doctor Sam smile, but Digger thought that most things did. "A short cop? Yes and no. Short for a police but not for a woman."

"A woman?"

"Ta police officer was a woman, ta one dat I saw. She had a last name dat started wid a 'Z.'"

*Zoro?* Digger giggled.

"You are in good humor, good!" concluded Doctor Sam, sliding his hand mirror back to a pocket, glancing once more at a clipboard attached to the foot of Digger's bed, and then moving toward the door. "I will see you again soon, and soon—tomorrow, I tink— you will begin terapy. Some food tonight, too. We will soon fatten you up."

Digger thanked his doctor's back before the room emptied again. Only questions filled the small space. With the image of a bullet lodged in his own head, Digger thought for the first time about the person who had put it there. Had he run into another killer during the time he could not remember, his lost year? Could Paul Smith have escaped or been let out of prison? No, impossible! Mr. Morbid had killed two people, just seven years back, or eight, or maybe ten. Time danced about in his mind, like fat, powdery moths, confusing. Simba had helped him to defeat Smith, to fight for life, and now where was his beautiful dog? The shelter—that's where she and Snodo went. His dogs could *not* have been euthanized, not while Sarah Palmer knew where they were, not while their owner actually lived, even if his life was just a long sleep with a bullet nestled in his noggin. No, the authorities would have kept his dogs alive, if not out of ethical concerns then due to judicial ones. Digger had never sued anyone or even thought about doing so, yet he did now. *Nobody* had better have made the decision to kill Simba and Snodo!

At that moment of righteousness, which felt good (made Digger feel strong for a change), a woman appeared in the doorway, not peeking around the corner like young Ana Cepatos, but standing directly in the middle, straight and sure, as though barring exit. She was dark and attractive and obviously a cop. Digger thought again of Detective Doyle, who had become a friend or at least a peer ten years ago. *Ten years!*

"Professor Diggerson," said the woman in the door, and her voice was not high and not low. *Balance*, thought Digger.

"Where are my dogs?" he said, noting that he had sounded demanding and then feeling fine with that tone. When the woman said nothing, he added, "Simba and Snodo. My dogs. If I was shot at home, then my dogs would have been there, and when I was taken to the hospital, they would have been taken care of too, right? So where are they now?"

"We will find out about your dogs," said the woman, and Digger thought, *Who's 'we'?* Did no one want to say 'I,' to take responsibility, or were they taught to use the plural? Were they hiding behind a pronoun?

"Do you know Detective Doyle?"

"I know of him," the dark-haired cop responded, and Digger was glad that she had not said 'we.' "But he is no longer part of the OVPD. Now, Professor Diggerson, we have been told that you cannot remember the past year and that the bullet cannot be removed. That is unfortunate."

The memory loss? The unmovable bullet? *Unfortunate* for whom, Digger or the police. *The latter, probably.* "A little more than that," he said. "About fifteen months."

"Then you will not remember talking with me."

"No."

"You obviously do not remember, then, who tried to murder you."

"No. Do you have any suspects?"

The female cop hesitated. "My name is Detective Zorn," she said, but she did not offer her hand in greeting. Digger felt a little self-conscious about his thin fingers, anyway. "We met on two occasions to discuss two prior murders, two women who were connected to you." *Connected?*

"Two women *connected* to me? Who? How?"

"The first was a professor, what you would call an adjunct, named Johna Adams. Do you remember Johna Adams?"

*Joan-uh Adams?* She sounded like a Founding Father, or Mother, but history had recorded no Founding Mothers that Digger could conjure up.

"I have no memories of a Joan-uh Adams. None. But she was an adjunct at Ocean View? I must have hired her then last year, or the year before last. I just don't remember."

"Then you also probably will not remember a Valerie Walt, whom you apparently met at the grocery store."

*Walt?* At the grocery store? "I don't ever remember meeting any women at a grocery store. That doesn't exactly sound like me."

"You told us so yourself, and after you met her, she was murdered."

"Somebody shot her?"

"She was strangled, the same M.O. as Johna Adams. The same killer, we assume."

Digger had an unsettling thought. "You don't think that I killed these women!"

"We know that you did not shoot yourself, Professor Diggerson.

We think that you were meant to be the third victim."

"But why? Why would someone kill these two women, Joan-uh and, uh, Valarie, and then try to kill me? I'm a writing teacher!"

"You gave us a motive, Professor. Jealousy, envy."

"I don't follow you." Digger felt tired, his head full of words, too many fragments and questions. Someone was jealous of a writing teacher?

Zorn added more. "Both women seemed interested in you, and you thought that maybe someone did not want you to be happy."

"But why me? Why would someone care that much about me?"

"You said that maybe the envy had something to do with your books?"

"Did you say 'books,' plural?"

Zorn checked her phone, tapped it, and Digger realized that she was not rudely making a call but checking notes. "*Composition Murder*," she read and then "*Murderous Mistakes*."

*Murderous Mistakes*? He had written and published a second book? Vaguely, he remembered the alliterative title, but only as a note, a possibility. He felt suddenly as light as a feather, matching his emaciated look. He giggled, bubbles floating toward the sun.

"Apparently I giggle easily now," he said to the stern policewoman, adding, "I remember my first book, but not that second one. I'm a two-time author!" This dark woman had brought light to the room after all.

Yet she seemed unimpressed, and then she changed the topic completely. "You gave us a list of suspects, colleagues. Would you like me to read them? The names might help you to remember."

The word 'colleagues' had darkened the room again, for some reason, and Digger suddenly felt very tired. *Where was Anna?* Where were Simba and Snodo? Who really cared about a second book?

"Honestly, Officer Zorn, I'm too tired and too, uh, uncaring about all this. Could you come back later? Could you find out where my dogs went, where they are?"

The woman tapped her phone and slid it into her shirt pocket.

She had no coat. *It must be summer*, thought Digger.

"Officer Zorn, could you tell me the month? I keep forgetting to ask people."

"August," said the serious cop. August second."

"My birthday," said Digger in wonder, and then he giggled.

Again, he slept, dozed, kept half waking and then slipping off again, weighed down by the myriad questions. When his eyelids opened again, Anna filled his sight, so beautiful, so light, but then he noticed her tears. Anna was standing at the foot of his bed and crying.

"Matt," she said. "I found out about your dogs. Snodo was adopted out over a year ago, to an old couple, apparently, and Simba—oh, Matt!—Simba was so old and broken that you had your vet put her down. Simba is gone!"

# Chapter Three:  Pathos

The ability to evoke an audience's emotions is often an arguer's most
effective tool, one that allows him or her to position readers or listeners
and to establish points, often ones lacking in supportive evidence.
Feelings are powerful forces, so an arguer who can elicit sadness,
concern, fear, derision, anger, or especially guilt is one who can usually
win an argument.

Matthew Diggerson was on fire. He remembered a pain like this
once before, back in high school when he had tried to defy genetics
and his skinny body by lifting weights with a bigger friend, too
many weights and for too long. He had awoken the next day with
his arms locked, perpendicularly, as though he were reaching out
to accept a solemn gift, perhaps a folded flag. Now he had done
the same thing, and once again he could blame only himself and
vanity, his embarrassment and concern over his stick-like arms.

Lying in his Breezy Sea's bed, Digger tried not to move any
upper-torso muscles, failed, and moaned, a strangling sound, the
call of a conscious cow in an abattoir, causing Ana Cepatos to
straighten up from her sweeping duties.

"I overdid the dumbbells," Digger said slowly, knowing what
the young aide's response would be, and there it was.

"O-oh-o!"

Usually, this reaction made Digger smile, even giggle, but
somehow in the context of his current pain, the sound seemed
inadequate, almost the equivalent of "You don't say!"

"Could you get Nurse Addie?" said Digger with clenched lips
because moving even a millimeter caused cascading sheets of pain.

*This must be how back patients feel,* thought the stiff man, concentrating on remaining rigid. When the pain inevitably came, it ripped up his arms and down his torso, but not down his legs. Those big muscles, he had not over-stressed, just his skinny arms, which made him think of concentration-camp victims, old men, old before their time.

Frozen, Digger seemed to wait for hours, but then Nurse Addie appeared. "You overdid it, didn't you?" she said reproachfully, as though she were the teacher and he the recalcitrant student, which, of course ,was true. "What did I tell you about those dumbbells!"

"I'm the dumbbell," said Digger, one word at a time, a breath between each, and that made him think of Eliot Gladstone, the Breather. It had been nice of Eliot to drop by, to show so much concern about his health and memory. In fact, a handful of his colleagues had appeared during the past couple of weeks, each a surprise, a gift given for no special purpose, but Officer Zorn had not reappeared. With his shadowed memories, Digger was apparently not worth much to the cops. He did not want her to return, especially at the moment. He expelled a drawn out, descending "Ohhhhh," far less pleasing than Spanish Ana's exclamation.

"You've been in therapy for just one month," lectured Nurse Addie, "and these things take time."

"Dese tings," said Digger.

"Yes, just as Doctor Sam says, 'dese tings' take time. You can't rush your rehab, or you end up like this, frozen in bed in pain. *Now* you're going to have to take some time off."

"I can still walk," said Digger.

"Yes, I suppose so, but what's your big hurry? Going somewhere?"

"I need to get Snodo, or at least to see my dog. Anna says that she met the old couple and that they love Snodo. That she has a good home. But I need to see her myself."

"Oh, I thought that you were pining to get back to the classroom."

"That, too," said Digger, thinking of his new plan for assignments. Little changes, revisions, made teaching exciting, and his plan to use paired assignments (instead of two versions per paper) had him yearning to teach again—but not so yearning as his desire, his need, to see Snodo. And Simba's grave. Sarah Palmer, his vet, had visited him almost a month ago and told him all about that day in his backyard. She had said that it was "beautiful" and that she had never done that before, eased away a dog's pain out in the elements. Sarah had told him about the grave she had seen, the hole actually, and she told him where it was. Digger pictured the spot, just to the right of his spruce tree and the bird pole. No birds would be visiting Simba, though, not without seeds and bread pieces spread out. He wondered if the sparrows missed making off with Simba's thick fur.

Anna had told him that Snodo seemed very happy, that the little white beagle-ish dog had sniffed her over completely and then punctuated the inspection by licking her calf. "She whined when I left, too," Anna had said, adding, "I think that she could smell you on me, Matt!" *Maybe*, but any happy creature would be attracted to Anna.

Anna couldn't visit this weekend since with the coming of September, school had begun again. She was teaching three sections of Intro to Art at Cape Cod Tech, and each section had its full quota of twenty-five students because the course was required for Graphic Art, one of the technical college's most popular programs. "Everyone wants to be a graphic designer," Anna had told Digger, and he had responded, "Maybe so, but not at Ocean View, unless things have really changed in my lost year." Most OVC students seemed interested in business or criminal justice, even psychology, a word that always made Digger think of Professor William Watkins.

Had Watkins walked through his door, Digger would have been surprised indeed, just as he was when Gwena Schmidt had appeared, especially when she filled him in on part of his lost year. She brought him copies of both his books (he didn't let her know that Anna had already brought them and cooed over them, having been informed of the novels' existence months ago by his mother), and Digger and Gwena had a good time talking about Billy D. Wilder and discovering what he was up to in the second book, which seemed to be based loosely on Tobias Mann's and Dan Pinsky's murders, in other words, on a killer like Paul Smith. Less enjoyable was hearing that Gwena's husband, whom Digger remembered as being stately and capable, was now in a nursing home full-time, his Alzheimer's being too much for a wife to handle alone at home. "Is he here?" Digger had asked, meaning Breezy Seas, but Gwena had said no, that he was closer to their home, in a place called The Willows. "Who invents names like that?" Gwena had announced. "They all sound like cemeteries already!"

Other old colleagues had visited, too. Lou Knightly, the Lip Licker as named by Digger (but he told no one this little nickname), had been first, and Lou too had talked about Digger's first book, *Composition Murder*, but not about the second one, a little fact that pricked at Digger after the tall, thin man had left. Diana Pell, the literature (specifically poetry) teacher, had come next, and then old Eliot Gladstone, whom Digger learned was now the department chairperson, his old job. "I did not want the position," the Breather had informed his younger colleague, "but somebody had to step in." Neither of these old peers talked about either of Digger's books, but both had asked what Digger last remembered. To be fair, everybody who saw Digger for the first time asked this same question: "What do you remember last?"

And Digger answered it the same way: "I need to hire two new adjuncts." And although apparently that had been bad luck for one of them, this repeated answer always led to a giggle, which usually created some silence, which sometimes led to another giggle, which Digger now accepted as a part of him, a quirky characteristic for Born Again Diggerson, the man who lived for five decades, fell asleep for a time, and rose again on his own birthday. Upon hearing that, everyone said the same thing, too: "That's quite a birthday present" or sometimes "God's birthday present" or something like that, some reference to a heavenly gift. Digger supposed that they were right because life had once again become a shiny present—when Anna came, anyway, which was often or had been in August, before the fall semester. But even when she wasn't present, she was. *Anna was back!*

He had overdone the dumbbells for her. He had wanted to get back to normal for her. He wanted to get Snodo and to go home, for them all to go home.

"You can't go home yet!" scolded Nurse Addie, who then mentioned all the problems that overdoing things could cause, such as swelling, bleeding, and even migraines or seizures. And, of course, muscle pain, which she labeled 'spasticity.' Seeing the poor man with his arms stuck up, as though beseeching the Heavens, Nurse Addie shifted, her frown reforming into empathy, or to be more precise, the eyebrow 'V' stayed the same but the woman's lower lip rose into the upper one, changing her expression completely. "The muscles, given time, will relax on their own, but I can give you two extra pills for the pain, and this cream will help, too. But you will simply have to wait for a few hours for your muscles to release. I'm sorry about that, Professor Diggerson, but we can't give you too many pain relievers."

"Call me 'Digger,' Nurse Addie. After all, you've seen me at my worst."

"Your worst! As Ana says, Digger, you've been nothing but an angel."

"My Anna or yours?"

"The aide Ana. Yours has been an angel herself." Digger thought about that, felt warm despite the pain that even smiling caused him. Then Nurse Addie changed the subject. "Doctor Sam has told me more than once not to let you overdo your therapy. Small steps, Profe... Digger." Then the nurse put two white pills in her patient's mouth, one at a time, and lifted a plastic water cup to his lips. When Digger moved, his arms and then upper body launched into spasm, and the composition teacher could never remember feeling pain such as that scalding blanket.

"Oh, god!" he whispered, and then "sorry."

"Go ahead and curse," said Nurse Addie, squeezing some cream onto Digger's arm, which immediately felt cool but which hurt like hell again when she began to spread it around. His upper arms still looked like sticks leading to knobby elbows.

"Oh god!" he said again, partly because he hated thinking about his incredible thinness, mostly because the word just felt good.

"This cream has anti-inflammatory and pain control in it, so you should feel some relief. Sleep for a bit, and you will awaken much better." The nurse got up and headed for the door, just a few steps, but then she turned. "Don't touch those dumbbells!" she admonished, and Digger giggled in response—and then grimaced in pain.

Despite his current muscle aches and the shadow of his lost dogs, Matthew Diggerson did feel happy, 'born again,' light, sort of floaty and elated, and Nurse Addie said that such feelings were to be expected due to the rush of nutrients through his hungry body, to the serotonin released via the ever-increasing therapy, and to his thin body itself, the utter lack of fat. "Your body, not mine," she would joke, and, of course, Digger would giggle at that self-recrimination. Giggles and jiggles.

Nurse Addie was correct, of course, yet Digger understood the real roots to his awakened joy:  four simple letters, almost mirroring his four-note giggles, in fact. 'A,' 'n,' 'n,' and back to 'a.' Anna's light had nurtured him for all his sleeping years, especially the last, when her voice had drifted into his veins and cells, illuminating the shadows and even forcing Digger's black river—that stream that gurgled just above his dreams, that dark flow where all his doubts and guilts and black feelings rolled by and occasionally belched themselves into consciousness—down, down, down, so no wonder the man felt lighter than air almost, rooted to reality by the warm weight of future hopes and present contentment. Just perhaps not the immediate present.

Digger liked seeing anyone come through the door, even when

they held needles or other prods, even the aide Julio, who wandered into room 21 occasionally just to talk, curious about what Digger remembered before the coma and even during it. Not a lot, that was for sure.

The somewhat furtive aide appeared now, always strolled right through the door, never peaking around it like Ana Cepatos. "Heard you was feeling some pain," he said, and the rumor seemed to entertain the fellow. With his arms bent and frozen, Digger could understand the humor.

"Those five-pound weights were too much for me," he said.

"Five pounds!" exclaimed the wiry man. "Then you're the record holder around these parts!"

Digger thought of all the elderly patients down Ward C, the sleeping or sometimes moaning souls he passed whenever he walked the grounds, a few times every day. Sometimes one of the old people—often a woman—would be wide awake and just staring, so Digger would visit the wisp of a human and listen to broken tales that always involved family members. Family members were always *coming*, but none ever *came* by the time Digger exited those rooms. He had trouble making fun of his Ward C 'peers,' but still smiled at Julio's little joke.

"No pain, no gain," he said to Breezy Seas' only male aide, who wasn't listening. Something down the hall held his gaze, and Digger waited to learn what it was. "Cop!" Julio said, and then he was gone. Digger giggled, but he also wished that he could move that quickly. He wondered why Julio feared the police. Maybe he was an illegal alien.

Within half a minute, Officer Zorn appeared, stopping in the doorway and then bringing her dark beauty into the room, along with a touch of sadness.

"Professor Diggerson," she said, seating herself beside Digger's bed in the room's only chair. "Now that you have been awake, conscious, for a month, and now that you are much stronger and alert, we had hoped that you could aid our investigation." Then she added, "We have not solved the crimes."

Digger tried to sit up straight, making his upper body spasm. "I don't remember anything of the last year, or I guess it was two years. The time I was in the coma or the year before it. Nothing. I remember needing to hire two new part-timers, and apparently I did so, or at least one, since she was the first person murdered, right?" Talking hurt.

Zorn was clicking away at her phone, which she then held up to Digger's face, just as Nurse Addie had done with the water and pills. "This is a photo, supplied by your university, of Johna Adams. You do not recognize her?"

To Digger, the woman in the picture, which seemed to be her ID photo, looked *normal*, for lack of a better word. Dark haired, not long or short, regular features, none standing out, a nice smile. The woman had been attractive.

"I don't remember Johna at all," Digger said to Detective Zorn, who went back to pecking at her phone. It made Digger think of his students, many of whom seemed addicted to the devices, drawn to them, pulled into the little screens as though beholding something magical, perhaps a turtle beaking its way from a small egg. Digger could never understand how they could type on such small devices, but maybe even he could do so now, now that his fingers looked like uncooked spaghetti strands.

Zorn stretched her phone out again to Digger, who now saw a different face, an even more attractive one, raven haired and green eyed and very much alive, perhaps due to the background, a beach scene. "Valerie Walt," said the policewoman.

"The second woman murdered, right?" said Digger, studying the face. He had supposedly met this woman at Stop 'n Shop and more or less *picked her up*. That didn't exactly sound like him!

The detective transitioned from the victims. "Professor Diggerson, we have a list of names, suspects, colleagues of yours. You gave us their names in support of your theory regarding envy over your book." She tapped her phone and then added "*Composition Murder*."

Zorn announced a name from her phone, one that Digger

recognized, of course. "Lou Knightly."

One of Digger's suspects? *Lou!* "No way," he told the officer. "Lou would not kill anyone. Did I really give you his name? Why?"

Zorn looked at her screen and frowned for the first time. "Something about lip licking," she said, and Digger giggled, picturing his colleague's odd mannerism.

"Eliot Gladstone," continued Zorn, and Digger laughed inside again but didn't erupt in a four-note giggle. *Eliot?* The Breather!

"Look at me," he said. "Even in this state I could no doubt outrun Eliot. He doesn't have the, what, strength, youth, whatever, to kill a young or fairly young woman."

"Both victims were middle-aged," said Zorn. "And both appeared to be rendered unconscious before they were strangled."

"Rendered how?"

"Struck. Head wounds."

"So an *old* guy could have hit the women and then strangled them?" said Digger, and he thought of Eliot again. Anna had called him Professor Happy Rock, and that made him smile, which again caused a ripple of pain due to his overworked arm muscles. "Why did I suspect Eliot?" he asked Zorn, who again looked at her phone. Digger concentrated on staying still, motionless, so that his arms wouldn't seize up and scream.

"Showed extreme jealousy," she said, adding "something about a famous writer and graduate school. A David Reed Winslow."

Digger knew the name, of course. What English teacher didn't! But he failed to see a connection between the famous literary giant and Eliot Gladstone.

"We looked him up," said Zorn. "He did attend the University of New Mexico at the same time as your colleague, Eliot Gladstone."

"And I told you that Eliot was jealous of David Reed Winslow and that that jealousy had been transferred onto me, and that Eliot had then gone around strangling women who knew me! What kind of a theory is that? Does Eliot even own a gun?"

Zorn went back to her phone, pecked a couple of times. "No registered weapons," she announced. "But 22-caliber guns are often not registered, especially old ones."

*Family heirlooms?* Now Digger transitioned topics. "Paul Smith, he's still safely locked away, right? No furloughs or escaped road-side duties?"

"Paul Smith is not eligible for either. He has been accounted for."

"Who else is on my list, Detective Zorn?"

She checked her phone, clicked. "Jay Moore, an adjunct, a, um, blinker."

"Did you say a 'blinker'?" asked Digger, adding, "and an adjunct? We have no part-timer named Jay Moore. Unless, of course, he's the second adjunct I hired—he and Johna Adams."

"Correct," said the policewoman.

"Does Moore still teach at OVC?"

"Three scheduled fall classes," read Zorn from her phone. "One a night class. Johna Adams was killed after a night class."

"Adjuncts often teach night classes, which most full-time faculty want no part of," Digger said, and then he added, "After a night class? Do you, or did we, suspect a student?"

"You mentioned one student, a boy named Twitch, actually Michael Whitman, but not as a suspect." *Twitch?* "This Twitch talked to you about the second murder at a time when certain information was not divulged, and apparently Twitch had received it from one of your colleagues."

Nothing made much sense to the composition instructor, and the name 'Twitch' held no memories. It was extremely odd to be given notes that he had supplied but could not remember in the tiniest detail, not even a vapor of a memory.

"I just can't remember!" he said at last. "Anything! Twitch? That's a strange name. Everything's strange." His biceps, what was left of them, rippled and froze, and Digger grit his teeth.

After a few seconds that seemed like minutes, he could talk. "Detective Zorn, do *you* have any suspects?"

Still seated, the policewoman paused, no doubt determining what information to disclose. "So far," she said, "the perpetrator has been very lucky. No useful forensics at any of the three crime scenes. At Johna Adams,' too much trash strewn about, at Valerie Walt's, too clean, and no fingerprints at your own home except yours."

"The bullet," he said. "Still in my head, but is it needed? Would it help you to find the killer?"

"Probably not," said Zorn. "If a similar bullet had been matched to a previous crime and if the gun were in fact registered, then, of course, it could help quite a bit. But the doctors tell us that it cannot be removed."

"Detective Zorn, the murders have stopped, right? I mean, it's now been, how long, since the last actual killing, close to two years?"

"Two years," said the woman, adding, "September for Adams, December for Walt."

"So could the murderer have gone away, left town, got out of Dodge? And have you discovered any OVC employees who have recently left the school, since last December, or the one before that, I mean?"

Zorn nodded, sort of bobbed her head. She found her phone again and typed away at it, several clicks. "William Jacobs," she said.

*Bill!* Digger said nothing, gave nothing away, but he thought of his long-time colleague, bearded and angry, a suspect in Tobias' and Dan Pinsky's stabbings, a person whom Digger had named to the cops, to Detective Doyle, that little big man. But Digger had been wrong back then, wrong to suspect Bill. Could he be right now? How had Bill reacted to Digger's book, its pending publication? He couldn't remember. Yet Bill Jacobs did seem the type to be resentful, reserved (at times), even jealous, a green-eyed monster. Could Bill have been jealous enough to kill?

"You know for a fact that Bill has left Ocean View College, that he retired?"

"He retired," said the policewoman, adding as she rose "Please contact us, Professor Diggerson, if you remember anything."

"I will."

After the policewoman left, Digger wondered what her first name was and thought about all those named suspects. Despite the dark past and current muscle pain, he slipped into the peace of sleep.

And September passed, all those long days, Digger's muscles getting used to exertion, his stomach accustomed to more and more food. His face had definitely started to un-hollow, so much so that Digger no longer avoided the mirror when he stood to brush his teeth in the corridor's common bathroom. He still felt absurdly skinny though, and whenever Anna came (on weekends), he made sure to roll down his long sleeves. "I look like the Ghost of Christmas Yet to Come," he would tell her, and she would respond, "You look great, Matt."

With a walker, then crutches, then one stick, then a simple cane, the professor took long walks around the grounds of Breezy Seas Rehabilitation Center, and he reveled in the still-warm days, the full green foliage—a month yet from turning—and the occasional cold but soft winds that whispered "fall." Near the month's end, on yet another glorious New England early-autumn afternoon, Digger heard a honking from above and located a dozen fleeing geese. The flying 'V' passed right above him, quite low to the earth, too, as though the birds were avoiding radar, and he watched the 'V' flatten as the flock receded. They seemed to be going east, not south, and as usual the flying 'V' made Digger think that the animals were dragging something across the sky within their formation, but what? Did birds have hopes, dreams? Were they simply honking and flapping due to instinct, to sparks sent forward in time through DNA? The geese appeared so meaningful, a community joined by the dreams of a warm future, of an empty beach and soft sands, of *home*.

And his own dreams? Anna, of course. Anna and maybe Snodo,

definitely Snodo, too. Too bad that Shyla had run off, disappearing after her sister. Maybe more cats would appear on their porch. *Theirs!* Anna had not talked about moving back, and Digger had not mentioned it. He was simply existing, and he pictured those fat seals that seemed to do nothing but lay about all day in the sun. True, he was a very skinny seal, and the waters beyond the sun held great white sharks. No matter, not now.

Since 'September' meant school, the beginning of the fall semester, Professor Matthew Diggerson did feel a tinge of guilt about lying in bed and wandering aimlessly beneath the sun and soon-to-fall leaves, but not much. He planned to contact Eliot before long about spring courses, maybe just two of them to start, perhaps just one—and not a morning class either! *Eliot Gladstone, a killer?* He had replaced Digger as chair, but that meant nothing. Eliot had never been the chair; it had been his time for that responsibility.

*Anna, Anna.* Digger's mind returned continually to his ex-wife, who had stolen his heart long ago and then left without giving it back. For nearly a decade, he had lived on the scraps of a heart, until a killer he *could* remember, Paul Smith, had tried to take even that pitiful, tattered organ, an attempt that had backfired on Mr. Morbid, for Digger had discovered a will to live, a strength buoyed by memories of Anna and the frenzied barking of Simba. Simba. *My lion dog.* Gone. Digger pictured her grave often, despite the fact that he could remember nothing of the dog's euthanasia. Simba, in his backyard, near the blue spruce, its arms thin like Digger's own, the bird feeder empty, the heavens motionless.

On one weekend in late September, weeks after Digger's muscles had unlocked and stopped spasming, Anna announced those dreaded words that "they had to talk," and Digger's mind seemed to contract into a repeated cry of "Not again! Not again! Not again!" But what she needed to say involved her, not him, for she tried to justify her leaving all those years ago, almost two decades now, saying that she had done so to see if she could do so, to survive on her own, to grow, to find something within herself, some confidence or purpose that had been taken from her as a little girl, or perhaps simply had not been implanted in her then by a gone-away father and a selfish mother. Anna told him that she had been drawn to art in order to find herself, that painting and taking art-education courses had been a path not taken, one that needed to be trod, that needed to be walked alone.

While he had wanted to say "Why?" again and again, Digger did not interrupt his somewhat stumbling ex-wife, and he had tried to understand, to not be at all critical even though he yearned to yell that he would have walked with her on any path. "I guess that when we're young," he said when Anna had finished or seemed to, "we try to understand everything, and especially ourselves, and then when we're middle-aged, we try just to survive."

"And when we're old?" Anna asked.

"Who knows! I guess we'll find out, Anna."

"Hopefully, when we *are* old, we'll understand, and we won't have to struggle just to survive."

Digger laughed then and said, "I *am* old, Anna! Apparently I turned fifty last year and didn't even know it!"

Anna didn't laugh, looked pensive instead, and Digger waited. "I suppose I'm old, too, Matt," she said, looking from wherever her mind had been and back into his eyes, "because I'm beginning to understand."

At that assertion, Matthew Diggerson wanted to ask "What? Understand what?" Yet he swallowed the question, smiled at the woman, who seemed so small and so incredibly beautiful, and allowed silence to settle and comfort. He thought that he knew what Anna had meant, and feeling exactly the same way, he responded in a silence born by love and just a touch of fear. He did not want to learn if her answer differed from his own.

# Chapter Four:  Logos

The third point on the rhetorical triangle, logos, means logic—i.e., clear, valid points and unbiased, relevant evidence supporting those claims. However, a dark side of this appeal exists, fallacies in logic, best described as twisted reasoning, trickery, manipulative tactics. To understand rhetoric, you must know logical fallacies.

Diggerson had looked dead. What with that little hole in his head, the blood, the flung back arms, the echoing silence. The sound of his father's 22 had still echoed thinly around his colleague's living room, trying to find a way out of the little house, an escape. The white dog had run off at the gun's bark, but it had come back before the shot's echo merged into silence. He could see its white snout peeking around the door to the kitchen, its eyes big, brown, and blazing. Condemning. *Let Snodo out.* Diggerson's last words.

And he had. He had been a man of his words, nobody could dispute that! The little white rat fairly shot out the back door after he had cracked it open. *The neighbors?* One peek out the side window had told him that they were no obstacle since the side of the house next door was dark, had been dark. The dog was in the fenced-in backyard, no doubt dancing a jig to the moon with that wacky black cat. He had had to admit to himself that the cat scared him, seeming to be more than just a feral feline. Still, he was a full-grown man, a professor, a powerful taker-of-life, and with those mantras in mind, Eliot Gladstone had slipped out Diggerson's back door into a young night, looking back once to check that his peer's ghost was not following and then creeping across the unkempt patch of yard to the creaky gate, the sea grass, and then the beach.

While he had waited in the cottage, the stars had come out, and they blazed away above that night, which usually seemed so long ago and sometimes only yesterday.

Out on the beach, Eliot had stopped to listen to the winds playing about with the bay waters, poking them into the shore like a nasty cat. Somewhere someone had a flag out, and it was dinging continually. *Weren't you required to take those things down at night!* He had looked back at Diggerson's cottage and seen two dark shapes at the gate, maybe. They looked like bowling pins, but he had known what they were. That cat and dog, together, linked up now. Well, he had saved the dog, anyway. He had kept his word. Then the twin shadows had disappeared, or seemed to. He definitely needed glasses. Why put it off anymore. Pride, vanity. Why, his brother wore glasses, had for decades, and his father, too. *Good old dad!* That drunken bastard! Time for the youngest Gladstone to take a step into old age. Glen's glasses didn't look too bad, though, sort of stylish. They reminded him of John Lennon's. Amidst the darkness, under the stars, surrounded by ocean sounds and scents, Eliot Gladstone had decided to see the ophthalmologist *tomorrow.*

The stubby gun had made itself known, expanding and contracting. In the darkness, he had not been able to see the deadly little thing, his father's gun, one of them anyway. Glen had taken the others. His big brother loved guns, and like their dear old dad, he didn't mind an occasional scotch either. 'Glenlevit,' his father had called the boy, and the littler boy had thought for years that his brother's full name was that, Glenlevit, until years later he realized that his father had been partial to that brand of scotch and that he had been making a drunkard's joke. Everything was a joke to a drunkard, for a while anyway, and then everything was very serious. That's when you had to sneak away, when things got serious.

His father's stubby 22. *Thanks, Dad!* Out on the beach, the son had stood and felt the unsteady ground and thought about putting a bullet in his own head. Right in the temple, just like Digger's.

Then the cops might think that someone else had done the dirty deed, had killed both composition teachers, along with that earlier one, that woman, the adjunct. The other woman hadn't been a college professor, but what the hell! A little variety, a little *spice*. The bay's water beckoned, sinuous and thick and icy, too. *Come on in, Professor Gladstone!* The gun breathed into his palm. He had been holding it like a tennis ball, clutching it. It had grown so heavy in his hand, he remembered fearing that it was stuck there, that he would not be able to shake it loose.

And maybe the gun would crawl back! That thought had burrowed a hole into his brain. Maybe it wouldn't disappear at all. Who could know what the bay's bottom looked like? Would his revolver shake into deep silt like a starfish and vanish from human sight or squat knobbly like a damn crab on hard sand, ready to be snatched up by a police diver? Why could he never make up his damn mind! Back then, now, ever!

He had hurled the gun into the sea. He had meant to throw it further in, had heaved with all his might. But nothing was quite satisfying, nothing!

Diggerson *had* looked dead!

But he looked anything but deceased now, gallivanting about the grounds of the rehab center, the nursing home! Eliot had seen him exit the front door not ten minutes before, and now Diggerson was off somewhere behind the place, enjoying the sunny autumn day. Out in front, in the little parking area (reserved for whom, insignificant employees, the types with old cars, unappealing ones?), Eliot had found the perfect spot to watch and wait. Amidst the old-model sedans of moppers and cooks, his big SUV stood out, stood up, but who would really notice yet another SUV? Everybody had one now. Why, GM had even quit making sedans since nobody wanted them anymore. Gas prices were down again. *Not low enough for these moppers and cooks*, thought the OVC professor, grimacing at the white and tan and dark blue cars lined up along his. Where the hell was Diggerson!

Eliot hid behind his big, black SUV and his prescription sun glasses, which really did look like John Lennon's, those black circles. Both of these possessions made the man feel bigger, but he didn't need propping up anymore. He was Chair of Humanities now, the conjurer of schedules and fixer of problems, not that many people came to him with those, *thank god!* Why, he had even hired his own brother, a retired lawyer, as an adjunct even though Glen didn't act like a part-timer, didn't show that certain deference to the chair, still treating him like a little brother, actually, saying things better left unsaid around his colleagues, laughing at him. Ah, but that's what big brothers and fathers did, make fun. Eliot could *fire his ass* anytime he so desired, but he wouldn't. Glen would always be above him, that's just the way life was constructed, and they did have a bond.

Eliot had begun to write again, too, and he had to admit that Diggerson had played a role in that, Diggerson's Dream Board, where seemingly every composition teacher had added something: a poem, an editorial, a scholarly piece, a scene from a play, a summary for a book. His own *novel*, a psychological thriller, told from the perspective of the killer, a pillar of the community, a respected educator. Diggerson had told him once, "Write what you know," and he had been correct. *No doubt*, and now Eliot's tome was half completed, or maybe just a third, two murders anyway and a couple more to go. *Into the Fire*. Destined to be a best seller, much more popular than Diggerson's little mysteries about that Billy D Wilder fellow.

Why, Diggerson didn't even remember his second book, and that was a riot! After having visited his colleague last month, Eliot had had what the news related confirmed to him: his colleague remembered nothing of the shooting, had no idea that Eliot was to blame, didn't even remember who that Johna Adams lady was, let alone the whore from Stop 'n Shop. "You don't remember writing a second book?" Eliot had asked his skinny peer, who had looked like a holocaust survivor, and the dumb man had simply giggled, as though not remembering something like that had been of no consequence. Something like that! He had told Glen about the visit, and when Eliot related that Diggerson could not even remember writing a second book, Glen had said, "And you can't forget not writing a first!"

Glen was a bastard, no doubt, DNA slithering down from the family tree, but his older brother was a confidant, too, as well as a wise man. He understood things. During his visit with Diggerson, Eliot had talked about OVC, about hiring Glen, the retired lawyer, the logical angle of both jobs creating a link. "Somebody had to take over after you, uh, became unavailable," the newly bespectacled man had told his prone peer, who had giggled again and said, "I'm glad that you took over, Eliot, but it's a pretty precarious position. Tobias murdered eight years ago—or nine, or is it ten? I keep forgetting to add years to the date. Tobias's death and then mine almost. You might be safer being a first responder!" How damned skinny he had been, but how happy! Why so happy? "You seem pretty upbeat," Eliot had said to his victim, who had responded, "I am" and then, "I guess it's like when you first recover from a cold or the flu. You know, you're just so happy to feel good." Eliot never got sick, and he had said so to Diggerson, who had giggled.

Watching from his SUV, from behind his Beatles' prescription sun glasses, Eliot Gladstone thought about those damn giggles. Were they cause enough to finish off the inexplicable man? *Maybe.*

Somebody else popped out of the electronic front door of Breezy Seas: a man, and he headed straight for the little parking lot. Eliot picked up the newspaper and pretended to read. The damn thing had cost him two bucks. Two bucks for a newspaper! It wasn't half as long as a paper had been back when he had regularly read them, and the paper itself seemed different, harder but cheaper, the ink refusing to stay on the page. Eliot looked with disgust at words that now stretched across his palm, and he bent down to read, raising his chin to view the text through his bifocals, an action that he took unconsciously now. Little black words, something about a fire "that had started in the attic." Eliot Gladstone smiled at that, knowing that fires always started in the basement, down in the dark.

The man passed him without comment or concern and drove off in some piece of junk. He had looked like a janitor, Spanish too, so Eliot's conclusion about the parking lot was now supported with evidence. *Moppers and cooks!* He half crumpled the newspaper and cast it back to the passenger seat, rubbed his palms, watched for Diggerson. Maybe he had fallen on the path.

A car pulled into the spot vacated by the mopper, so Eliot snatched up the nasty paper again, pretended to study it, but his eyes behind the shaded circles swiveled to the newcomer, who drove a white sedan, of course. A pretty woman, recognizable, who? It couldn't be Diggerson's ex-wife, what was her name? Eliot had seen her once, long ago, approaching the Faculty Offices Building with her husband, newly full-time then and full of himself. Eliot had watched the happy couple and then closed his office door. Later, he had heard them chattering as they passed by, and then clucking some more as they left. This woman looked like the image in his memory, and wouldn't that be funny? So sad for poor Diggerson to see a woman who looked like the one who abandoned him. *Oh, Digger was in for a shock!*

The blond woman glanced his way as she passed but didn't slow down or say anything. She didn't look back at him as she headed the forty yards or so to the front doors, which soon parted like the Red Sea and swallowed her. Not for long, though, because then she appeared through the sliding doors again, looked both right and left, and then headed down the path taken twenty minutes before by Diggerson. Could she actually be looking for him? Oh, if only he could see that meeting!

*Wait!* There was Diggerson, walking pretty quickly and with hardly a limp toward the blond woman, and then they met and hugged. Quite a long hug at that. *My god!* Could that be Diggerson's run-away wife? No way, *no fair!* He had lost *that* woman, and what was lost could never be returned.

Arm in arm, the woman and Diggerson were returning to the building. The doors slid open and in they went. Gone but not forgotten. Eliot Gladstone shifted in his raised seat, thought about things, about actions taken and not taken, not for a long time now. *Into the Fire*. His protagonist could sit in a car like this—no, an SUV—and watch his next victim. He could even read a raggy newspaper like this as he waited—for what, though? Inspiration, a plan. Eliot sat and made some decisions, in light of the new facts.

Inside Breezy Seas Rehabilitation Center, Digger and Anna had just reached room 21.

"Just a little more rehab," said Digger, "and I can go back home. What I'll find, I'm not sure."

"What do you mean, no electricity and a fridge full of mold?"

"A fridge full of mold!" repeated the man. "Thanks for that image! No, I want to find memories of Simba, maybe her harness, her dog bowl, her chewy toys, her grave. I want to remember Simba. How can I mourn for an event I can't remember?"

"You don't mourn the event, Matt. You mourn the absence."

"I know all about that, Anna"

"Maybe you won't find a gross refrigerator," said Anna, but she didn't tell her ex why she was smiling, that in fact she had gone to 111 Cottage View repeatedly throughout September to clean out the fridge and get the place cleaned up, having hired a carpenter to fix the living room window. She had even had a quick conversation with the next-door neighbor (what was his name? Greg?), who looked confused (probably couldn't remember her) but glad about Matt's progress. He had said, "There's a big black cat that will be very happy to see him," but Anna did not see the creature out back. She loved cats. Going to the cottage was her secret, and she planned to accompany Matt home when the time came to surprise him with a clean, welcoming house.

"At least the gas and electricity should still be on, right? I mean, I pay my bills automatically, so nobody would shut anything off. I have direct deposit, too, and Eliot told me that OVC paid my salary all last year."

"Professor Happy Rock?"

"Your name, Anna. You remember! Even though you never even met him, right? Yeah, Professor Happy Rock was here a month or so ago and told me a lot about stuff I can't remember. Apparently, I had a bulletin board put up to showcase everybody's writing."

"Including your own!"

Digger giggled at that and then looked over to the narrow table against the wall, his eyes landing on two books, one cobalt blue, the other green. *His books! Composition Murder* and *Murderous Mistakes*. Billy D Wilder, and his dogs. Digger thought of Simba, of Snodo.

"I'd really like to get Snodo back, but that probably wouldn't be fair, would it? I'd have to find her, and would the pound even tell me who had adopted her? I doubt it. And Snodo was more self-reliant than Simba, who was stuck to me by a sort of desperate intensity and joy. My lion dog."

Anna stayed quiet, but she smiled inside, knowing that *yes indeed* the pound would tell him, just as it had her, about the dog that lived, about the old couple who had adopted Snodo. She knew because she had already contacted them. Had he known about all her efforts, Matt would have called her a 'Busy Little Bee.'

"Matt, you're really walking well now, and you look much, um, fatter!"

"My father's DNA will never allow me to get fat, but it's nice of you to notice my non-stick-like appearance."

"Wow, you were thin!"

"One of my high school friends, Joe Brown, I think, used to tell this joke about being skinny, something like 'If you were any skinnier, you'd fall through your sphincter and hang yourself.' Of course, he didn't use the word 'sphincter.'"

"I remember that joke."

"Who knew it was actually true!"

They sat quietly for a moment, thinking their separate thoughts, about jokes and old friends, about Digger's recent weight loss, his proximity to death. Then Anna looked at the wall and said, "You need a window. Can't you get a different room than this?"

"I keep thinking that I'll be out of here soon enough, so why take the time to move all my stuff." They laughed at that because Digger's 'stuff' consisted of his two books and a scattering of get-well cards. "Plus," he added, "I've grown to like my little den."

"I love that cobalt blue cover and that stormy water," said Anna, gazing over at Digger's propped-up books. "The Whirlpool, does that spot really exist?"

"It does," said Digger, "or so I've heard. I've never gone down to the shoreline off OVC, but students have told me about it. The jetty sticks right out into the bay, and supposedly the Whirlpool's right there, at the end, where the bay turns up and goes inland."

"But why a whirlpool? What makes it?"

"Currents, I guess. I'm going to go take a look at it one of these days. I'll take a trip to OVC to spark some memories. An entire year lost, more than a year! One colleague visited recently and said I was unhappy with everyone's response—or lack of response, he said—to my first book, but I don't remember that at all. Or writing the second, for that matter. And Simba, I remember that she had been growing distant, sort of separated from me, for she always was so close; we were always connected. She wouldn't take a step without looking to see that I would join her or lead her, and she was so happy with every step I took, so full of joy, but now she's gone, and I can't remember any path, or much of one, from my lion dog to her grave."

"Maybe that memory loss is a good thing."

*Maybe*. To forget a year of pain, he just had to give up another, via the coma, and forget another. Two lost years to avoid one painful one. The sort of a deal that only the Devil would make ("I will take away your sorrows for but years of your tomorrows!"), and Digger found himself thinking that he would take that deal without much thought at all, perhaps offering even more years for the lessening of past pains.

"Maybe," said Digger, "but it's vexing, too."

"Let's go to the cafeteria to get some food," replied Anna.

"Then we can come back and maybe read a bit."

"Read a bit? You're up to something, Anna. What is it?"

"Me?" she said, smiling.

What were they up to in there? In this paltry parking lot, he had sat out here for hours, *for what?* For some scraps of facts, evidence that added up to what? Should he kill Diggerson just because his wife seemed to be back (maybe a look-alike replacement)? Snuffing out the mystery writer, that old fire had gone out. Who cared about Diggerson's happiness? Let him write his little who-dun-its, forgotten tales almost at the moment of their birth. *Into the Fire! A novel!*

Beneath the dark circular sunglasses, Eliot Gladstone smiled with his lips, but the feeling wouldn't quite stick. He felt it dry up, evaporate. He was hungry and a bit sore, sitting in the same position for so long. He should leave right now, perhaps drop by later in the week to visit his old friend and colleague, just to see if any memories were surfacing or forming. At that moment, an old car caught his attention, and in his rearview mirror he saw it pass, a pale green Subaru, one of those little station wagons, and in it a couple of old people. Too old to be moppers or cooks. Eliot turned his head and watched the long little car pull into one of the few remaining spaces within the ignoble car park, right in the far corner. The old woman got out first, from the passenger side, and she had some rope in her hand. As the old man rose slowly from the driver's side, Eliot realized that his wife's rope was in fact a dog leash, and with a start he recognized the animal through the back window, a little white thing with big, dark, probing eyes, an intelligent looking creature. The dog he had saved. The puffy woman opened the back door, hooked Diggerson's dog to the leash, and let the lively thing hop down to the pavement. Eliot turned away, frozen in fear. Scared of a little dog! *How Glen would laugh and laugh!*

The trio was approaching, was behind his SUV, was passing alongside it. The old couple seemed to be concentrating on their direction, so Eliot chanced a glance to the left, catching the dog's attention. It stopped on the spot, staring at him, and the old couple halted, too. "C'mon, Snodo," coaxed the woman, but the damn white dog wouldn't budge, just stared up at Eliot with the unmistakable glare of recognition and loathing. *The dog loathed him!* "Snodo!" said the old man, as though accustomed to the animal's stubbornness, and that tone reached the frozen animal, who showed her teeth and growled, eyes still locked on the man in the dark SUV.

"I'm so sorry," said the old woman. "I can't imagine what's gotten hold of her. She's a very friendly dog."

"Snodo, come!" said the old man, and that broke its spell. Eliot half smiled at the woman, and the trio continued on their way, waddling up the sidewalk the way old people did, trying to avoid pains. Every dozen feet or so, though, the damn white dog stopped them and turned back, and Eliot was almost sure that he could see teeth and hear that low growl.

*New plan*, he thought as he started the vehicle and shifted it into reverse. Diggerson's safe for now, but *that dog must die.*

Lunch had been pretty tasty. Turkey and mashed potatoes and green beans. More like a dinner than a lunch, and Digger ate everything, including three rolls. "I love canned green beans," he had pronounced, his mouth full of them.

"You don't need to tell me," Anna had laughed. It had been a good lunch. Back in his windowless room, Anna seemed preoccupied, kept looking at her cell phone, at the *time*, Digger thought. The turkey had made him very sleepy.

"You can go, Anna," he said for the third time at least. "I need to nap anyway. Too much turkey."

"I'll stay until you rest," she said, but he was asleep almost before Anna finished the statement. *Golden slumbers*, his mind conjured as he drifted down. "Once there was a way," he sang or somebody did, "to get back home." To get back home, you had to sleep, but that wasn't true. He was getting there, getting back home in his waking world. *Golden slumbers!*

Digger dreamt. He was in a golden room and Anna was reading a book, his book, *Composition Murder*, and they had 'space in time,' as they always used to call those hours when work was done and time held no responsibilities. Light was coming from somewhere, maybe from Anna herself, and then Digger heard a scuffling, a scream, but the dream was still beautiful for the stark noise came from joy, and suddenly he felt his face being licked and licked, and wasn't this some dream! A wide warm tongue, like a washcloth, that left a tingling chill, almost like a nice breath mint, and Digger suddenly thought, "Snodo bubbles!" And then Digger was awake, and the beagle-sized dog was dancing on his chest and pummeling his face with that tongue and that cold black nose and cooing and making hooting noises, and Anna and a couple of old people were hopping about trying to get Snodo to calm down, but Digger was just laughing and saying, "Snodo! Snodo!" and then he was crying, weeping for his lost time with this incredible dog and for Simba, for that sweet hole in his heart, and crying too for happiness. *Weeping for joy*, that oxymoron.

Snodo's older sister, Simba had uttered basically one sound, a muffled "woof" asserting a happy agreement: "Yes, let's go for a walk!" or "Certainly, this morning's going to be a fine one!" or "Too true, it's time for a meal!" Snodo, on the other hand, had always created a grab-bag of noises to fit her moods: a series of sharp, deep double barks to announce the presence of an intruder (95% of the time being the mailman); a single higher bark of glee, such as when Digger was lowering her replenished food bowl to the floor; a repeated three-note, one-quarter series of low assertions ("raow, raow, raow") that signaled curious interest; and a soaring rise and fall showing unbridled and uncontrolled happiness, a sound that greeted Digger at the back door whenever he came home. However, her noise at Breezy Seas, as she snuffled and licked his face, was beyond any of these prior vocalizations: a guttural glee that rose and fell like storm-tossed waves, that peaked like lost hope found, that reached even higher like deferred dreams delivered. Down the hall in room after room, old gray heads cocked and rheumy eyes cleared, smiles forming, a last light of day breaking at last through a clouded sky going dark. At the foot of Digger's bed, the old couple looked in wonder at each other, the man's eyebrows rising, the woman's bunching together yet falling, for the brain behind them had already recognized and accepted loss.

"Snodo!" laughed Digger again, and then "How? What?" He simply didn't know what to say.

"Well, I guess she's your dog," said the old man, who then laughed at his own joke. The old woman looked at the happy dog and then shook her head.

"Yes," she said. "She's still your dog, Professor Diggerson. My name's Annie, and this is Len, and I'm very glad that we never changed Snodo's name. We love Tolkien, too."

"Annie's read all the books," said Len.

"We saw you on the news, of course," said Annie. "They always show your picture, your Ocean View faculty one, probably, because you look dressed up and very smart. Snodo saw you, this was a year ago at least, and she perked right up. The TV never interested her before, not even when that video showed dogs doing silly things, but your picture brought her right to attention. When the screen changed, Snodo just lay her head down and closed her eyes, and she wouldn't budge, didn't even perk her ears up to the word 'treat!' She seemed depressed for days. But then she became her happy self again. We've never seen a dog so full of life as Snodo."

"But how did you know I was here?" Snodo had lain flat upon his chest, her nose almost resting on Digger's chin, but she was far from quiet yet. Her chest still pushed noisy breaths into the room.

"She told us," said the old man, Len, pointing at Anna. Then he said, "This pretty lady. Anna here." *Anna here!*

"Anna," said Digger. "You've been busy!"

"Len and Annie couldn't have been nicer, and I loved Snodo on first sight, too."

"She took a real liking to Anna right away," said Annie, "so I should have known."

"Known what?" asked Digger, looking from the old couple, to Anna, and then into Snodo's eyes, their darkness lit by a thousand stars.

"That we would lose her," said Annie, and then she cried, absolutely bawled. Len and Anna each put a hand on the sobbing old woman's shoulders, where she had so much to bear at this moment, and even Snodo swiveled her head around to gaze at Annie and her great woe.

"Look," said Len. "Snodo doesn't want you to cry, Annie." That didn't help.

Twenty minutes later, the old couple left Breezy Seas, walking even more slowly and in silence toward their old Subaru.

"It's for the best, Annie. We could never have kept her after seeing her reaction."

"I wish we had never come," said the old woman.

"No, you don't, you don't wish that. You saw how Snodo reacted to that man, and you love her. You wouldn't want to stand between that."

"Yes I would!" said his wife, but both knew that she was just letting out some steam, some grief. When they drove from the grounds of Breezy Seas, neither noticed that the black SUV was gone nor mentioned the silent man who had made a happy dog growl.

# Chapter Five:  Exigency

This somewhat fancy (Latin) term basically means a motivated self-awareness, a need, an "emergency"—i.e., the reason an arguer decides to don armor and launch an attack. If an audience detects personal reasons, sometimes those will engender unity and fortify the debate while at others they will render the communication petty and narrow minded. An argument can be a fragile thing.

Each late October afternoon, as the sun gave into its fall and dropped below the horizon, room 21 at Breezy Seas Rehabilitation Center darkened despite its lack of a window since its now open door took in less and less light. Yet to Matthew Diggerson, sitting cross-legged in his narrow bed, the Crypt had never been brighter. With Anna sitting at the bed's base and Snodo's back-and-forth enthusiasm over the two humans, the room simply glowed.

"Look at Snodo's eyes," said the man. "Have you ever seen a dog with a deeper stare?"

The woman laughed. "It's actually a little unnerving!"

"Yeah, that's what I first felt at the pound when she willed me back to her cage. But those big eyes, they don't hold a cold stare of aggression. It's more of an open stare of wonder, full of stars, the whole spinning galaxy in those depths."

"You and your images, Matt!"

"The spinning earth. That's my usual one. They tell us that the earth's spinning, what, 96,000 miles an hour, or is it a second? Could something go that fast? They tell us stuff like that when we're young so that we take it for granted, so that we can't dispute it. All that spinning. It's the craziest science *fact* we ever learn."

"Not my favorite one!" Anna agreed.

"What if we were Australians? Would they tell us that we were standing upside down? Is that what they learn *down under*?"

"Doesn't seem likely. Think what it would do to a kid, to be told that they're living upside down."

"But what other conclusion could the little Aussies reach, Anna, when they see images of the earth? It has a top and a bottom, and they're on the bottom. Wouldn't they have to be upside down?"

"Matt, you worry about Australian kids but not about who shot you!"

"That seems less interesting." In fact, Digger almost could not care less who had shot him, for shadows simply had no chance when Anna was present. And now that Snodo was back, Digger felt in possession of Galadriel's vial of eternal light. He was living in Lothlorien. Yet one little worry kept knocking. Snodo was back, but he was still at Breezy Seas. He somehow doubted that the staff would approve of his roommate.

"You need to figure out who shot you, Matt," lectured Anna for the fifth or sixth time that day alone, as she had been urging since his coma awakening. "If not for you," she added manipulatively with a smile, "then for this little girl here, for Snodo."

Digger nodded, and as if on cue, Snodo swiveled her head and checked to see what Digger was up to, that he was still there. Then she turned back to Anna, who seemed to infatuate the white unicorn. Once again, Snodo began batting with her left arm at Anna's knee and then checking the woman's face for a response. Anna ruffled the white head.

"I can't get over that scruff of hair on her head," she said. "It goes right down her back, like a Mohawk."

Digger giggled. His insides felt all outside, but safe, warm, nice. He, Anna, and Snodo were all in a bubble. Only Simba was missing. "I'm going home," Digger suddenly realized and said aloud.

"Going home?" said Anna. "You mean back to the cottage?"

"I mean today, tonight, now. I'm going home with Snodo!"

"But, can you? I mean, you're still recuperating, and don't you need to sign out or something, some official release?"

"I'm not in prison, Anna, and this is America, land of the free to do whatever you want, and I want to go home, right now, in fact."

Snodo liked his tone. She had squiggled her body around to face him, her body releasing a drawn-out groan sigh. "You see," said Digger, "Snodo agrees. She's tired of this place after an hour, and what will Nurse Addie say when she comes in and sees Snodo? 'No dogs allowed,' that's what."

"I can take her, Matt, while you finish recuperating."

"I can finish at home, you know. I know what to do, and you can't take Snodo because of school. She'd be all alone while you were away. Think about how that would make her feel." Digger thought about how that last statement would make Anna feel and added, "It's nice of you to offer, but I can't be separated from my dog now."

"What about the old couple, Matt? They could keep her for a couple more weeks."

"No way, Anna! Remember that old woman's crumbling face when she left Snodo here? She'd keep her the next time, that Annie, so I have no choice but to go home, now."

"Let me go ask the nurse," said Anna, jumping up and exiting before Digger could say anything.

Digger's determination hardened as Snodo began to snore, sounding remarkably like a human, but when he eased from his cross-legged position off of the bed, her one visible eye opened, then slowly shut again. Digger took the three steps required to reach the set of drawers beneath the narrow table, glancing at his books as usual, yet the drawers revealed nothing but his keys and wallet. Not a bad start. Then he closed the door half way to reach the tiny closet behind it, finding enclosed just some sheets, another pair of white pajamas (like the ones he currently wore), and some slippers. He slipped into those, which would have to do. *Dressed for success at Breezy Seas*. Going back to the narrow side table, he gathered up his books and put them on the bed. "Look," he said to Snodo, and the white dog stretched out her snout to nose them, then lost interest. *The blessing of the nose.* Anna told him that she had read both books to him while he 'slept,' and Digger had read both to himself since his awakening, the "new" second one first. Quite an experience to flow through the one he could not remember, to not know what the next paragraph held.

Anna came back and said, somewhat ominously, "Nurse Addie's coming." *Uh-oh!*

"Let's make a run for it," laughed Digger. "Look, I found my keys and wallet, and these slippers. You can escort me out the door in my white suit." Anna's frown seemed to be hiding a smile.

Then Nurse Addie entered, talking. "What's this I hear about *leaving*, Professor, uh, Digger?"

"Nurse Addie, I *am* going home, now, soon, tonight, with my dog, and my ex-wife is taking me." When nobody said a thing to this, except for Snodo's making little cooing sounds at Nurse Addie, Digger added, "Thank you very much for all your help."

"*All our help* is not over, Digger! You're simply not ready. This is a real situation you're dealing with."

"Nurse Addie," lectured the teacher. "I know that my situation's 'real.' I have a bullet in my head, and what's more real than that? That could even be a cliché, you know? As real as a bullet in the head!" That made him giggle, but neither woman joined in.

"Matt!" said Anna.

"Professor Diggerson!" said the nurse, resorting to her comfort zone, formality. Both women had V's above their eyes, so Digger giggled a second time.

Snodo said nothing, for she had once again fallen asleep.

The troops arrived an hour later, in the form of old Doctor Sam, who repeated Nurse Addie's decree, just with less pathos: "Dese tings take time." However, the Indian doctor knew when he was beat, so he repeated past advice, which Digger wrote down or pretended to. Anna's little notebook was fast losing pages. Doctor

Sam advised Digger to eat lots of fish and eggs, lean proteins, to not neglect spinach and kale, complex carbohydrates, and to take extra vitamins E and D, antioxidants, to focus on salmon for vitamin D and sunflower oil for copper. He talked about the pain and various possibilities for reducing it, such as musculoskeletal manipulation to reduce nerve compression

"That cure sounds more painful than the disease," said Digger.

"Not bad," responded the good-natured man. "Very nice. We stretch your spine. And we have aquatic rehabilitation to replace weight bearing or even electrical stimulation."

"He won't like any of the electrical stuff," said Anna.

"Makes me think of Frankenstein," said Digger.

Doctor Sam laughed at that. "No monster," he said. Then he advised walking often since sunlight provided natural vitamin D and suggested that Digger continue with the anti-inflammatory drugs to reduce pain and the anabolic steroids for weight gain. "Must reduce steroids gradually," he warned.

During these instructions, Nurse Addie occasionally popped into the room, frowned at Digger, and left with no words spoken. Snodo mostly slept, but a few times, a big light-brown eye opened and an ear cocked, just to make sure she was missing no important information.

Doctor Sam was about done: "You will be fine, professor, back to yourself in no time. Already, you have added much weight, dat is good."

Nurse Addie appeared in the doorway, just her head and upper body, her feet firmly planted outside the door. "What about the police!" she declared and disappeared. Doctor Sam, Digger, and Anna looked at each other, and then they all laughed. Snodo cocked an ear, wagged a tail.

"If you need information or have trouble," said Doctor Sam, rising from the bedside chair, "you come back, yes?"

"Yes," smiled Digger, and then the smile sank through him and expanded because he realized that he was about to leave—with Anna, with Snodo! "Thank you," he said one last time to his doctor, who nodded and left. Digger wanted to shake hands but let the man go untouched.

Nurse Addie took his space in the room. "Well, I suppose you're leaving now," she said, and Digger thought that he saw a bit of a tear in one eye. "You be careful, Profe ... Digger. Don't forget that someone shot you!"

"As real as a bullet in your head," smiled Digger, adding, "Have you seen Ana, your Ana? Is she working today? I'd like to say goodbye to her."

"Oh, she's around here somewhere," grumbled the nurse, accustomed to complaining about aides.

"Maybe I'll see her on the way out," said Digger, getting up from the bed and causing Snodo to lift her head and then pop to her feet, wag her tail. "Ready, my Anna? I have my own private chauffeur," he said to the older woman.

"You're a lucky man," she responded.

"He bosses me around," said Anna.

"That's why she left me," said Digger, but he was smiling.

"Learn your lesson then, professor," said Nurse Addie, heading out the door again. "I'll look for my Ana."

"Ready?" asked Anna.

"Not much to take, is there?" Digger put his keys and wallet in the white pajamas pocket, held his two books and Anna's notebook, and helped Snodo to the floor with his other hand. "Ready, Snodo?" The white dog was patting the tiles as though playing bongos, making flapping sounds.

"She's doing a little jig," laughed Anna.

"A touch of the Irish," said Digger, and together they all walked down the hall. Digger looked right and left, but none of the other patients were awake enough to respond to his farewell waves. "They don't get to leave," he said to himself as much as to Anna.

Outside Ward C, in the square foyer that led to all three wards at Breezy Seas, Digger said so long to the security guard, Davino, and then heard a noise that might have been a word or a cleared throat. Ana Louisa Maria Consueala Cepatos was standing behind them.

"You are leaving?" she said.

"I am," smiled Digger. "I have my own beautiful nurse and my dog, too." Snodo took a few steps and began to sniff around Ana Cepatos' feet.

"She licked my foot!" said the young aide.

"You have been blessed!" said Digger, who then bent forward and hugged the human who had gone out of her way to talk to him during his long sleep.

"O-oh-o!" said Ana Louisa.

Ten minutes later, sunk into the passenger seat of Anna's white Honda (a newer version of the car Digger had once known), Matthew Diggerson saw "Cottage View" up on a pole where the road angled to the left, chasing the bay. It was unreal. *Anna, Snodo, going home.* He had defeated Time at last.

When she pulled into the driveway alongside his little house, Digger saw his black Toyota Yaris. "My car!" he said. "I'd forgotten all about it. I wonder if it will still start?" Anna thought that it would. His backyard didn't look so good, needed a mowing, but then Digger thought of Simba. She was out there, the lion dog, beneath the unkempt lawn, in the sandy soil. When he opened the car door, unhooked Snodo from her leash, and let her shoot off, the white canine darted from spot to spot out back, like a bee high on nectar, and then ended up at the gate, staring out toward the beach and the water. This was her place, too. Snodo gazed out at the distances—the sand, the bay, and maybe even the distant shores— paying no attention to Simba's grave. Apparently, the lion dog's scent was gone, but Digger saw where he had buried her since the ground was churned up even more than usual back against the fence, right in the middle. He would have to get a stone.

"Thanks for bringing me home, Anna. Do you want to come in? I'm sure you have stuff to do, and tomorrow's a teaching day, right? What day is it?"

"It's Sunday," laughed Anna, "and tomorrow *is* a teaching day, but I have some time. I'll see you home!"

Snodo wanted to get inside now. She had beamed from the gate to the back door without Digger's noticing. Digger fumbled with his keys. Inside, the air smelled a little stale, but not as bad as Digger had expected. Anna was smiling.

"Seems in good shape," said Digger, looking about the kitchen. "I don't remember cleaning it like this, but maybe I became more domestic during my forgotten year ... two years!"

Anna just smiled. Digger opened a cupboard and told his dog that she still had food. Still smelled good, looked okay. Then he picked up her water bowl and filled it from the tap. Snodo drank loudly.

"I'm afraid to look in the fridge," said Digger, but when he did, he cried, "Look at this, Anna! It's empty! Completely cleaned out. I thought I'd find layers of old food and mold. Who cleaned this out?"

"I did," said Anna, laughing. "I stole your keys weeks ago and came over here. Your neighbor saw me, and for a minute I thought he was going to call the police. I cleaned up the place, wasn't hard. It was basically clean anyway, but all the food had to go. Don't worry, I recycled what I could! And I got someone to fix your living-room window, too."

"My window? Oh, that's right. The cop said that whoever shot me broke in through a window."

He went into the living room, followed by Anna, followed by Snodo, who began to sniff about—at the couch, at a chew toy on the coffee table, at corners. *She's looking for Simba.*

"Snodo's looking for Simba," said Digger, and the two people watched the dog as she travelled through her memory scents before hopping up on the couch, doing the circle dance that preceded canine sleep, and then flopping down to rest. Digger stroked her head, flattening the dog's funny Mohawk, and placed his two books and Anna's notebook on the table.

"The cop said that I was shot on this couch, but I don't see any blood."

"I did do a little scrubbing," said Anna, "if you can believe that! The police left a bit of a mess."

"Thank you, Anna. Which window was broken, this side one? Looks good."

"I got help from Ocean View Hardware. I was going to get you a security system, too, but I thought you'd want to pick that out."

"Do you think I really need it now? If someone were still after me, wouldn't they just have done away with me at Breezy Seas? After all, I was out in the open, walking around, all this month."

"Better safe than sorry, right? And now you have this little girl to keep safe, too."

"Ah! You're using rhetoric, Anna, manipulation, pathos, my love for Snodo, if not concern for myself. Sneaky motivation!"

"When you're married to a writing teacher, you pick up some skills," laughed Anna, and then she told Digger what she had learned about security systems, all the new technology and choices. Mostly what he heard, though, was the word 'married.' Anna was astounded to learn that he owned no cell phone. "That will limit your choices," she said. "Oh, and the guy suggested that you get a motion-detector light out back. In fact, he persuaded me to get it installed, so you already have it. We just need to plug it in out back."

"Wow, Anna! I owe you a lot, some money, too."

"I really enjoyed my little surprise, and helping you these past months. I liked being needed, and I definitely don't want money, Matt."

"You're definitely needed, Anna," said Digger, but he stopped there, didn't trust himself to block the torrent of words that might pour out in support of that point.

"I do have to get back to the Cape tonight, Matt, but I'd like to stay until you get settled. We need some food, maybe some wine. Can you drink with those pills you're taking." Digger giggled at that, and the two slipped away from the sleeping dog and headed toward the back door.

"I'll start my car, hopefully, while you're gone and let the battery charge up. Where are you going for food?"

"What would you like?"

"Nothing that Doctor Sam recommended!" laughed Digger, adding, "Surprise me again, Anna."

The black Toyota Yaris started right up, after just a momentary small squeal, but that didn't surprise Digger much because the car had always been dependable and because the man couldn't remember losing an entire year—two, for that matter. He kept forgetting to add the coma year, focusing instead on the time lost when he had been actually living life, hiring adjuncts, picking up women at the grocery store, dodging a killer. None of it seemed real.

He let the car run and walked across the yard to the spot that looked like it might be Simba's grave. He would have to mow down these grass tufts and maybe even re-seed, or attempt it. The sandy soil wasn't conducive to a green lawn, and pesticides weren't allowed this close to the bay, or were they? Digger couldn't quite remember, but he wouldn't use pesticides anyway, not with dogs using the yard, *a dog.*

"Well, hello neighbor," came a voice. *Graham.* The man's head soon appeared over the six-foot fence dividing the two properties. *Up on his ladder.* "Digger. Donna and I saw on the news that you had *arisen.* We would have visited, but we weren't sure it was allowed."

"The cops were keeping everyone away, Graham," said Digger, even though that wasn't true. He was just giving his neighbor an out. "Apparently, somebody tried to kill me."

"The police thought I did it, some female cop, or that Donna had done it, out of jealousy or something. They grilled us but good, but you know, Digger, we never saw anything that night. Remember those swastikas?"

"*That* was a long, long time ago, those swastikas, but yeah, I remember them. I just don't remember the last year or so."

"Really? Nothing? You don't know who tried to kill you?"

"I don't remember any of it, any of those murders. I have a

bullet in my head."

"No kidding! Wow! Well, at least your car still starts. And you know what else? I saw a woman cleaning up your place a few weeks back. She had someone come in and fix your window. I would have done it, but I didn't want to tamper with evidence, you know?"

"I know."

"But what I wanted to say was that this woman, she reminded me of your ex-wife."

Digger giggled at that. Graham laughed, too. "What's the last thing you remember?" Everybody asked that question.

"I remember needing to hire two part-timers."

"Oh. You had another cat, you know? A big black one, but it left after you, uh, got shot."

"I had a cat?"

"A stray again, like those little black and white ones you had long ago, but this was a big one, big black head. I don't remember what you called it. Maybe 'Blacky.' It was a strange cat. Used to just sit at your gate and stare at your house." At that, both men looked at the back gate, which at their angles framed nothing but a square patch of sea grass and sand. "Maybe it will come back, now that you're here again."

"Did you see me bury Simba, my brown dog?"

"Yeah, Donna and I were sad about that. You were really shaken. You sat out with her body just like it was a wake. You had the vets come and put the dog down, right there in the middle of your yard, and later you buried her near the fence. We were worried about you, the way you were just sitting there, like you would never move. A storm had been coming. We thought you'd get caught out in the rain."

The two men talked, over the fence, the way that neighbors do, until Anna pulled back in behind the Yaris. She was holding one big brown bag and one smaller, thinner one, obviously a bottle. "Hello," Anna said to Graham.

"Well," said the neighbor. "I'd better get going, see what

Donna's up to, and let you two eat." Then he looked back at Anna and said, "I can see why Digger likes you. You look just like his ex-wife!"

Everybody laughed at that, Digger realizing that it would be a joke between Anna and him from now on, that she looked *just like* his ex-wife.

They ate at the kitchen table, spaghetti and eggplant with garlic bread and white wine (just one glass for Digger), and outside night fell, coaxing the stars to appear. Time had ceased to matter, but then Digger thought of his mother. He should give her a call. Anna said that it was his mother who had asked her to visit him, that Jean had been beside herself with worry and frustration that she couldn't go to him, that she could find nobody to take her, and that she had pleaded for Anna to help. "I had seen what happened on the news, of course," Anna told him, "and then I'd called your mother to find out what was happening. We talked repeatedly over this past year, and I remembered why I liked her, liked Jean. So different from my own mother."

"Deena," said Digger. "How is Deena?"

"The same," said Anna, "and that's both good and bad."

The two had had this conversation before, at Breezy Seas, but repeated conversations could be comforting, like re-reading a book or re-watching a TV series. Old friends.

"Do you miss not teaching?" Anna asked out of the blue.

"Not yet, really, but I will soon, I expect. I'll get cabin fever before too long, and you know that while I was in that coma I was apparently thinking about teaching! I told you about my new dual-assignments plan, right? I must miss teaching more than I even realize if I dream about it."

"I have a student this semester, at Cape Cod Tech, who paints nothing but nighttime starry skies. They're beautiful but cold, very chilly looking, and when I asked her why she loves those cold starlit skies, she said that they reminded her of her grandmother, who had died fairly recently. 'Why?' I asked, and she said that her grandmother had told her that stars made a night colder. 'Why?' I asked again, of course, and she said that her grandmother had said, 'Because they're dead.'"

Digger wasn't sure how to respond to this anecdote. "That's quite an uplifting tale," he decided to say, and they both laughed. Under the table, Snodo made a grumbling noise. She seemed to be catching up on lost sleep.

The two humans did some 'remember when' trading, laughing at the past, and suddenly Time was up. The microwave said 10:08. The other clock, over the sink, had read 2:46 the entire time.

"You know," said Digger. "I'm really happy to have you sitting here, to have Snodo snoring under the table, to have everything back. But I'm still a little sad because Simba's not here. Isn't that human nature, to have it *all* but have it not be *enough*?"

"From all that you've told me about Simba, I feel as though I knew her, and, of course, from what I've read. Billy D Wilder's two dogs, Belle and Holly, they're obviously Simba and Snodo, right?"

"Write what you know," said Digger.

Snodo rose up then, putting her front paws, her hands, on Digger's thighs, her hair plastered down by sleep. "Hello!" said Digger, and Snodo looked from his eyes to Anna's, to that strange woman who seemed so familiar, surrounded by the same light as 'her human,' the same warm tranquility.

"I'd better go, Matt. Classes in the morning."

"You have a long ride to the Cape. Are you awake enough? You could stay here, you know?"

"I'm wide awake. I'll be fine. I'll call this week and see you soon. Are you going to call Jean?"

"Too late tonight, but I'll call her in the morning. What about coffee? I guess I can go out for some."

Anna got up and went to the cupboard to the left of the sink, opened it. The shelves held some cans, one of them being a pound of coffee. "Welcome home!" she said.

"You, Anna, *are* an angel! Let me walk you to your car."

Snodo had wanted to go out, too, but it was too dark. Her white face appeared in the lower corner of the door.

"You should plug in that motion detector, Matt. I'd feel better if you did."

Digger found the chord and stuck it into the outside socket, lifting the cover first. The light blinded both humans. "Wow!" said Digger.

"That light definitely works," said Anna. "It should go off if anybody enters your backyard."

"Any killers, you mean!"

"Yes, any *killers*, Matt." The repeated word made both smile, but then drew two pairs of eyes toward the shadows beyond the light. Gradually, their pupils blossomed like a night flower, and at the same instant, both Diggersons saw the shape beyond the gate.

"Is that…" said Anna, "…a cat?"

They had both investigated but found nothing beyond the gate, and Anna had left for home soon after. Digger had waved to her from the driveway and then returned to his living room, followed by Snodo, his little white shadow. The dog hopped up on the couch, did her twirling dance, and flopped down. Digger smiled at his remaining friend and then closed his eyes, listened to the silence, an empty sound that for more than sixteen years had been so heavy, such a burden, especially those first eight before Paul Smith had tried to put him down but instead raised him up. It had happened again, too, right in this very room. Death had come and taken its shot, literally this time, and once again the result had swung strangely, leading to a great improvement in Matthew Diggerson's life. The silence was light now, just a flight of violins far off, no longer the drowning hammer of a thousand distant cellos.

Just one cello thrummed now. The Simba string. Her absence. Digger opened his eyes and then closed them again to find his lion dog, to hear her sweet single "woof" of communication, to see her mouth break open into that wide corgi smile. The dog could easily be in the bedroom, sprawled across the bed, just waiting, or perhaps laying like a cow on her chest and looking out the back door, or maybe sleeping beneath the kitchen table, dreaming of food and of him. One cello amidst all those dancing violins. Snodo had accepted her sister's absence already, but perhaps a dog's mind did not stretch so far, did not contain so many shadowed rooms, even for a hound as smart and aware as Snodo.

Digger walked slowly, but with no limp or hitch at all now, back to the kitchen, followed sleepily by his white shadow. The dog probably feared to lose him again. "I will never leave you," the bending man said into the sitting dog's face, and then he ruffled Snodo's hair, raised the Mohawk, and giggled, the noise awakening the animal, causing that bongo pitter-patter. Digger felt bigger than life, huge under the heavenly cover of the galaxy, so despite the late hour, he brewed a small pot of coffee, strong java (Breezy Seas had offered a weak brew!), and then ambled out to the back porch with his cup and pup to look and listen for Simba's presence. Would her essence lie closer to her bones?

Snodo bypassed that possibility and darted straight to the gate, igniting the motion detector, which cast a blinding light that took ten seconds or so to extinguish. Gradually, Snodo appeared, then the empty doorway to the beach, no cat. The black feline had vanished earlier when Digger and Anna, cooing, had approached the rickety opening, or maybe they had both imagined the creature. With Anna's being gone from the cottage, Simba from the known world, Digger felt both big and small under the dome of night, beneath the ever-present wind, the dinging of a neighbor's flagpole, the death twinkle of the tiny stars. His memories of burying Simba were as deep and unreachable as his beloved pet. It seemed inconceivable that Simba was buried out here and that a killer had crept across this yard with a gun. *Who?* Apparently, Digger had suspected various colleagues, once again, but what about his neighbors? Maybe Graham had blown a fuse, and what about that local kid who clacked around all day and night on his skateboard and under a hoodie? In fact, what about Anna, the ex-wife? She had returned, and weren't the two victims women known to Matthew Diggerson? Anna seemed like an obvious suspect, yet because the female cop had not mentioned her, Digger had clearly not suspected Anna back then—nor now! Stupid to tread that path! Had Anna wanted Digger back, he would have broken up with any other female on the planet, without so much as a pause.

Somebody, though, had wanted those two women dead and him as well. Was it just a coincidence? What did that even matter, the coincidence? Somebody wanted *him* dead, even if somebody else had dispatched the unfortunate women. Yet it did matter, Digger realized, for the truth was bound around that connection, wrapped logically in someone's mind. The women's killer was his own potential undoing.

As that fact dawned, the motion detector did too, igniting the shadows, sending a wave of sharp light down on the porch and away across the backyard. *Damn wind!* Cry wolf! The wind had set off the motion detector, nothing more. Maybe it could be tightened somehow, but he doubted it. Digger tried to screw the bulb in further, and when it wouldn't move to the right, he tried the left. As if on cue, the wind howled, and the bulb blazed right into Digger's face. *Damn thing!* He bent and blindly unplugged the chord. Much better. Without the light's violence, the night could settle in and rest, the stars sparkling. *Dead already.* That's what Anna's student's grandmother had said. Maybe so, but despite their demise, the stars still managed to cast their communicative light to the heavens and to the earth. *Not cold at all*, thought the newborn writing professor, alone in the poignant glow of the night. If the shadows hid a killer and provided free passage to his door, so be it. Matthew Diggerson was happy again, starlit, so what did death matter? And he was not alone anymore, either.

"Snodo! Do you see a cat?"

The white dog had turned at the sound of her name, but then she twisted back and resumed her vigil against the night and the beach and the entire endless dark. Her job was to protect this house, this yard, and this human. Instinct had immediately reminded her of this fact, and she was more than up to the job. Out there, out in the darkness, danger waited and watched—danger and that cat!

"C'mon, you nut! Let's go to bed."


Since his awakening, Digger had talked by phone to his mother dozens of times, but not from the harbor of his own home, so he especially enjoyed hearing her phone ring on the first morning back at the cottage. The phone rang four times. *Unusual.*

"Hello!" Jean Diggerson's voice finally cried across the wires. As usual, his mother sounded a little put off at having to answer the phone.

"Have you been out jogging?" Digger said, deflecting the anxiety of his mother's greeting.

"Oh, Matthew! Out jogging? Don't be ridiculous. I have not jogged for years, although I could certainly run quite quickly as a young girl. But how are you? Are you keeping up with your exercises?"

Jean Diggerson could transition from thought to thought like a computer, and this deft progression caused her son to giggle. The mother was no fan of this new response. "Matthew, as I have mentioned before, it's not polite to laugh like that.

"But I can't help that giggle, Mom. I woke up with it. It's a bullet-induced giggle." He had to suppress another release.

"Well, I don't know about that, but it certainly occurs at strange times. It makes you sound a little, well, deranged."

That word choice, of course, caused another eruption, but the conversation smoothed out soon. Jean Diggerson was not only a great talker, but a skilled listener, a rare combination. Most humans could use one of those head holes but not the other. Although his mother loved to complain and was certainly old enough to have collected a trunk full of negative topics, the eighty-three year-old woman also asked appropriate questions and clearly enjoyed hearing about other people's lives. *That's how she collected her data,* thought Jean Diggerson's son. She especially loved to hear about Digger's teaching and his writing, wanting to know all about

Yusef from Digger's first book, especially whether the characters were based on real people, and from the second book, she waxed poetic about Billy D Wilder's dogs. She chastised his scoundrel, the killer Ned Dunlap, and enjoyed hearing all about the fictional character's alter-ego, the very real Paul Smith.

"Oh, your father would have loved these books!" His mother had made that announcement almost as often as the declaration of her own age, yet the son didn't mind anymore. Matthew Diggerson was in a very good place now. Nothing bothered or worried him, even the potential of a gun-toting murderer creeping beyond his windows.

"Have the police learned *anything*?" she inquired, accenting the last word to show her attitude.

"Haven't heard from the cops."

"What are they *doing*?" Jean declared, again pounding on the final word. "But if you're not worried about who's trying to kill you, why should I be?"

"That's very logical, mother," said the son, waiting, waiting.

"Well, I am worried!" exclaimed the old woman. "I'm your mother, and it is a mother's right to worry about her children."

"Guess what? This kid's at *home* now."

"At *home*? You mean the doctors let you leave the hospital?"

"You mean Breezy Seas, the nursing home. But yeah, I'm home, back at the cottage."

"With Anna? Did she take you home? The doctors *said* you could go?"

"Yes, Mom, yes. The doctors signed off on everything. The whole team of them, so there's no need to contact Breezy Seas, and especially not Nurse Addie!"

"Oh, I liked her, Matthew. She and Anna, how often we talked while you were, uh, well, not awake."

"Anna brought me home last night, and guess what else!"

"I am almost afraid to guess, Matthew."

"Snodo's here, too! I'm here at home with Snodo!"

"Do you mean that your dog was there all this time, just

waiting? Who was feeding her? Anna told me that she was cleaning up your place for you, as a surprise, but she did not mention Snodo."

After Digger explained about the old couple and Anna's efforts, Jean Diggerson said, "Anna has certainly come through for us, Matthew, hasn't she?"

"She's been unbelievable, and it's almost as though the years have been sewn together, as though no time has passed at all. Except for Simba, of course."

"I will miss that dog. Simba. She was so loyal and happy. And *calm*. You still can't remember her passing or who shot you?"

"Nothing. A big dead zone there, my lost year."

"When will I get to see you? Can you drive?"

"I feel as though I could leap tall buildings, Mom, and I'm planning a visit early next month, before Thanksgiving, way before."

"That will be nice," responded Jean Diggerson, adding, "Bring Anna." With that, the conversation ended. After Digger hung up the phone, he giggled, the four notes having been hammering at him for release. His mother's anxiety was actually sort of humorous. As usual, attitude was everything.

# Chapter Six: Kairos

Timing is everything, right? Arguers must understand the rhetorical situation and strike while the iron's hot (lot of clichés here!). In other words, sometimes a persuader must wait until the audience (even an entire society) is ready to accept a change in attitude, a new way of looking at an issue. A mistimed argument is doomed to fail, so kairos (opportune timing) is essential.

November came, and its breezes plucked the leaves from the trees, saving some Maples for last, their leaves burning, turning, and falling, not unlike the lives of men, for that matter. Less impeded by furry branches, the winds whipped about, whispering of winter, causing beach walkers to duck heads into shoulders and to don woolen caps. In Matthew Diggerson's backyard, the accent blue spruce tree lost none of its color, but the winds agitated it, causing its branches to swing and poke at the air, as a man would swipe at a hidden mosquito. The chickadees returned, the blue jays remained, and the cardinals stood out even more, even the dark green females. The sparrows spent most of the time roosting in the arborvitae bushes, dreaming of Simba's fur clumps, no doubt.

On the back porch, the mysterious black Tom cat ate its food and kept watch, too, just like Snodo. Digger could already pet the cat now, having been doing so for weeks, first out at the gate, then halfway across the backyard, and now on the porch. "You'll be inside soon, Bumper," he had told the cat more than once. Two weeks past, he had named the golden-eyed cat, for it had pushed up against his hand as Digger leaned down to pet the big, black head, the size of a softball. "You like to bump, don't you?" he had said back in October, and in response the black cat had raised up on its back legs to push against Digger's hand, reminding the man of the brontosauruses in the first *Jurassic Park* movie. On the phone, he had told Anna about the name, which she applauded. Just this past weekend, the black cat had showed off his name with her, but Anna would not be able to visit again for a couple of weeks—too busy at Cape Cod Technical Institute with her art students and their projects.

Strange to be home all day in early November, not to be grading papers or tweaking lesson plans. Strange just to be. Out back, Bumper was now licking his paws clean after dinner, first one and then the other. The cat then turned those golden orbs on Digger, standing in the kitchen doorway, and blinked his thanks for the food and the camaraderie. Digger blinked back.

Cracking open the door, he said, "Want to come in, Bumper? It's a little cold out there. Winter's coming, you know?" From nowhere, Snodo appeared and slipped out the door, but Bumper had for weeks grown accustomed to the flurry that was the white dog, who always stopped respectfully short of the cat and simply nosed her. "You like Bumper, don't you, Snodo?" Digger said, watching the two fascinating animals. Snodo had run down the steps to pee in the yard and to scout about, a white flash in the shadows, making sure that no changes had occurred in her domain. Almost motionless, Bumper watched the dog and then turned back to Digger, and blinked. "C'mon, Bumper, come inside tonight. You'll like it in here." The cat turned back to the great outdoors and stared at Snodo, herself staring out the gate to the beach and the great waters, which were gray beneath this twilight and flecked with white, pecked at by the winds. Digger shivered, Snodo ambled back into the cottage, yet the black cat remained on the porch, undisturbed by the elements.

Digger called to the cat one more time. "Are you sure you don't want to come in, Bumper?" But in response, the cat simply sauntered down the steps and disappeared into the darkness of the yard. Maybe he had gone into the old dog crate behind the holly bushes. Digger looked up and saw that the stars were prominent, twinkling even. *Spirits in the material world.* Then he felt the winds fingering their way into the kitchen, so he closed the door, glad that the motion detector was not screaming its warning against nature.

Out on the beach, a tall shadow appeared, headed toward the back gate, but staying low, in the darker shadow of the dunes. A lurching black mass, unbalanced.

Diggerson was a creature of habit, same as all *creatures*, so he would let the dog out back around nine, just as the moon would launch itself free of the horizon and float skyward. Eliot Gladstone had seen this scene before, many times back then, having watched his peer's brown dog who had died and the little white bitch who soon would spill out the lighted doorway as though Heaven awaited, their frolicking joy a sad image to the shadowed man. Happy and stupid, canines. *Unhappy and stupid!* That's what dear old Dad used to say about clients. What would the old man say about his youngest son's nocturnal outings? "Don't get caught," probably, or more likely nothing but a snicker. The old man could snicker with the best of them, the worst. Snicker and sneer. Sounded like a Vaudeville team, an ugly pair of midgets. Glen could snicker and sneer, too. Armor and arms. Shields and weapons. *Meet the Gladstones!* Lawyers all but he. Staunch defenders of the law until five p.m. or so, until the door to the family estate closed, when the law began to morph and twist. W*hat memories!*

Diggerson's father had been a lawyer, too, if he remembered right. They had talked about that connection once, long ago, but listening wasn't one of Eliot's human strengths. And everything seemed *long ago*, twisted by time, until who knew what was true anymore? *This* was, crouched alone beneath the night on a beach, holding a club and planning to use it. Nothing was more real than *this*, the adrenaline, the power of being present, being the protagonist in one's own tale, a tragic hero, but still!

Had Diggerson's father also been a scotch aficionado? That 'old man' had perished in a car accident (right?), and was it not liquor that always lubricated those exits? Car accidents and domestic ones, such as accidental shootings, and Eliot thought of his brother, a chunk off the old block in many ways, but not a drinker, not much. Neither Gladstone boy had traveled that worn path. *Glen Gladstone.* All that separated a little brother from the great blue sky above, parentless for decades, just Glen, and he had not been around much either, not until now.

The little brother looked up and found a moonless night full of stars. Orion's Belt, easy to spot, and the Big Dipper, probably anyway. And *there* were the Seven Sisters, or at least five of them, a couple apparently having passed away, their lights extinguished. He could hear the wind repeatedly banging a flag line against its pole, the most common and haunting of seaside sounds. With some effort, he could also hear the little smackings of the sea against the shoreline, like a cat's licking. *Ugh!* Eliot had never liked cats, and none of them had ever rubbed itself against his long, hard legs, either, at least not more than once.

Lonely sounds, the wind and the water, but pleasant in a masochistic way. Even the stars seemed to hum a bit, almost beyond human hearing, but maybe that whine was just adrenaline racing about his veins. Energy pulsing. Sound traveled slower than light, that's why lightning always led the grumble of thunder, so mankind would not be able to hear the stars' lament until each speck flared out. Then the sound would fall from the heavens, from the total darkness. Eliot thought of that sound, brass or wind instruments? It would be terrible either way, but nourishing, too.

How alone and alive he felt under the speckled night sky and relentless ocean breezes. Not a bad loneliness, better than the feeling in a classroom surrounded by old teenagers or in a conference room amongst a circle of colleagues, each with nothing to say and too many words to say it. Diggerson wasn't so bad, though. Ironic. Diggerson was actually more likeable than the others, yet he had shot the man and killed off women who might have made him happy, and now he was planning to crack his remaining dog's skull and do what? Toss the furry thing into the bay. Repulsive and invigorating. What would his old colleague say, the great David Reed Winslow, David Two Last Names, the star who blazed and fell so spectacularly? "Nothing really matters," probably. What else would someone who had *hanged* himself say? And what about dear old Dad, drink in hand? "The bastard deserves it," probably, for when the scotch level fell, the *bastards* always deserved it, and everybody was one.

Outside Diggerson's yard, the sea grass sprouted dead and spiky from the dunes, and that's where Eliot Gladstone sat and thought and waited for backdoor sounds. If the man came out, too, as he often used to do, then Eliot would simply return another night. He could even remember Diggerson's waving a flashlight through the darkness, and at first the pale ray of light seemed to be searching just for him, crouched below the dunes. But then he had realized that Diggerson had been worried not about himself and the presence of his doom, but about wild creatures that might hurt his dogs. One night, the man had even yelled to his hounds, "No skunks, Simba? All set, Snodo?" or something like that. Snodo was a hobbit's name, *that idiot, Diggerson*. To love fictional characters and dogs, what a pale life indeed.

Eliot raised his head up, like a periscope, and felt pain in both knees. The backyard remained shadowed and still, so Eliot lowered himself with a sigh. Was he getting too old for this sort of activity? Was the risk even worth it? What could the white dog do besides growl at him? It couldn't point a finger, couldn't put emotion into words. But Diggerson would bring it to work, and sooner or later he would wonder why the little bitch loved everyone but Eliot Gladstone. Tail wags for everyone but him. Eliot ran a hand up the little baseball bat cradled beneath his coat. So smooth and cold and strong. It gave the crouching man strength and purpose. With just one clonk, women were useless, mere rag dolls, so why balk at a little dog?

That was the plan, to listen for the canine, to see that it was alone in the yard, to sneak up and open the gate, to coax the animal into the dunes, and then to complete the bonking. That would do the job, no doubt, but then he would have to hurry away with the body, toss it into the waters way down the beach near the parking area, and then simply drive away, leaving that smug bastard to come out calling the dog, happily at first and then with more and more anxiety. He pictured Diggerson's finding the gate open and searching the beach, calling the dog's name and then losing hope, maybe finding the soggy white bundle in the waves, and crying, crying. *Wah! Wah!* The man would blame himself, of course, for leaving the gate open, and wouldn't that be satisfying?

"How did the dog get out of your yard? Oh, and why was the gate left open?" He would ask these questions of Diggerson one afternoon next semester, each interrogatory a knife to be inserted and twisted.

Eliot Gladstone listened to the night. *That damn flagpole!* Then he heard the bump and squeal of doors being opened, and the stalker rose on painful knees again to see Diggerson in the doorway's light and a flash of white in the yard. *The dog!* He noticed immediately that the back light, which had never extended beyond the little patch of sand and grass anyway, failed to ignite, and Eliot saw that as a sign that tonight was indeed the night. The night of Maxwell's silver hammer, and he swung the bat back and forth, like a grandfather clock's pendulum, the command of time. Diggerson remained in the doorway, watching through the half-closed opening, and Eliot realized that the cold breezes were another ally tonight. *Yes*, the silly, hobbit-loving man retreated, and the door closed. No head appeared in either kitchen window, either, so Diggerson must have returned to the spot that should have ended his life a year and a half ago. Eliot pictured the small living room and the couch, his peer splayed out, blood flowing.

He moved up the narrow path through the sea grass to the little gate, bent over a bit to hide his approach, but the dog had seen him anyway. Probably heard or even smelled him, *but not for long*. The white animal was poised barely ten feet away, almost within reach, and it had one paw raised to come even closer. Like one of those hunting hounds signaling a downed duck. Then the animal emitted a low growl, the same sound Eliot had heard outside Breezy Seas when the couple had brought the bitch back to Diggerson. It was a soft yet rumbling warning, and for a moment the low sound frightened the approaching man, made him freeze and listen. *The little bitch!* That's why the creature had to die! It couldn't stay quiet, and Diggerson would soon be bringing it to school, as he always did with his damn dogs, and somebody would say, "That cute dog sure doesn't like you, Eliot," and people would laugh and laugh, but then they would start to wonder why the dog growled *just* at him, that perhaps the dog remembered something, the stupid little beast!

The gate had a simple latch, and Eliot reached through the wire to push the lever up and release the hound, so to speak, keeping his eyes on the motionless animal, urging it not to bark, not to call its master but to come to *Him*, so the focused man was completely blindsided by the black fury that raced through the shadows, up the gate, and onto his head, which exploded suddenly in light and pain.

*The cat!* That strange black son-of-a-bitch was stuck to his head like a scab, clawing a chunk out, too, and Eliot Gladstone dropped his little club and rose up to rip the animal off. It was like one of those furry Russian gargantuan hats rimmed in barbed wire, and it wouldn't let go, just deepened its claws. *Auugh!* Then the beast detached itself as suddenly as it had pounced, and a staggering Eliot heard himself breathing and the dog barking, not growling now but full out howling, and it was time to *get out*. Son of a bitch!

He scrambled forward on knees and hands until he found his silver hammer, *couldn't leave that*, and then he turned and ran as quickly as the heavy sand allowed, ran for his life, ran without shame, through the knee pain, because only if a man lived could he fight another day. His father had said that, and Eliot could hear him now beyond the wind, laughing and telling his young son to *run*, and his shoes felt like cement in the sand but he was getting away. The flagpole line dinged and screamed, and his father's laughter was joined by Glen's. The Gladstone boys sure liked merriment. Not his mother, though, she never joined in. But she never *stopped* the fun, either, never did a damn thing.

Halfway down the beach, the youngest Gladstone stopped and gently touched his forehead, felt the sticky blood and pain. The dog was still barking, but it was muffled by distance now, by darkness, too, and Eliot searched the shadows for a panther, but found only himself. He touched his head again and then moved down the sloping beach to the shoreline, where he bent and cupped cold water into his hands. Splashing it into the pain, he felt the icy heat and the flared agony of the wound. Slightly salted, but that was good, painful but good. Cats carried all kinds of *poison* in their claws, that's what he had learned long ago, and that's why he had never been kind to cats, or at least that's what he had always told himself, even as a boy, when cats were easier prey than even him.

He searched the empty beach again. This cat was definitely not normal! Black and nasty! He would have to wash out his wounds carefully, with alcohol, and then do some replanning. All teachers were revisers, so Eliot had already accepted his failure, acknowledged the taunting from the other Gladstone men and from David Reed Winslow, too, that *talented bastard*, and the silence from his mother. Words could be armor but so could silence. Eliot knelt on painful knees and splashed more icy salt into his wounds, into the slashes. He would be scarred by this night, but what did that matter? What was one more scar?

On the couch, Digger listened to Snodo's barking and smiled at first. His little unicorn took her job as security quite seriously, with gusto! But then he noticed the urgency in the sound and thought about his neighbors, Graham and Donna, who would no doubt soon be searching out their upstairs window to discover yet more commotion in their *crazy neighbor's* backyard. Snodo's barking would get them up or keep them that way, so he raised himself— with no pain anymore—from the couch and looked out the backdoor. He saw what he expected, a white shape planted at the back gate but nothing else, no intruders. When he opened the door, he immediately felt the cool breezes push past, so he called Snodo right away. "C'mon, you nut! Let's go! Where's Bumper?"

The barking cut off but still echoed down the beach, and suddenly a black shape appeared on the porch. In the light spilling through the half-opened doorway, Digger saw golden eyes surveying his face, calmly, in peace. Bumper actually looked somewhat pleased with himself, and even when Snodo came racing up the steps and stood sniffing at the black cat, Bumper just sat motionless before turning his attention to the inquisitive white dog. "You see, Snodo. Bumper's a friend." Apparently finding no troubling scent, Snodo lost interest and then trotted through the door, and just as Digger was about to bid the feline a good night, Bumper moved forward, too. And that was the night that 111 Cottage Road became an even fuller home, richer, one filled with another layer of joys and dreams.

# Chapter Seven: Slippery Slope

As the name implies, this fallacy warns that taking one step will cause a person to "slip" to another less desirable one and then to another, falling helplessly down a "slope" to philosophical and usually societal oblivion. Nuts like to use this fallacy to brandish their Constitutional rights.

The drive to his childhood home took Digger three hours normally, but like a weekend hiker, he allowed repeated rest stops on this trip. The first, to an old but large cemetery off the rural highway connecting to Interstate 86, was for Snodo, a pee stop, but Digger stayed amongst the tombstones and trees for close to an hour, walking to rub out the cramps, closing his eyes for a power nap in the car. Fine with Snodo. Like Simba, the white tufted beagle liked just about all of Digger's actions and choices, except for bath time. In the muffled quiet of the rural graveyard, she simply curled up on the passenger seat and threw herself into more active dreams.

When Digger awoke, he stared at the forest for a few seconds, wondering where he was, but his memory hadn't been affected *that* much. Snodo was snoring softly and sweetly, but Digger could also hear the winds whistling almost silently, passing more easily than they had mere weeks before when with each breath the leaves would shake and shout. By mid-November, the breezes had swept off most of the trees' stylish garments, and to Digger the woods looked lovely, not too dark, and definitely deep, rolling away and disappearing as was the want for New England's forests, the land that obscured all horizons.

An hour later, he pulled off the exit into a McDonald's and

consumed a chicken sandwich, fries, and a Coke, enjoying especially the French fries and thinking happily of Anna's frown over "health food" such as this. He had a secret for her. Nobody knew it, not even his mother, a secret that he had kept for a dozen years, in part because the subject rarely arose since Digger ate nearly all meals alone—just with his dogs. The secret was that Matthew Diggerson had not eaten a mammal in over a decade. And while he knew that this decision, this spiritual act of sacrifice, had no doubt aided his arteries, health was not the motivating factor. Partly, it had been Simba, a mammal, smart and kind and loyal and loving, and if she could display such ethics, why not cows, pigs, and sheep? Mainly, though, he had said, "never again" after watching an afternoon showing of the classic movie *Silence of the Lambs*, or specifically the scene when Jodie Foster's FBI character told the monstrous Anthony Hopkins about hearing the lambs *screaming* as the farmer (was it her father?) slaughtered them. The ensuing 'silence.' Alone with Simba in his living room—probably it had been a January afternoon, winter break—Digger had been struck dumb by the scene, and his shock had not gone unnoticed by a previously slumbering Simba, who had sat up and stared at him, cocking her head to find the answers to her great friend's sudden anxiety. "Never again," Digger had said into the dog's open face. "I'm never again going to eat another mammal!" At that, Simba had wagged her tail and broken into her customary wide corgi grin, thinking that Digger had said something about a "walk." Snodo was like that, too. Like Eskimos with 'snow,' both dogs seemed to have many words for 'walk.'

Anna would soon enjoy this tale, which she would find hard to believe. While being a dedicated health nut, Anna knew that Digger had been raised on meat and potatoes, so she would shake her head and smile. Why was he waiting? One reason was simply that he had gotten used to telling no one. Digger had given up animal meat for himself, for ethics, for the cows and the environment, not so that he could preach and attempt to convert others to an anti-factory-farm cause. Also, he thought that the subject fit Christmas, the most spiritual of days, when he and Anna would have hours together (space in time) in the cottage, for they had made those plans already. "No expensive gifts!" Anna had declared, and he had reluctantly agreed. A book or two, maybe a Tony Hillerman one, and maybe a nice sweater, chocolates, but definitely no jewelry, not yet. Perhaps just a shiny bracelet.

He had asked her about accompanying him to his mother's house, of course, but she was still ensconced in Cape Cod Technical Institute's fall semester. Digger wondered, too, if such a trip, to his mother's no less, seemed too soon for Anna, too symbolic. *Meet my mother!* Jean and Anna had obviously met many times before and talked many times by phone recently, but now everything with Anna seemed new, fresh, recognizable yet exciting.

His *never-again* decision would show Anna that he was willing to change (if need be), that he was better than before. Maybe he would also tell his mother, for wouldn't that be a funny anecdote for Christmas? He knew what Jean Diggerson would say, one word: "Ridiculous!" Then she would embellish that judgment with something like, "No wonder all we ever eat when you come here is salmon!" Digger smiled as he drove, thinking of his mother's reaction. She was right, of course. For the past several years, Digger had cooked for his mother, turning the tables at last, and nearly every time he offered the same meal: salmon, a sweet potato (or maybe baked), and some vegetable, often asparagus. "You can't overcook salmon," he would always jokingly explain. Maybe during this trip he would tell his mother why they always ate like grizzly bears, but doing so would require some bravery. Jean Diggerson's son tried never to elicit a 'ridiculous' maternal response, because that word cut him too easily, opening a path to his black river, where he kept life's miseries and doubts submerged and hidden.

Since his birthday reawakening, that sluggish stream had really evaporated, sinking so far down that Digger rarely heard or felt even a gurgle. Maybe the bullet-releasing giggles now kept the black ooze from rising, or maybe it was his extended vacation, the lack of responsibilities, such as papers, lessons, meetings, advisees, and more meetings. But mostly it was Anna, her sweet glow, her golden aura. She had read his books to him as he slept and kissed his forehead as his face had grown gaunt. She had cared for him and prayed and loved him, cementing the link that most divorced men would have declared gladly broken, but that had instead nourished Matthew Diggerson for decades, providing a little flicker in the dark, a single star in the night sky, a link that Digger had never allowed his black waters to consume.

Only Simba's absence caused the river to erupt and rise, but Snodo helped in that regard, the canine angle. The white dog, too, had been connected to Simba, so Digger had no trouble seeing a brown shadow trailing his energetic, humorous Snodo, as the lion dog always had, never quite able to keep up with her younger, smaller, more athletic sister, but always trying, always smiling, her shepherd ears bouncing a bit, her corgi body see-sawing. How easy it still was to picture two dogs, not just one, especially when that *one* was a white bouncing blur, a being with energy to spare, enough for two dogs, especially when one was but a ghost.

"Has she calmed down at all?" Jean Diggerson had asked during their last phone conversation, for Snodo had always been a bit too active for an elderly woman. And because Snodo was not Simba. That's why his mother had asked the judgmental question, for other than he, nobody would mourn more for Simba than Matthew Diggerson's mother. He loved her for that, and more.

The usual three-hour trip had taken closer to five this time, but finally Digger exited I86 and connected before long with Connecticut's hidden gem, Route 8, and then went west again, passing little hills and quiet streams, house after house until he reached his childhood dwelling, set on the end of a cul-de-sac with little but an army of trees on three sides. Here, alone, his mother had lived for six decades, but she was not house-bound, not yet, not for years. Jean Diggerson was eighty-three, but she was feisty, the typical New England matriarch. She could call the plants by name and label a bird by just its sound. The seasons were friends, not obstacles, yet she still liked to complain about them—the cold, the heat, the rain, the "blah" of November, as she often referred to this month. His mother could make four negative announcements in a row, with nary a transition, but then end with this: "But we have to count our blessings, right?" To Digger, this house, this woman, was New England.

And he knew, too, where he would find her after entering through the side door (the front was mere ornamentation) into the kitchen: seated in the window at the big circular table, where once many had sat and ate and laughed and enjoyed being a family. Now Jean Diggerson sat with only memories and her one remaining cat, Rachel.

"Well! Here you are! And here's little Snodo. No, down, down, little girl!" Snodo was squiggling, squealing, and trying to jump into his mother's lap—or perhaps right through the elderly woman. Rachel the cat was nowhere to be seen.

"Down, Snodo. Come! Hi, Mom. Snodo's certainly happy to be here."

"That dog's happy to be anywhere, I suspect. Now, sit, Matthew. Tell me what's going on. Have the police found out anything about who shot you?"

"I'm happy to say that I have talked to no cops since they grilled me upon my reawakening, or maybe it was a little later. Things are still a little fuzzy."

"You still can't remember the last year, before your coma, I mean?"

"Nada, nothing. I have no idea who shot me. I can't even remember Simba's passing or writing my second book."

"Anna sent me a copy. I can't use a damn computer! Amazon! They seem to be selling the world, but I'm not connected. I'm eighty-three years old, you know!"

"Eighty-three years young," smiled Matthew Diggerson. "And you're not missing much by not having a computer. All I do is grade papers, answer emails, and check basketball sites about the

Celtics. That's fun, though, I have to admit."

"I wouldn't know the first thing to do, online. I'm so uneducated." Digger had heard this refrain before, and those repetitions carried on from one decade to the next, making his mother seem unchanged by time. Yet now Digger did see change. His mother's face revealed fine lines running parallel in many directions, out from the eyes, down from the mouth, all across the cheek even. Fine lines as though sketched by a talented artist illustrating a tired old woman. Anna could no doubt doodle such weariness. His mother's jaw stood out, too, as though operating on creaky hinges that wouldn't quite close, and Digger thought sadly of Jacob Marley, of the cloth rope tying his chin to his head. *She is old! As we age,* Digger thought, *our infrastructure begins to show, ribs and skull,* but he decided not to voice this realization.

"Mom, you're a reader, you read everything, and college is still mainly all about reading. You're probably the most educated person I know."

"Oh, you don't know everything, Matthew. Why, you always have to explain all those grammar rules to me. I don't know any of those."

On every trip, Digger had had this same basic conversation. Soon, mother and son would cover national events, and Jean would lament the sorry state of the country, the same as old people everywhere (they just disagreed on the sources of the "sorry state"), and then they would talk about her neighbors (their antics), about Digger's two aunts and one uncle, each a source of intense anxiety for his mother (and of deep comfort, too), and then about his book (books!), his teaching. While Jean Diggerson could command a conversation like no other, she was also a skilled listener, asking specific questions, nodding, really paying attention, and Digger did not take this interest for granted. He found it nowhere else in the world, except with Anna, always with Anna, and with Simba and Snodo, too, their sparkling eyes, cocked heads, wagging tails.

Much of the mother-son talk centered on Simba, on memories

and the disbelief that she was actually not present, not sleeping beneath the kitchen table, one of her favorite spots in the world. More than once during the three-day visit, Digger glanced beneath the table to find his lion, but the space remained empty. Snodo tended to sit at the table herself, up on a chair, where she would curl into a white ball and raise her head upon occasion, perhaps thinking that she had heard the word "walk" or maybe "dinner." With her head up and body hidden by the table, Snodo indeed resembled a meerkat. Emma, his long-gone sister, would have enjoyed that comparison. Not so strange that Digger felt closer to her and to his father here, where his world had begun.

Jean talked often of Anna, too, of her having "saved" the situation, of her effort and love. "Are you two seeing each other again?"

"We are," answered Digger.

"And does that mean that you two are in visual proximity of each other, or something more serious."

"More serious, Mom. You might say that we're 'dating.'"

"Well, that's fine. Your father would be very happy. Back when you two first met, you told us that you were just friends, but we knew better. We knew that Anna was different."

"Yes, it's like it was before, so *easy* with her. I have no shields up." Digger had once read that love was like a tempest, a rush of adrenaline, a knocking off of one's feet, imbalance, but for him with Anna it was just the opposite, not a hurricane's tumult, but its eye, a circle of peace and calm and wonder, of safety within the ring. With Anna, Digger had immediately felt at home, safe, as though he were by himself but with another, sharing the journey. He had read that twins often felt that same way, in tune, that after sharing the security of the womb for so long, they just extended that connection through the waking world. He had felt like that with Anna, right from the start and still did right now.

"Do you have shields up with me, Matthew, your mother? I would hate to think that."

"Just some little ones, Mom. I have to deflect all your age

references, and the word 'ridiculous,' too." He giggled.

"Well, I am eighty-three, you know, and I suppose I keep saying it so that I won't forget! And how can I *not* say 'ridiculous' when the whole world is just so, so, chaotic!"

Threads between family members interweave like this, thought Digger, creating and clearing paths, some bright with bird song, some dark, all meaningful to the conversants. His mother's cats had also peppered every conversation, but none of them had enjoyed Digger's visits since Snodo's arrival. Snodo had outlived all but one, and although Rachel was rarely seen during any of the three days, when she was, Digger tried to befriend the old but beautiful calico cat, Jean Diggerson's main topic of conversation.

"So pretty that I named her after Raquel Welch," she said, and although her son had heard this tale dozens of times, he just smiled and nodded. "But for some reason I kept calling her 'Rachel' instead of 'Raquel.' I suppose that 'Rachel' was easier to say. And then that name just stuck. If you call an animal one name for more than a week, it pretty much becomes that name."

"I wish she wouldn't run off whenever I'm here, or Snodo, that is."

"That little dog has such an intense stare. If I were Rachel's size, I would stay away, too. Usually, she sits here right in my lap, and we watch the birds. Occasionally, she sneaks out, but I don't trust these woods anymore, Matthew. Coyotes and foxes. Why, I even saw a bobcat recently, a beautiful creature."

Digger could remember foxes but not coyotes, not bobcats.

"It walked right across the yard, not more than ten yards away. Trotted, totally unafraid. The squirrels didn't appear again for hours."

"I'll bet." Digger could empathize with the squirrels because apparently he had been one (was one?), stalked by an unknown bobcat. It didn't seem real to him, though, and usually only late at night, when anxieties sometimes held their parties, did he think of the bullet at all. Because he had no memories of either murder victim, they troubled his sleep not at all, less than the killings on every newscast since those were 'real.' Even his mother admitted that his temple looked normal, that she would never have known that he had been shot. If not for his long coma, that shooting would have seemed as fictional to her as the two women's strangulations were to Digger.

More than once during his visit, Jean asked about her son's new cat. "He just appeared in your yard, Matthew? Cats used to do that around here, too, before the coyotes."

"My neighbor, Graham, says that Bumper was around during the time I can't remember, that lost year, so maybe he's not even a stray. Maybe he just likes my house better than his own. Graham's going to feed Bumper, too. I left him out back. He wouldn't want to be inside all day and night, alone."

His mentioning a 'neighbor' evoked the typical response of the Greens.

"Oh, Jan Green! She seems much happier now that Tom's gone, and I never see Karl or Kurt. She tells me how busy they are, of course. She'll probably be down here one of these afternoons. She just barges right in, whenever!"

Digger had grown up with both Karl and Kurt, and he remembered their mother, Jan, as a devout Catholic. Every Sunday, while Digger was out with his football or basketball, Karl and Kurt would stand around looking uncomfortable in their polished shoes and slicked back hair. Raised Protestant and none too devoutly, the little Digger couldn't comprehend his friends' once-a-week transformations.

"Did you know, Matthew, that Catholic masses used to be in Latin, all in Latin, so that the masses wouldn't know what was going on, so that they would stay in their place."

"Well, to be fair, Mom, I think *ritual* was and is part of most religions, and there must have been something soothing about all those Latin words. The romance languages flow so nicely."

"Ah, phooey! Jan says that nobody can fall asleep during mass because the congregation has to get up and down so much. She used to call going to church her 'Jane Fonda Workout.'"

Digger giggled. He had always liked his childhood friends' mother, even though 'Mrs. Green' had been sort of direct, for lack of a nicer word. "So going to church is physically healthy, too."

"Mumbo, jumbo! Church doesn't make a person good or ethical. I think Jan Green's glad that her husband's dead! Your father and I weren't like that. We liked each other's company."

"Dad always seems to be about here, doesn't he? He's just upstairs, taking a nap, or maybe downstairs, tinkering with some project."

"I talk to him every day, but don't tell Jan Green that your father's 'downstairs' or she will get symbolic about that. You like to get all symbolic, too, don't you?"

"Maybe I'm a closet Catholic."

"Oh, no, Matthew. You could never stand to wear shoes."

During this second-day conversation, Digger was startled to see flecks of white drifting down behind his mother. "Look!" he cried. "It's snowing!"

"Oh, God!" said his mother.

"Oh, boy!" said her son. The flakes were spaced out and gentle, each taking its own path to the earth, none encumbered or prodded by any winds. "It's beautiful!" said Digger.

"It's a big pain!" said Jean Diggerson, but then she conceded that the snowflakes were pretty but that she "wasn't quite ready" for winter.

"I love the first snowfall," said Digger. "It's always like this, too, so slow and peaceful, and it won't add up. You won't have to have *this* snow plowed."

"No, but it's coming, Matthew."

"I'm going to visit Dad's and Emma's graves today, so I hope it's still snowing. Do you want to come?"

"No, but you go. I'll stay right here, and you can tell me what your father and sister have to say."

"Simba used to love that cemetery, the prettiest one I've ever seen, with the big rolling hill and all the trees. Did you know that out west the tombstones are just plaques in the ground, all white squares in flat green or brown fields?"

"That doesn't sound very peaceful."

"No, but the skies at night, the stars, the sunsets, that's when you get the New England cemetery feeling. Depth and eternity."

"Now you're getting too symbolic, Matthew. Remember that I am not an educated woman."

The cemetery stretched out just a pair of miles from Digger's homestead, an easy walk when he was growing up, but, of course, he drove there now. A half hour after it had started, the snow turned off, the clouds traveled on, and sunshine actually reigned by the time Digger stood before his father's and sister's graves, side by side near the top of the hill. His father's stone was a bit larger, for it held two names, his mother's having decided to have hers added (the year of her birth and then a hyphen) when ordering her husband's stone. Digger wondered if his mother had felt strange seeing her name poised for eternity like this. Probably, she did not come here often. The slope itself provided an obstacle for any elderly person.

The sunlight created shadow shafts behind the two-foot tall stones, and Digger could almost see the dark lines moving, reaching, stretching out and up the hillside. Indeed, the sun set quickly in New England, for the hills made hiding easy. Digger knelt and put his hand out, touching the quarter-inch slots that announced his father's name, Robert Diggerson, a legacy to Time chiseled out of rock. The son ran his fingers along and into the tremendously small ravines, just wrinkles really, listening to the silence beneath his fingers, feeling the nothingness and urging it into something tangible. *Absurd!* What could be more of a dead end than a hole in a rock, two elements that led nowhere! Where are you? What happened that night? Can you hear me, hear Mom? Do you talk with Emma? But the holes did not whisper, for nothing, not even wind, could draw a syllable from the gray stone.

After saying goodbye to most of his immediate family, Digger walked down the hill, passing Tom Green's newer gravestone and pausing to say hello for a moment. Tom and his father were *still* neighbors.  Tom's stone announced just his name, though, not "Janet Green" and then a space for an ending.  Glancing back up the hill, Digger watched Snodo trotting down, her investigation afield apparently successfully completed. Above his dog, a solitary black bird (a left-behind starling?) zipped in a line across the sky, as though late to an appointment. In a distant tree atop the hill, a big maple or maybe an oak, a half dozen crows waited (for what?). *Crows and cemeteries.* Silence and timelessness. Was anything colder than a tombstone, a hillside of crooked teeth? No matter the time of year, even in August, even bathed in autumn sunlight, the stones were always cold, especially in November.

And in that moment, Matthew Diggerson realized, perhaps for the first time since his awakening, that someone, maybe a 'friend,' had tried to put him into that cold, that silence.

Driving back to his mother's house, beneath the now sunny skies (New England weather!), Digger had lost that dark reality once again, and not even his mother could resurrect it.

"All those students, Matthew. All the years. Do the police think that a student tried to kill you?"

"No, probably not. That would mean that a student killed those two women, neither of whom I can remember at all. The first one I actually hired, and she was killed after a night class, but I don't think that the cops considered a student. And apparently I never did either, because this one cop told me about my suspicions back then. I didn't suspect any student, just some of my own colleagues."

Was *that* true? Digger tried to remember what that cop Zorn had said, something about a student with a strange name, and then he remembered the surly George North, whom Digger had once suspected of killing Tobias Mann. But Digger decided to keep this information to himself. No need to add extra worries, extra wrinkles, to his mother's eighty-three-year-old brain.

"I remember, Matthew. You were not thrilled with your

colleagues' response to your book. You complained about their lack of interest. You were hurt, of course. Shame on them!"

"You know, Mom, I can't remember any of that, any of that hurt. It's like I have a clean slate. I wake up *without* any resentments and *with* Anna. With Anna and a giggle."

"Hmph, that giggle, Matthew. It is ridiculous. Oh, there it is again!"

"I'm going to giggle every time you say that word, Mom."

"Oh, oh, oh! Why are people always trying to *kill* you, Matthew?"

That change in topic elicited no giggle. Digger took a sip of coffee and grimaced because it was only lukewarm. Snodo's head popped up at that. The white beagle was curled up on a chair at the table, waiting for dinner probably.

"Paul Smith, several years ago, or I guess it's up to ten now, he wasn't really trying to kill me. Only after I figured out that he had murdered a couple people in our building. Tobias, the chair, and Dan Pinsky, the janitor. The cops suspect, and apparently I did, too, that this new killer's jealous—of my book, books, of my happiness."

"But whom could that be, Matthew? It would have to be someone close to you, don't you think?"

"Someone bitter, I would think. Someone who feels that life hasn't been fair, someone with a dream deferred. There's a poem that talks about dreams being *deferred*, and one reaction is an 'explosion.' Maybe that's what happened to this person."

"You know I like Robert Frost, Matthew."

"Well, then, think of this person as having taken the road less traveled, I guess."

"Do you think that they're still on that road, Matthew, that you are still in danger?"

"No, definitely not, Mom. No worries. All that stuff's behind me. Ahead is just sunshine and Snodo and Anna, and visits home, of course."

"Well, that sounds good, but you're not getting any younger, you know? You're fifty-one years old yourself."

"Are you sure? Last I recall, I wasn't even fifty."

"Don't be ridiculous, Matthew!"

After another day of such conversations, the topics looping, being re-examined and released, Digger began the long ride from his old home to his new one, but before leaving, he stopped just outside his mother's driveway to study the impressive stonewall built by his father (and by Tom Green on one side) back before Digger was even born. Time and New England winters had shaken the lines of stones, toppling many, squashing the wall in places. Digger pictured his father's holding each stone, placing every one carefully, and he vowed to fix up the wall next summer. Maybe then he would tell his mother about not eating mammals, too. By June, he would have more strength for the stones and for Jean Diggerson's reaction.

Only two stops were needed on the three-hour drive home, the sun eventually setting in his rearview mirror. Bumper appeared suddenly on the back porch as Digger unlocked the door, and without a word, the black cat slipped right past Digger to enter the cottage. "After you, Bumper," said Digger. Snodo entered last, having investigated the small backyard for any new smells and squatted briefly over a suspicious spot or two.

Once inside, Digger fed both pets and then stood at the sink with a Bud Light and watched the stars twinkle above the bay. He was tired but content. He thought of Anna and then of the time. The microwave announced 7:39, so he punched in her number on his wall-mounted landline. "It's me," he said into the phone. "I've survived another trip home!"

"Congratulations!" said his ex-wife, who asked about his mother and then said, "I've been online, Matt, researching coma victims, for one thing. Did you know that coma patients often remember a white tunnel? Did you see one of those?"

"No white tunnel memories for this coma patient. That sounds sort of like a white light, you know, a pathway to heaven."

"I thought so, too, but none of the people made that connection. Some said that they remembered feeling trapped in their bodies, and some mentioned feeling as though they were in another country. Isn't that odd? Did you feel that way?"

"No, Anna. I just remember waking up and feeling your presence. I was tired but basically happy. My muscles hurt."

"Online, coma patients said that they woke up confused and scared. They said that being in a coma wasn't restful at all."

"It was for me. I woke up with a giggle."

"You're not normal, Matt! Did you know that?"

"Who wants to be normal? You're not normal either, Anna. You're far better than normal."

Anna ignored this compliment and instead changed the topic. "I've also been looking up feral cats, how to determine their gender and whether or not they've been fixed. Is Bumper there?"

Digger looked down and saw that Bumper had finished her kibble. Snodo was nosing the cat's dish, but Bumper had disappeared.

"He, or maybe I should say 'she,' but I think it's 'he,' is here somewhere. There's something not normal about that cat, too. The way he appears and disappears."

"When you find him, flip him over and take a look," said Anna. "Apparently, testicles can disappear as a male cat ages, especially if they've been neutered. But you can still tell the gender. For males, if there's more than one inch between the anus and penis, then the cat's been neutered. You can identify gender, too. The urinary tract opening and anus are much closer for females"

"I have a ruler right in my kitchen drawer, Anna, so the next time you're visiting, have at it." Digger giggled.

"Funny man," said Anna. "Also, some vets will tattoo the cat's ear or even make a little clip. Are Bumper's ears uneven?"

"Not that I remember."

"The vet might tattoo the belly, too, so check for that when you check Bumper."

"This is a lot of information, Anna, so I might just wait for you when you come next. Before Christmas, I hope. Oh, no! I'm beginning to sound like my mother."

"Don't say that, Matt! I don't want us to become our mothers. But back to Bumper. I wrote all this stuff down, of course. Here, if the fur on Bumper's belly is short, then probably he was neutered, even if you can't see a tattoo. And does he pee in the house ever."

"Never, thank God!"

"If he sprayed in the house, that might suggest that he's not neutered, and how about the smell? Is it pungent?"

"Hmm? I'm not a very good pee detector. Maybe I'll leave that up to you, too. It's nice to have something to look forward to, isn't it?"

"If I'm going to be smelling urine and studying your cat's privates, you had better provide some nice wine and a great dinner."

"I can supply the wine anyway," laughed Digger.

"That will work," she replied and then changed the subject. "How's your motion detector working?"

Digger felt a little guilty when he answered, "Just as I always wanted."

"It still works? I like knowing that nobody can sneak up on you again."

Digger looked out at the darkness. He could just barely make out the gate that separated private from public space. The beach was completely shrouded on this moonless night. He would have to remember to plug the motion detector in again before Anna's next visit.

"Everything's beautiful," he concluded, and soon the two ex-spouses bid each other a sweet goodnight.

November passed, completely sweeping the trees of their colorful coats and the air of any summer memories, and Digger began to think of Ocean View College and of his new idea to pair assignments. Eliot had given him one afternoon professional writing class, three days per week, an easy shift back into work, and Digger was grateful to the Chair for that simple schedule. Last he remembered, Digger was himself the Humanities Chair, but he did not want that job now and did not resent Eliot's having it. With coffee and his computer, Digger set up his class' site by rewriting directions sheets and updating models and other materials. He would begin with two letters and logical fallacies, requiring that students read a piece (he chose an article by Rush Limbaugh and then a narrative essay by Doctor Richard Selzer), analyze the writer's use of fallacies in logic, and then write directly to the author to explain those fallacies. He would begin with Limbaugh since the reading was easier.

After this paired assignment, Digger would shift to reports, doing a couple on problems and solutions (involving lists of fictional employees), then a couple more on actual topics chosen by students. Each first paper in its pair would count as just 5 or 10% of the course grade, but each second would balloon to 15 or even 20% of the overall grade. Thus, the students would be more responsible for their grade: if they confronted their paragraphing and sentencing issues the second time (for each paired assignment), then they could really raise their grades. The theory sounded strong; soon Digger would discover the reality, but he was hopeful. He could not believe that it had taken decades and then a coma for him to think of this paired approach, which seemed to reflect the way that humans actually learned.

Besides working on his teaching, Digger spent more of that November with old friends, such as the novels of Tony Hillerman, the poignant characters of Jim Chee and Joe Leaphorn, the beautifully lonely setting of the desert southwest, the four corners region, all that space, the fullness within the emptiness. Late at night, alone, both Snodo and Bumper lost in their dreams, Digger would sit up and read about the Navaho cops' adventures. Outside, the November winds would begin to moan and sometimes to howl, and it was not unpleasant to dip his thoughts into loneliness and his own insignificance, into Simba's absence and the lack of emails from his colleagues (apparently, *nobody* was still reading his books).

Late at night, with heavy rain drumming on his roof and against his windows, Digger could feel his black river moving, for it was still there, despite Anna's return to his life. The black river would always be there, for death had been its builder and *it* always came calling, whispering, sometimes even walking in the "real" world. Maybe that's what old Catholics felt, alone with looming eternity and their own black rivers, rising, rising, lighting their little candles with wrinkly, trembling fingers. The fullness of faith and belief in a Holy payoff for an empty, dark, silent ending. Nights alone. A little white candle trembling, too, almost snuffed out but flickering back. Metaphors within metaphors. *Human life!* As simple as rain, as complex as the forces above squeezing water from the sky.

# Chapter Eight: Faulty Emotional Appeal

Children learn this fallacy before they even know how to magnify it through words since simple tears often get them what they want, and some adults never seem to grow out of this tactic, one devoid of reason (points or proof), a reliance on emotions alone. Note that when a person can make an audience feel guilt, the argument tends to be won.

On the somewhat long walk from the faculty parking lot to the Faculty Office Building, Digger expected some sort of greeting, but nobody noticed him. The students all seemed to be new, as though all whom the writing professor had known had been swept away, graduated and gone. Apparently, that was half true. Passing the Administration Building, Digger half hoped to see Doctor Powers, the LD Specialist, or maybe Don Domberg, the head of Tutorial Services. How long would his shovel beard be now? What about the administrator Omar Johns, who had gone on and on at Danny Jones' memorial? Forever in Digger's memories, that's where Omar Johns would be found. But nobody emerged from Admin except a flock of female students, happy in the circle of their traveling world, jabbering like the sparrows beneath Digger's bird feeder.

Above, the sun was shining cold, and hundreds of other small birds, possibly sparrows but probably starlings, were swirling and dancing about, turning the pale blue heavens into art. The birds made shapes, nets, as they shifted directions and swam through the air. Who was leading them? One bird must be orchestrating it all, but which and why? Digger stopped to watch the sky show, chin up, looking as though he were conversing with a higher being. He was. A blossom of confetti, blown into life and then into pieces, memories. Then the head of the flock raced northward, the rest madly following. Shoppers at a going-out-of-business sale. And the inevitable few left behind, racing one by one across the sky, desperate to find their place in the heavens. *That used to be me*, thought the stationary man. The left-behind starling.

Matthew Diggerson resumed his journey, passing the Psyche Building. What would he say if Professor William Watkins were suddenly to appear? When had he last seen the prickly professor? Ah, suddenly Digger had spotted a more inviting face! Diana Pell was on the path and heading his way. "Digger!" she said, and her smile blossomed with the word, taking a decade from the old woman's appearance.

"Diana! You look good. Ocean View looks good. I'm back!"

"It's great to see you outside your hospital bed, or that place, Breezy Seas."

"I left a couple months ago. I've just been home, getting stronger. I'll be back this spring, teaching just one course. Eliot gave me a great schedule!"

"He will, no doubt, *observe* your class, even though you're his peer. Eliot has been on a quest to stick his nose into everyone's classroom so that he can strengthen our teaching with his own dazzling observations."

As the Chair before his "accident," Digger had not done any classroom observations, but he thought that they were meant for part-timers, for adjuncts.

"Do you mean that Eliot is sitting in on *your* classes, Diana, on Jolie's and Lou's?"

"That's his plan, but so far he has just observed adjuncts, I think. He seems hesitant to enter some of our colleagues' classrooms, certainly mine anyway. I plan to scare him off with a scowl."

"I'll just make him part of the class, that's what I did back when I was a part-timer being observed."

"Good, Eliot will hate that! By the way, by the spring, your full-time status will be reinstated, one course or not. More than just a few of us have been fighting with the administration over you, you know!"

"I'm very grateful, Diana."

"It wasn't hard until this summer, before you awoke. For the first year, the pencil pushers were very loyal and agreeable, but when one year began to shift into two, they took some convincing. Quite frankly, if you had remained in that coma, they would have cut you off."

"I woke up just in time."

"I'm having a party in a couple weeks. In early December. I would have invited you via email, but since you're here, I'll do so directly. You are partially the cause of this party, that Dream Board of yours and my renewed writing. I'm publishing another book of poetry, Digger, called *Seasonings*, and I'm throwing a party for myself!"

"That's great, Diana. Congratulations! Where can I read the poems?"

"Oh, most are on the Dream Board, but I will get a copy for the library, too. And, of course, it's available on Amazon. What isn't?"

Digger thought about mentioning his own books being on Amazon, too, but he stopped that thought, saying instead, "I'm looking forward to seeing this Dream Board, which you told me about last August or September, I can't quite remember when you visited."

"August, but almost September. You still don't remember the last year, before your coma, I mean?"

"It's perplexing! In fact, I'm visiting OVC today to see if I can spark some memories. It would be nice to remember the poor woman who was killed, for one thing. I hired her, after all, so I should feel a little guilty about that, but I don't really. Maybe a little. Guilt likes to be felt."

"That just means that you're a New Englander, Digger, and I hardly remember the Adams woman either. I never really had a chance to know her. Now, I have to get going, but I will email you the details of my party. I don't think that you've ever been to my house."

"No, and good, Diana. Hey, can I bring a guest?"

"Your dogs are always welcome, Digger."

Digger giggled. "I actually know some people, Diana, not just dogs."

"Two legged or four, bring whomever you like."

Diana Pell walked off. She had been OVC's welcoming party for him, and Digger renewed his trip to the Faculty Office Building with a lighter heart. This was *home*, too.

From his office window, Eliot Gladstone watched Diana Pell leave the Faculty Offices Building and walk off on the upper path, toward the Admin Building. One of those idiots was coming the other way, too, and Eliot wondered if Diana and the administrator Omar Johns would stop to chat. *Everybody did.* The campus would be much more pleasant without all these people. He watched Diana and Johns slow and speak, but apparently neither had much to say because the great poet just kept going and the fat-head did the same, in opposite directions. Where was Omar Johns headed? *Anywhere but here!* Eliot pictured how that round head would look if he gave it a nice bonking. *Bang, bang!* Eliot's own head began a playful tilt right, left, right, left, leading the melody or letting it lead him, perhaps. *Bang, bang, Gladstone's little club comes down upon his head.*

In the window, had Omar Johns decided to look up, he would have seen that Eliot's round glasses, on left head tilts, caught the sun's fire and became shiny silver dollars, over and over, as the drum beats sounded and then flared away into darkness when the chair's head shifted to the right. *Bang, bang, Gladstone's little club made sure that he was dead.* Behind the fire and shadow, the long-time composition teacher watched Old Pumpkinhead scurry toward him but then veer off toward the water. *Good!* Then he saw Matthew Diggerson approaching, looking all around as though he were a high school student on a tour, or the king of the ball searching for the queen. Eliot's forehead began to itch, and he ran a bony hand across the three white lines there, each rimmed in red.

Time beckoned, his noon class, but if he left now, then he would run into Diggerson, have to say a few words. *Unless he took the stairs?* Diggerson would no doubt use the elevator after all his physical problems, so Eliot would just need to get down the corridor fairly quickly. He grabbed his workbag, passed by several closed doors and the one open one, the adjunct faculty office, noticing that somebody was in there but not caring who (since he knew it wasn't his second hire, Beverly), nodded to the big-haired secretary, and headed left down the stairs. *Safe!* Then he ran into Diggerson on the second stairwell.

"Eliot," said the former chair. "I thought you usually took the elevator."

"Diggerson," nodded the other. "I thought you were not scheduled until next semester."

Eliot's round glasses made Digger think of John Lennon and then of Harry Potter. Neither matched Eliot, who also had a little beard below his lip. What did people call those? *Soul patches.* Eliot had a soul. Digger reached out to one of his former suspects and shook his hand.

"Good to see you, Eliot, and thanks for giving me a nice spring schedule. One class will be a nice, smooth re-entry. I thought I'd just visit today, reacquaint myself."

"You look far better than when last I saw you, in that place." Eliot seemed to be searching for a spot on Digger's head. *Ah, the bullet hole.* Eliot's chest was going up and down, big breaths, making Digger think of his label for this odd man, the Breather.

"It's still in there," said Digger. "The bullet. The doctors were afraid to move it."

"When I heard that you were shot, I could not believe that anyone would shoot a composition professor. For what reason? A bad grade? Perhaps just a burglary? What did they steal? Do you still remember nothing?"

Both men were studying each other's heads. Eliot's sported a triple white line above his right eye, slightly red and raised, as though he had tousled with a tiger lately, a small but determined one.

"Nothing much, but what happened to your head, Eliot? That looks like a really nasty scratch!"

Eliot reached up and rubbed the spot again, but the lines remained. "The neighbor's cat, a vile thing. You can't trust cats. I tried to pick it up, and it went crazy. I should sue."

"The cat?" Digger giggled.

"The neighbors!" Eliot did not giggle or even smile. "You have dogs, don't you, not cats?"

"I have one dog and one cat, who has recently adopted me. She's a bit of a watch cat."

"Do not turn your back on that cat, trust me. Duplicitous. By the way, your office is as you left it. Others wanted that space, but we kept it for you."

"Thank you, Eliot. Diana told me how you fought with the administrators to keep me in the ranks."

"Administrators!" Eliot said, leaving not much unsaid in that one word. "Goodbye, Diggerson. I will see you next semester, unless of course you visit again."

Off he went, down the stairs, no doubt then turning left and taking the lower path, probably to the Classroom Building, where most of the writing classes were held. Digger watched the tall, thin man descend. Eliot could walk pretty fast for a guy who breathed so heavily, down a stairwell, no less. Digger thought of the Breather's scratched forehead and then of Bumper, who would never unfurl his claws like that. Would he?

Up the stairs, on the third floor, he found and greeted the Humanities Secretary, Gloria Swanson, seated behind her desk.

"Matthew Diggerson!" the gregarious woman cried, rising from her desk and giving Digger a hug. "Why, just look at you! You look good! A little thin perhaps, but quite colorful."

"Not my pale self, you mean?"

"Not at all, Digger. You seem to be glowing. You must be in love."

"Well, I just saw Eliot, and before him, Diana."

"I can't imagine Eliot Gladstone putting a glow on anyone, so it must have been Diana. What are you doing here?"

"I'm on my magical memory tour, but so far nothing magical has happened, at least in terms of remembering anything."

"What do you mean? What memories have you lost?"

"I lost a year in my coma and about a year of memories before it. Can you believe that?"

"You have no idea who shot you then? What about the adjunct who was killed? You must remember Johna Adams."

"Nothing, nada, zip! But maybe you can help. Let's check out Johna Adams' bio, if it's still on our site and if you have the time."

They went behind Gloria's desk, and she sat and typed in the school's Web address: OVC.edu. Shifting aerial pictures of the school appeared, no doubt taken with a drone.

"Wait," said Digger. "This is something new. I don't remember these aerial pictures on our site."

"We're forever improving the place," said Gloria sarcastically, but she was just joking. Gloria Swanson loved OVC.

Digger saw the drone's view of the Administration Building, then the library, and then one of the clock towers, closer up. They didn't show both towers, Digger thought, because the clocks were never synchronized, but he stayed silent. Then the bay was stressed, and Digger saw the spot that he had written about but never actually visited, what students called the Whirlpool, the camera's zooming in on the jetty from across the waters, a dramatic view.

"Ah, that's the Whirlpool," he said, adding "Have you ever gone out on that jetty, Gloria?"

"Once, and once was enough. Not a whole lot to hang onto out there. I'm surprised that the powers that be don't tear it down or build it up better." Then she said, "Ready?" and clicked on "Faculty" and then "Humanities." The Whirlpool vanished.

"I had my character, Yusef, be killed at the Whirlpool, in my first book."

"I can believe it."

Gloria scrolled past pictures and short paragraphs, biographies. Then she stopped on Johna Adams. Digger looked at the picture and then the name below it. "Looks like 'John-uh,' but the police told me that it was pronounced 'Joan-uh.' I wonder why she spelled it that way."

"She was sweet on you, Digger."

"Well, I don't know about that, but the cops have a theory around those lines, because of the other woman, the other victim, someone I guess I met at the grocery store, a Valerie something."

"Will you get your memory back? What's the last thing you remember?"

"Having to hire two adjuncts! And no, probably not, not with this bullet still in my head."

"That's awful! I didn't realize that it, uh, the bullet, was still in your head. I thought it had, I don't know, passed through."

"Whoever shot me used a 22. Wasn't strong enough to blast through, so it's still bouncing around in there."

Digger giggled, and then silence reigned as both people thought about the bullet.

"That bio of Johna," said Digger. "It doesn't spark a single memory. I just don't remember that woman."

"Was it the coma or getting shot? Your memory loss, I mean?"

"I'm pretty sure it was the bullet." Johna Adams' smiling photo seemed suddenly wrong. "This bio, shouldn't we take it down, I mean the administrators, maybe Omar Johns, maybe Eliot?"

"Oh, Eliot Gladstone should do a lot of things, Digger, but don't tell anyone I said that. I'm surprised he hasn't *observed* me and written up a report."

Digger giggled. "I won't, but why do you say that, just out of curiosity?" Digger thought of how he had told the woman cop about Eliot, about how he had suspected him.

"Eliot's been observing the adjuncts."

"No, I mean the part about him doing a lot, or should be doing a lot. Why do you say that?"

Gloria looked toward both corridors, right and left. Both were empty. "He's just not a good chair, puts things off, and hires strange people, too, like his brother. Have you met Glen? No, well prepare to get the creeps!"

"You know, Gloria, if we weren't so used to Eliot himself, he'd probably give us the creeps, too."

Gloria nodded and then laughed. "Even with that bullet, Digger, your brain's still working!" Gloria was scrolling down, photos of adjuncts sliding past. "Here he is," she whispered, glancing past Digger toward the Humanities hallway again, down which a decade ago a killer had stalked.

"Who?" whispered Digger. Subterfuge was catching.

"Eliot's brother, Glen. Take a look." The man did look like Eliot, sort of. He seemed older, a little gray, a sprinkling, but he had the same somewhat large head, the same round glasses, too.

"He's smiling," Digger said. "Other than that, he looks a lot like Eliot, especially with those round glasses, which Eliot now has, too."

"Glen's different that Eliot, bigger somehow, but that's no improvement. I probably should let you make up your own mind."

"I trust yours, Gloria." The two stared at the smiling, bespectacled Glen Gladstone, gone slightly gray. Gloria frowned.

"I can't remember how Johna Adams was killed. Was she shot, like you?"

"If something happened two years ago, I'm not the best person to ask, but this time I know the answer. After I woke up, the cops, a woman, came to see who shot me. She left disappointed, of course. She said that both victims had been strangled."

Gloria Swanson shuddered, and Digger realized that he had seen enough, that the photos had failed to illuminate the past.

"I'm going to check out my office, Gloria. Maybe I left some notes in there, something that will jog my memories, and I want to look at that Dream Board. Diana's told me all about it."

"That has been a big hit around here, Professor. I've been thinking of cleaning it up, but I don't want to remove anybody's work. Maybe I should send out an email about taking some stuff down. Let me know what you think."

"Okay, and thanks, Gloria, for your time here and your smiling face. I feel at home again."

The Humanities Secretary said that "it was" his home, and Digger smiled, turned away. None of this 'family' mentioned his books much. At all. He shook away that nagging thought.

From the end of the hallway, Digger could see the Dream Board right away. It looked thick even from a distance, and the writing instructor kept his eyes on it the whole way. Nobody else seemed to be present, all doors closed (even the adjunct faculty one), and Digger felt sad remembering how lifeless this corridor often felt. At least he remembered that! The Dream Board pulled him back into the more pleasing present, and maybe more boards should be added along the way, too. Yes, that's what was needed, not a clearing out of the Dream Board but its expansion. Maybe one board for poetry, one for short stories, et cetera. As usual, Matthew Diggerson was trying to solve problems.

Before examining the board, he turned his office doorknob and found it locked, as expected. Digger unlocked the door and peeked inside, finding no new memories there. The small space looked even cleaner than normal. He left the door open and went back to the Dream Board, reading "Share Your Dreams," which he had apparently typed, cut out, and pinned to the board, which was big: wider than he had expected, at least a yard wide and tall, square. The pins were red and blue and green and yellow, the colors adding to the board's appeal. His colleagues had been busy since three or four layers of work were displayed. As he dug through the pages, Digger thought of a tree's internal rings showing time's passage. Maybe he could locate his many hidden months in here? At the bottom, he found his two book covers, the cobalt blue *Composition Murder* and then the other book, the forgotten one, *Murderous Mistakes*, which was green with a gun-toting shadowy figure.

Unconsciously, the writing instructor rubbed his temple where the bullet had burrowed in and now slept.

The board, though, made him smile. He saw a handful of Diana Pell's poems, imagining each resting in her new book, and many songs by Jolie, too, and at least two editorials by Lou Knightly, and what looked like scholarly articles, one from the stately adjunct, John George, and another by Mary Bowens, the department's brainiest member. Todd Thomas had added what looked like an article about squirrels, and Digger wondered if mid-western squirrels were the same as New England ones (he would have to read the article, but not now). Eliot had added what looked like part of a novel, *Into the Fire*. Why hadn't he mentioned this? Maybe he had not finished the project, or maybe he had told Digger all about it during his lost year. Looked like just a few pages, though, far from finished, perhaps now forgotten.

Digger fingered his way through more layers. Drama, too, appeared on the board, one scene from someone named Jay Moore, and Digger dragged his mind to find that colleague, but no face materialized. Then he remembered the name from his talk with the cop. He had suspected this man of murder, Jay Moore, one of two adjuncts hired, Digger's last memory. He had hired two part-timers, one who would be killed and this guy. What had that cop, Detective Zorn, said about him, something odd? *A blinker!* Jay Moore was a blinker. What did that mean?

Beneath his second book's cover, Digger found a letter to the editor (to the *Gull's Call*, Ocean View College's monthly paper) about gun control (too much of it!) by Bill Jacobs, the part-timer who had given the school more years than even Digger had, but who had apparently retired without a ripple of recognition. Apparently, Digger had not suspected Bill—this time. He could remember telling the short cop, Doyle, about Bill after Tobias' murder. *Bill Jacobs*. Bitterness, pessimism, and a dry wit, hardly humor at all, really, and yet he missed the man. You could not share the same job with another person and periodically see him or her and not feel a sense of connection, of community. The man should have received a send-off, an email thanking him at the very least, yet Digger had seen no OVC emails about Bill that autumn. When full-time faculty and staff retired, the administrators opened the lounge in the Administration Building for a one-hour party, or they had an outside get-together such as the one for Gwena Schmidt. Gwena would have given Bill a party, but Eliot had not, and now it was too late. At this point, Bill Jacobs would no longer have access to OVC email, so that avenue was blocked. Maybe Digger could call him or perhaps send him a Christmas card. Gloria would have that information, but then Digger realized that he probably would not make the effort, that the time for connection had passed. Nothing mattered yet everything mattered. One of life's true juxtapositions.

"Digger!"

Jolie Matterson was moving purposely down the hall, all ninety pounds of her (perhaps that was an exaggeration). She was thin, that's for sure, and her hair was still short, as Digger remembered. "You've been writing songs, Jolie," said Digger.

"We need a bigger board because I have a couple more to add."

"I was thinking that we could add boards by genre, one for poems, one for songs, that sort of thing."

"Make it happen, Digger, now that you're back. Don't expect Eliot to do it."

Digger looked down the empty hall, reminding himself of Gloria's paranoia, and he thought about all the closed doors, which didn't necessarily mean that the rooms were empty. "You don't care for Eliot's managerial style?" he said quietly.

"He's more of a douche than usual," she replied in her normal voice, "but even more so. A douche with power. Did you know that he's doing classroom observations of full-timers? He went into Lou's class and then did a little write up of his opinions. What a douche! He's got that little fallen soul patch now, too, and have you seen his brother? They look like a pair of old pedophiles, a pair of bookends from the Adams Family mansion!"

Digger giggled, he couldn't help himself. "I wish that Eliot had emailed everyone about Bill Jacobs' retirement."

"Who?"

"You remember Bill, or maybe he was on an earlier schedule. Bill Jacobs, he had a beard and ..."

"Oh, yeah. That right-wing nut. He retired? Who knew?"

"Apparently nobody, and that's why I wish Eliot had communicated with us."

"You look good, not too thin. I'm really glad that you woke up, Digger!"

"Well, thank you, Jolie. I'm glad, too."

"You coming back this spring?"

"I am, but just one class. Eliot was good about that. Just one late afternoon class, professional writing."

"Eliot and 'good' in the same sentence! We'll have to agree to disagree, and I need to get going, Digger. I'll see you, glad you're back."

"I'll see you at Diana's party."

"What party's that? I haven't heard about it."

"She just told me about it an hour ago. She hasn't emailed us all yet, but she's going to have a party, a Christmas party." Digger thought that Diana should be the one to announce her new book, so he left that part out.

"Maybe she doesn't want lesbians to attend," smirked Jolie Matterson.

Digger giggled again. "Don't be stupid," he said good naturedly, wanting to say something witty, but nothing materialized.

Jolie stalked off up the hallway. Apparently, she had come down just to see him, not to dip into her office. *That was nice.* Before disappearing, though, she turned and yelled again. "If you see the janitor of this place, don't bother saying 'hello.' He's a surly bastard."

"A douche?" Digger yelled back, a little louder than he had intended.

"Oh, yeah! A douche," he heard through his own giggle.

With Jolie's absence, the corridor immediately seemed empty. Digger dipped into his open office and sat down. He still tired too easily, and his office chair felt nice. He spun around in it, enjoying the motion and the fact that this was *his* chair, *his* room. Outside his window, he saw that the clock towers both showed around five pm, two pale shadows reaching for the Faculty Offices Building, as usual. Digger remembered those extended shadows, but so far this trip had sparked no *new* old memories. Maybe he would walk the campus a bit, maybe even visit the Whirlpool to see if it was what he expected, to see if it fit his first book's scene involving poor Yusef, his fictional Danny Jones.

The hallway echoed silence, Gloria had left at least a half hour earlier, and the only soul Digger saw while leaving the building was the janitor, sweeping or more likely mopping down the hall on the first floor. Digger almost stopped to yell hello, especially since the janitor seemed familiar, even with his face turned away, but the composition teacher decided to just keep going, partly because of Jolie's parting comment. He realized that nobody—not Diana nor Eliot nor Gloria nor Jolie—had mentioned his books or asked if he were writing another, and that fact made the day a little darker.

On the lower path, the one Eliot must have taken earlier, students were making their way to the cafeteria, yet Digger recognized nobody. A couple said hello, and he wondered if they had been his students during the forgotten year. Maybe they thought him rude or a dope for not recognizing them, not calling them by name, but probably they were just being nice, greeting a teacher, an old guy. OVC students tended to be friendly. Soon, the students thinned, though, because he was sloping east, down to the bay, past the last of the residence halls. Why had he never come down this far? *Laziness, probably.* Digger reached a spot where the asphalt path turned back north but where a grassy dirt path led directly east, disappearing into a grove of stunted trees twenty yards away.

He took that path, passed through the little forest, and came out into another world, from civilization to the sea! Well, almost the sea, its throat anyway. The path became asphalt again for about five yards and then merged into a wooden jetty, which extended right out into the water.

Digger could see why Gloria Swanson had criticized the school for not making the jetty safer. He could picture drunk students toppling off into the water, but apparently none ever had. That's no doubt why the jetty had no safety railing, just some posts sticking up almost chest level every dozen feet or so. He walked out onto the jetty, kept walking. It was longer than he had expected. When he reached the abrupt end, he felt the winds, the wild of the water, saw the currents swirling and some lacy white froth. Digger felt goosebumps. A railing would definitely have helped, and he imagined Omar Johns standing out here. *No*, no administrator had ever stood out here, for if they had, then safety railings would definitely have been added.

Digger looked down and to the left at the water, at 'the Whirlpool,' the surface more turbulent, the waves churning in on themselves, and they made Digger think of a toilet, a flushing. He had the urge to throw something into the swirling mystery to see if it would be swallowed and wondered if students did just that, late at night, with empty beer cans and pizza boxes, using flashlights or just the moonlight to watch the waters eat.

Digger wished that Anna were standing here with him, the wind whipping her hair about. She would probably want to paint this scene, for he wanted to write about it. He was dumb for not having visited this spot before fictionalizing it because he realized how he could have personified the elements more thoroughly, the water, the wind, the gulls, the feeling of being above the earth and further from humanity. He turned to his right and gazed upon the towering Bay Bridge, the gateway to the Atlantic Ocean. The bridge looked even more gigantic from this low spot, this vulnerable angle, and he pictured Danny Jones way up there and then way down here. *The Bay Bridge.* He would cross that next. New memories could give rise to older ones, maybe push them to the surface.

The walk up from the Whirlpool to the faculty parking lot was fairly short, and again Digger lambasted himself for never having taken the effort to experience that scene. *Write about what you know.* Had he known more about that jetty's stark ending, about that hungry mouth in the water, he could have written a better chapter in *Composition Murder*. Well, he *knew* the Bay Bridge, or had known it. Before he could change his mind, he turned his Toyota Yaris south, not north to his cottage, and headed toward the bridge.

From this direction, the vast structure's ascent was longer and not as steep as the descent, making Digger think symbolically of life, especially of Danny Jones' short one. The quiet student would have been a middle-aged fellow today, still young, though, and Digger wondered what Danny would have done with the past seventeen years, where his footsteps would have led. Had Danny's little brother followed his older sibling's path to higher education, graduated, made his sad mother proud? A gust of wind took and shook the little car, bringing Digger back to his own trail, which was now the center of the Bay Bridge, just past the pylon that Danny had clung to, his last touch with earthly existence, a metal pole. That made Digger think of those poor little rhesus monkeys and their metal mothers (the psychological deprivation experiments), an image that stoked his coals repeatedly, that made his black river gurgle and expand, rise, but then the bridge's dip down snapped his attention back. *Pretty damn steep!* The winds grabbed more persistently on this side, seeming to not want Digger to proceed. This bridge was still a *monster*. Built by man, speckled with fairy lights, fitted with fencing, but never really tamed, the bridge growled and rolled, nuzzling the winds that frolicked and fought far above a sleeping humanity, lost in the distance and darkness below. Images were all!

Approaching the far side of the looming bridge, Digger greeted the fur trees, first their bony peeks, then the fuzzy middles, then the scruffy trunks, and with a simple left turn in the road, the winds ceased, and the Bay Bridge vanished behind him. Although Digger had left one ghost behind, he realized that he had not looked up at

Danny's pylon, that he still employed blinders, that sometimes ignorance was necessary.

Then he drove to Mario's, passing the Bayside Police Station and remembering his night inside, the friendly officers. All those old memories were easy to recall, yet his most recent year, the one before his awakening, remained shadowed. Frustrating! Digger empathized even more with Alzheimer's victims, and he thought of Gwena's husband, Richard Schmidt, slumped over and vacant in some nursing home, and Digger was glad that his mother still had her head on straight, even if her words could be a little sharp. Mario's was the same, and the pineapple pizza tasted so good, the fruit sweet, the sauce rich. Because the restaurant itself was too bright, the Formica tables too cold, Digger sat in his car to eat, listening to classic rock and sipping a coke. Anna would not have been pleased with this dinner, soda and cheese. Digger giggled. He decided not to tell her about it.

On his way home, the Bay Bridge let him pass unimpeded, the winds whistling elsewhere, perhaps down at the Whirlpool and up the throat of the bay, moving inland.

# Chapter Nine:  Ad Hominem Fallacies

Popular with politicians on the election trail, this fallacy tends to be personal—i.e., an attack on a person instead of his or her views. An ad hominem assault often comes with a side of generalizations, paired fallacies commonly occurring since illogic tends to attract like minds. How many right-wing spouses have left-leaning mates?

Digger was stuck, boxed in by the Gladstones. He looked about and saw more enjoyable colleagues in other conversational circles, no one available to rescue him. *Anna!* If only Anna had been able to come to Diana's party—or even Snodo. If he had brought Bumper, then Eliot probably would have shrunk back like a vampire beholding a cross. Digger giggled.

"Something amusing?" said Glen Gladstone. Both brothers were taller than average, with roundish heads and dark, short hair, going gray (especially Glen's), and both with little beards brushed across their chins. Eyes drooping to gravity, facial flesh, too, but not necks, both bony, as though flesh has been picked away under their heads. Neither man was attractive or ever had been, but both took up space. Long fingers, somewhat thin, as though everything in them gravitated to those digits and just kept pushing. No guts evident, no butts. Big ears and those droopy eyes, an old scuffed up golf ball on a tee. That was the impression Digger conjured. They didn't swing their arms much when they walked over to him, like a pair of motorized mannequins, and rarely gesticulated, as though afraid to use their bubble of personal space—or perhaps daring the unwary to enter it.

"No," answered Digger. "I'm sorry. That giggle just pops out sometimes, for no reason."

"That's a sign of insanity, Diggerson," lectured Eliot. "One best be careful."

"Eliot knows all about insanity," smiled the older brother. "He used to have a problem with matches."

"What child is not fascinated by fire?" Eliot retorted. "Weren't you, Digger?"

"A little flame, certainly," continued Glen, "but not to the point of burning down neighbors' sheds."

*Sheds, plural?* Digger looked at Eliot to see his response, but the light from Diana's yuletide decorations had ignited the lenses, making them blaze green and blue and gold and red, hiding the entrance to the man's soul. "I once almost burned down our woods," Digger admitted.

"You see?" said Glen, grinning. "Digger understands. You grow out of things, Eliot, such as pyromania. We certainly have."

Digger took another sip of beer. Diana had a sink full of Samuel Adams bottles, as well as wine, vodka, scotch, gin, all the mixers, all in the kitchen. Christmas lights were strung along the living room ceiling, too, and the other lights were dimmed, just as Digger and Anna always liked in restaurants. Anna would have loved this ambiance, and with her, Digger could have escaped the Gladstones, gone for a walk or something. Alone, though, he was trapped. *Where was Lou?* Lou Knightly would not choose to join this trio, but he could extract Digger from it. Where was the Lip Licker?

"You still detest cats, though, don't you, brother? You won't grow out of that!" Glen Gladstone had one of those smiles that people wanted to knock off his face, a cat-who-ate-the-canary smirk.

"Look at my head!" declared Eliot in response. "What sane human being would not detest those creatures?"

Both Gladstones scanned the room because Diana Pell had a cat, which had been making the rounds earlier just like a human, going from one group to another, staying a short time, rubbing against legs, of course, and then moving on. Digger wanted now to follow that cat, a big, bushy, brown and gold animal, a calico like his mother's cat, but he couldn't at the moment find it. Diana had named it Alfred, of all things ("After Prufrock," she had said to Digger earlier and then laughed).

"Where's Alfred?" Digger asked.

"Sheds and cats," said Glen. "Both failed to fare too well back in our old neighborhood."

Digger wasn't sure what to say to that.

"They just are not natural," said Eliot, enunciating each word while scanning the floor for the bushy-tailed cat.

"Eliot used to provide *treatment* for the neighborhood felines." Treatment?

"Ah, hah! There it is," declared Eliot, pointing toward the kitchen, and Digger turned and saw Alfred paused in the doorway, sitting on its haunches and swiveling its attractive head, surveying the scene. The cat froze its eyes on Digger and the Gladstones. "Not normal!" said Eliot.

Alfred lowered himself, settling down onto all four paws, and in defense of his colleague, Digger thought that the cat did look ready to spring, his eyes half lidded now. The man giggled. "Alfred does look a little supernatural, Eliot."

"It's watching you, Eliot!" Glen looked back and forth, from brother to cat.

"Treatment!" said Eliot.

What a *weird* scene! "He's just resting, Eliot. Remember that I have a cat, too, a feral one named Bumper. He's a sweetheart, wouldn't hurt anybody. Bumper and my dog are great friends now, or at least they tolerate each other's presence, and that's pretty nice between usual enemies, dogs and cats."

"Keep your friends close, Eliot," whispered his brother, who seemed to be enjoying himself.

"What's that you're drinking?" said Digger to Glen.

"Scotch! We Gladstones are scotch men, right, Eliot?"

"That damn thing's looking right at me!"

"Are you having scotch, Eliot?" said Digger, trying to distract him from thoughts of cats and *treatments*.

"Yes," said Eliot, returning his consciousness to the trio. "Scotch and a splash of water."

"These Sam Adamses are pretty tasty," said Digger. "A little stronger than my usual Bud Lights, but good." Neither Gladstone had a reaction, so Digger changed the subject before Eliot could lock eyes with Alfred again. "Eliot, I saw that you added a piece to the Dream Board, a novel excerpt, right?"

"That Dream Board is very interesting," cut in Glen. "A little left-wing, but interesting. I would not have thought the department to be so full of writers."

"It's a writing department," said Digger.

"But isn't it 'those who cannot do, teach'?"

Digger thought of Jolie, of her 'douche' pronouncement, and took a fuller sip than normal. His bottle, which had been fresh when the Gladstone brothers sidled up, was almost empty now. *Sam Adams! An escape!*

Digger tried again. "Are you writing a book, Eliot? I saw a title, *Into the Fire*, right? What's it about?"

"Serial killers," answered Glen, but Eliot cut in.

"Just *one* serial killer, and the story's told through his eyes. Into *his* eyes, into the 'fire.'"

"I like it," said Digger. "That's an interesting point of view. Sounds like a lot of research."

"Oh, brother's just making up most of it, aren't you, Eliot. He fancies himself a David Reed Winslow. He went to school with him, you know, down in New Mexico."

David Reed Winslow was a famous author, an intellectual, a writer of fiction, not simple murder mysteries. Not only the literary world, but the general public knew of David Reed Winslow. "I've heard of Reed Winslow, of course," said Digger, "but I've never read him."

"He and Eliot were great friends back in graduate school, were you not, Eliot?"

"I remember you mentioning that you went to school with Reed Winslow, but long ago. You mentioned something about it long ago."

"Well, it was long ago, long ago and forgotten."

"Eliot!" said Glen, with that sticky smile. "You will never forget David Two Last Names! Eliot used to cry about his success. Eliot can be quite the big baby, can't you, brother?"

"My brother is exaggerating," said Eliot to Digger. "I did go to school with him, as I have probably told you before, but I have no problem with his success, which apparently was not enough to make him happy anyway. Why would you envy anyone who took the easy way out, who hung himself no less?"

That was a good question, and Digger thought of the literary great, of Reed Winslow's sad ending. "Happiness isn't about reaching goals," he said. "It's about having them."

"You had better write that down, Eliot," grinned the older brother. "You can get it into your serial-killer book."

"Each path ends in the same spot," said the younger brother.

Digger ignored this extrapolation, instead asking Eliot about his south western experiences. "We should talk about grad school more, Eliot. I went to Arizona, you know? UNM, that's in Albuquerque, right? Tucson and Albuquerque must have been similar."

"Very hot," said Eliot, and again his round eye glasses flared as his head turned back to Digger.

"You know what I remember most about Tucson? The fires in the mountains during thunderstorms."

"I think of the desert as flat," said Glen.

"Tucson's flatter on the eastern side, but basically it's in a bowl, and the lightning would create little fires in the mountain's pines. From the city, the fires would look like lit cigarettes, the embers, you know? And it happened every time. The lightning, the trailing thunder, the orange glow as the mountains burned a bit."

"*That* is what you remember?" said Eliot. "You remember the fires?"

"And the monsoons, the faucets of water every afternoon in late summer."

"I think of the desert as dry," said Glen.

"Roads became rivers," said Digger, remembering. "From two in the afternoon until four, like clockwork. The raindrops were so big that they hurt your head! And the lizards all over the place, little brown ones in the trees. We have squirrels, but Tucson had lizards."

"Eliot's no fan of squirrels either," said Glen.

"And the stars at night," continued Digger, enjoying the reminiscing. "You must remember those, Eliot, from Albuquerque. Stars all the way to the horizon."

"What about the mountains?" said Glen.

*Definitely a lawyer*, thought Digger, who instead said, "You could get away from them and the city lights if you drove south out into the desert, toward Mexico."

"I remember the stars," said Eliot Gladstone, but he failed to elaborate. All three men stood and imagined celestial lights. Then the stars faded, the conversation died.

"I need another Sam Adams," Digger announced. "Nice to meet you, Glen, and we'll no doubt talk some more. I want to mingle a bit."

"Say hello to Alfred," said Glen Gladstone, but Eliot said nothing. From the kitchen doorway, where Digger knelt to pet a now slumbering cat, Digger watched the two odd fellows and wondered whom they would entrap next. Like a pair of macabre bookends, the Gladstone boys moved in, positioning themselves around Diana Pell's son, whom Diana had introduced to Digger as Michael. The son had not had much to say. Digger wondered what those three men would discuss. *Probably me*, he decided. Then Lou Knightly appeared. Alfred slipped off.

"Digger!" said the tallest man in the room, and after that announcement, the tongue made its prominent pass across the lips. "I saw you talking to the Gladstone boys. What lovely fellows, eh? Can't you see them at your local funeral home, one on either side of a coffin?"

"Jolie says that they look like pedophiles, but I agree with your image more. Funeral home directors, definitely. Did you know that Eliot hates cats? Seems to have a real phobia."

"That scratch on his head looks like a cat attack, and it's been there for a month!"

"Eliot told me that a neighbor's cat did it. When he tried to pick it up."

"If he hates cats, why would he pick one up? Probably his brother handed it to him. Glen seems like the type of person who would hand you a pile of dog crap or maybe an M80 and then walk away smiling."

"You don't seem to be a fan of our newest part-timer," said Digger, smiling.

"I like that guy you hired, Jay, and I liked Johna Adams, too. Too bad about her. Eliot hired his nutty brother and some other woman named Beverly, Beverly Douglas. She's a complete freak, Digger!"

"How so?"

"A total introvert. Will walk right by you in the hall without even looking at you, and if you say 'hello, Beverly,' she'll sort of flinch as though you just grabbed her by the throat." *The throat!* Lou paused, then added, "I don't know how she can be a teacher. Sure, we aren't supposed to lecture all the time, but we do have to talk!"

"Is she here? I don't see anyone new."

"Who knows? Check the corners. That's where Beverly will be lurking."

Digger looked at the corners. Alfred was now sleeping on a chair in one corner, and Digger noticed that Eliot was staring at the cat.

"We'd better keep an eye on Diana's cat, Lou," he said. "Just in case Eliot tries to pick it up!"

"Or Glen throws it at him. Glen's from New Hampshire, you know. Apparently, Eliot grew up there, too. Glen told me that his wife died, so he moved down here and stopped being a lawyer. Not sure why one led to the other, but here he is."

Digger and Lou watched the Gladstones and Diana's son, none of whom seemed to be saying anything. Digger thought of Paul Smith and his deceased wife, the reason for his loss of sanity. *The Morbids*. He pictured Paul Smith with his knife and the dance they had shared around his kitchen table. A decade ago.

"When did all this happen?" he asked Lou.

"I don't know, couple years ago. Glen showed up last fall. Eliot probably hired him to take some of your classes. You're coming back, I hear."

"Just one class, professional writing. Afternoons."

"That's the time you like. I'm surprised that Eliot gave you what you want."

"Having trouble with our new Chair?"

"Digger, he's a power nut! Did you know that he actually did a classroom observation of me? He barged into my class with his little notebook open, you know, to jot down all my mistakes."

"Why did you let him do it? I mean, the adjuncts, they have no choice, but you do."

"I figured just let him do it, if he wants to so bad. But nobody else has let him. Will you?"

"I'm like you, Lou. If he wants to observe my class, why not?"

"He sent me an official evaluation, said the lesson was 'sufficient,' whatever that meant. He recommended that I lecture more, can you believe that?" Like Digger, Lou Knightly believed in group work, active learning, and the two men often talked about lesson plans.

"I have an idea for my spring class," said Digger. "I'm going to have more assignments but fewer critiques, and I'll pair the assignments. You know, two papers on logical fallacies, for instance, the first paper counting as less than the second, so that students will fix the problems from the first paper and earn higher grades, and hopefully learn more by doing the same basic assignment twice."

"You mean, they'll write one paper on a writer's fallacies, and you'll grade it. Then they'll do the same assignment on another writer's fallacies, and that one will count for twice as much? Brilliant! I think you have something. Then you'll have two more assignments with the same directions, and then two more, right?"

"Right, I figure I can do seven assignments, one every two weeks. For the professional writing class, I'll have two reports dealing with problems/solutions, and then I'll have two more dealing with national and campus issues."

"I like it. I'm going to steal it, okay? I have a pair of introductory writing classes, you know, transfers and repeaters, and two 101's. They write about language and rhetoric, so I can easily pair assignments."

"I thought of it during my coma, apparently," said Digger. Then he giggled. "I woke up with the paired-assignments idea and a strange giggle."

"I like them both, Digger, but you can keep the giggle. I'll just take the assignments idea."

"It's yours, Lou. Don't forget what T.S. Eliot said: 'Immature poets borrow, mature poets steal.' Something like that anyway."

"Diana would love that," said Lou, followed by the passage of his tongue. "She named her cat after Prufrock."

Digger said that he knew and that he loved that poem. They looked over at Alfred, sleeping the party away. Although Digger was enjoying his talk with Lou, he envied the cat a bit. He hoped that nobody would sit on Alfred by mistake.

Digger saw that his colleague was drinking beer, too. "Good brew," he said, and Lou nodded in agreement.

"You used to have a little trouble with alcohol, didn't you, Digger?"

"Yeah, a little, but how do you know?"

"You told me! Did you forget that, too? And do you remember who shot you, by the way?"

"I have an image of a really tall, dorky guy," smiled Digger. "Tall and thin."

"Sounds like a Gladstone," laughed the other man, adding, "I'd place my bet on Glen. Although I don't know why he would shoot you."

"You know, I'm not that curious about it," said Digger. "Everybody else is. Anna, my mother, my neighbor, but I don't really care. It all seems *over* to me."

"Maybe that's why you giggle more now," laughed Lou. "But, seriously, you'd better watch the beer intake, don't you think? You used to tell me that you couldn't stop."

"That was after Anna left me, and, yeah, I couldn't stop, but only after I started, and I hardly ever started. I really didn't drink that much back then, and I never do now. I'll probably have one more tonight, just three total, three in about three hours."

"Hell," said Lou Knightly, "I'm going to knock back more than that!"

"Pretty soon you'll be telling everyone how much you love them, and then how much you hate them."

"Hah! Beers don't get me all emotional like that. Hard liquor maybe."

"Beer did it to me. Emotion squirming at the bottom of every bottle. Satisfaction after the first, then light love below the second, then heavier love waiting, then righteousness at the bottom of the fourth, anger topping off the fifth, and then guilt, and after that oblivion."

"You're a light weight, Digger."

Digger giggled and agreed. "Eliot and Glen are drinking scotch." Digger saw that Alfred was still nesting peacefully in the corner chair.

"Did you know that Eliot wanted your office? Not this year even, last! He argued that the corner office was the *Chair's* by rights and that you weren't using it. But Diana shot him down. She said that you'd be back and that your office should be outside the Dream Board. She really went for that board, Digger. Did you see my editorials?"

"Eliot told me a different tale, and, yeah, I saw them. Scathing!"

"I aim to please," said the tall man. How could Digger have ever suspected the Lip Licker as a killer?

"There goes Eliot." Digger motioned toward the stairs. "Upstairs bathroom, I guess."

"Must want some privacy, or maybe he's just snooping around. I'm surprised his brother's not going with him."

"Standing side by side."

"That is *not* a pleasant image, Digger!"

They watched Eliot's head, body, and legs disappear into the ceiling, at least that's how it looked with the stairway along the far wall in the big living room. Glen was still standing silently with Michael Pell, both looking as though they wanted to be elsewhere. Digger didn't really blame them, though, since standing around in circles with drinks wasn't his idea of time well spent. Still, he liked talking with Lou, who had a jovial sense of humor, the best one of his colleagues.

When the room's lighting brightened, Digger was momentarily confused, reminded of past bar days at closing time. Diana Pell was standing by the wall switch and waving to the twenty or so guests, holding a thin book, too. *Seasonings*, thought Digger, and he wondered how he had introduced colleagues to his second book, *Murderous Mistakes*. His brow furrowed. Nobody had yet told him that they had read that book, and what about his first? Maybe when he returned next semester, his peers would discuss those books. Of course, they would.

"Friends and colleagues," announced the host. "I'm throwing this little party for myself in honor of my first book of poetry in over a decade, well over!" The room broke out in applause, and with that sound of acknowledgement, Diana Pell smiled, her wide mouth rising and showing the old woman's youth—the joy of life in everyone, potentially.

"*Seasonings*," she continued, holding the thin book up. "Over thirty new poems, several of which you have probably read before, on the Dream Board down our corridor. That Dream Board! I want to thank Professor Matthew Diggerson for not only having that idea, but executing it as well. I know that we *all* have used and appreciated the Dream Board, and will continue to do so."

The room ignited again in applause, most faces turning to Digger. He giggled and made a little one-hand wave. Eliot's legs appeared on the stairs, then his torso, and finally his somewhat big, round head, and Digger wondered about his response to Diana's news. Eliot would probably not think much about a slim book of poems. *Into the Fire?* Digger saw that Glen was whispering something to his brother, who nodded once.

Diana Pell wasn't quite done. "None of you have to buy this book, of course," she said. "I will add a copy, or two, to the OVC library, and I will continue to add work to the Dream Board. Thank you for coming. Drink up, converse, the night is young!"

"That was a nice little speech," said Digger to Lou Knightly.

"All *little* speeches are nice," said Lou, and then his tongue punctuated that decree, peeking out, sliding left to right.

Diana joined them and said to Digger, "You really did spark this book, Digger, and I'm quite thankful. Writing again was like finding my youth, greeting lost friends. Incredible."

"I know what you mean, Diana," smiled Digger. "I feel the same way after waking up and finding Anna, another book, and then Snodo, my dog. Just like you said, 'finding my youth and greeting old friends.'"

"Digger's seeing his ex-wife again," said Lou to Diana.

"Oh, I know all about it," said Diana, smiling. Not at all the Reluctant Smiler tonight, thought Digger. Maybe her jaw hinges had simply been oiled by alcohol. "It is one of the wonders of age to circle back to youth and to sit with it for a while."

"That sounds like another poem, Diana," said Digger.

"It does, doesn't it? I had better go and write that down. I will see you both later."

"Uh, oh," said Digger to Lou. "Here come the Morbids!"

Eliot and Glen were crossing the room, heading straight for Digger and Lou, eyes locked like a pair of old vampires.

"Too late to escape," whispered the tall man, and the shorter one giggled.

"Well," said Glen Gladstone. "There it is." He smiled and seemed to think that everyone present understood his vague summation. "The reason for the party, the poetess' book. And I thought it was for Jesus."

"He's the reason for the season," said Lou, but only Digger smiled.

"What do you think of our illustrious host's announcement, brother?" continued the elder Gladstone. "Perhaps you should clap your hands and tell all those gathered here about your own writing exploits."

"At least I write more than court briefs," sneered little brother, and Digger applauded him for this retort. His brother was insufferable.

"How's that book going, Eliot? Do you know who the killer is? It sounds silly, but I didn't know who the killer was in my book until I'd written about half of it. Then I decided."

"What about your second book?" cut in Glen. "I have heard that you have doubled your output, published *twice*." With an accent on 'twice,' he looked at his brother.

Standing with these three tall men, Digger felt like a quarterback on his knees surrounded by looming teammates. Maybe he should call a play. "Hut, hut," he said and giggled.

"Is that the name of the book? Hut, Hut! Eliot never told me that, did you, brother?"

"No," laughed Digger. "It's just that you're all so tall that I feel like a shrimp here, or like a quarterback in a huddle."

"Sports analogies are trite," Eliot announced, and then he turned directly to Digger. "My book's protagonist *is* the killer, so I definitely know him already. *That* is my angle, Digger, the killer as protagonist, his motivations, his anguish. It must be quite lonely to be a murderer."

"I never thought of that," said Lou.

"Try being the victim," said Digger, and then all four men laughed. Digger thought that such mirth was as good as could be expected with this quartet, so he then excused himself and mingled for the rest of the party, talking with just about everyone present, even with the adjunct whom he had supposedly hired, Jay Moore, who arrived late, after Diana's little speech.

"Apparently, I hired you," laughed Digger.

"You did," laughed Jay Moore. "You were quite impressed by my knowledge and background."

Digger giggled, partly because Jay Moore blinked so much. Hadn't he said something to that female cop about a blinker? He had been right. The two men didn't talk long, though, and before long Digger said goodbye to Diana Pell and headed for his car, parked in a line out on the street.

"Leaving, Diggerson?"

Eliot was walking behind Digger up the driveway, about ten yards back, and Digger felt prickles run up his spine. Had Eliot held a gun to his head and then blasted away? Strangely, Matthew Diggerson didn't really care about the answer. Except for Simba, his life was so much better now that he almost wanted to thank the shooter.

"I've had enough of this party myself," the current Humanities Chair announced. "Diana, the poetess, she should try writing a real book, don't you think, Digger?" Eliot was breathing hard again, and Digger noticed white plumes billowing out of the man's nostrils and mouth. Then he noticed how cold it had gotten.

"December's here, finally," he said, adding "It snowed when I was at my mother's, just a little bit, that soft first snowfall. Did we get any snow here, a couple weeks ago?"

"No. No snow here. Of course, we're on the coast, so inland snow is just rain here quite often."

Thanks for the weather lessen, thought Digger, but he said, "I hope we get snow soon here. My dogs, I mean dog, loves the snow. Hates water but loves the snow."

"How did you get your dog back, Diggerson? Where was it? You were in that coma for over a year."

"Anna found her. Snodo had been adopted, and Anna found out

and went to see the couple, an old married couple, sweet, and they brought Snodo to the rehab place, and Snodo went a little crazy, and that was that. The old couple gave her back. I'm very grateful. I'm grateful, too, that the person who shot me didn't shoot my dog."

"So your ex-wife *is* back, that must be something. And you mean that white dog, right, Diggerson? Snodo, you say? I remember the brown one and the white one, but the white one didn't seem to like me much. Remember how it would growl at me?"

"To be honest, Eliot, I don't remember that."

"Your brown dog liked me, but the white one didn't. Growled every time."

"My memory's not the best. I don't even remember my *brown* dog's, Simba's, passing. None of it, and I don't remember Snodo's ever growling at you."

"Well, you will see it, no doubt, when you bring the white one to school. Are you planning to do that next semester, as you used to, bring the dog to work?"

"I haven't thought of it, Eliot. With just one class, I'll probably just leave Snodo at home. And Snodo has a house companion now, a cat, Bumper, as I mentioned, I think."

"Vile creatures!" spat Eliot Gladstone, fingering his forehead.

"Don't worry, Eliot. I won't bring Bumper to school."

Glen appeared then, shuddered in an exaggerated way, said, "Cold!" and added "Good to get out of that house."

Digger had to admit to that, but didn't. He excused himself instead, saying that he would see the two Gladstones "next semester" and headed to his car. A few of Diana's neighbors already had Christmas lights up, and the colors added even more ambiance to the sparkling heavens. Digger saw some white ragged cumulous clouds passing slowly like the ghosts of ancient armadas, and for a moment he stopped outside his car and simply beheld the wonder of the sky. Glen had been right: it was nice to be outside again, to be away from humanity, alone with existence.

Then he thought of Snodo and returned to earth.

As he drove away, Matthew Diggerson did not notice the two Gladstones entering Eliot's big, black SUV.

"Professor Pell was quite happy with herself," Glen told his brother.

"Yes," agreed Eliot. "Quite happy."

"Dear old Dad never liked that in people, did he? Happiness, people who were happy with themselves."

"That's no doubt why he liked Mom so much. She was never happy with herself."

"Arrogance is not an attractive quality, Eliot. Pop despised arrogant people."

"*Pop* despised everyone."

"And with good reason."

"Good reason."

"Did Diana Pell's book remind you of your old pal, David Reed Winslow? He was arrogant, too, wasn't he? That's what you always said. You were a little *hung up* on that fellow, wouldn't even use his name, called him David *Two Last Names*, correct?"

"He hung himself, Glen, so apparently he was not quite so arrogant."

"Pop would have approved."

Eliot did not respond, apparently concentrating on the back roads, the curves and stop signs, the way out. Then he said, almost to himself, "Did you ever notice that as you get older you mark time with death, no longer with life, with birthdays and accomplishments, but with deaths, with endings?"

"Eliot, that was quite a speech! What are you going on about?"

The younger brother did not answer, instead glancing at his sibling and noticing that Glen was smiling, showing teeth. Eliot thought of Diana Pell and her new book, of the big grin on that cigar Indian face, and then he thought of her fat cat, which also seemed to be grinning. Eliot Gladstone thought and thought. *Two birds*, he thought, *one stone*.

# Chapter Ten:  Positioning

As implied, this persuasive tactic relies heavily on audience analysis and quite often on emotional appeals. In the next "State of the Union" speech, pay attention to the special guests in the gallery, to how and when each is introduced. When positioned alongside such remarkable citizenry, Americans will feel better about the country.

When Matthew Diggerson awoke, his first thought was "Christmas," followed quickly by "Anna," then "coffee," then "Snodo," a name always shadowed by "Simba" these days. The white dog was curled up at the base of his bed, but her head had popped up, apparently sensing his change in consciousness or maybe her name in his thoughts. "It's Christmas, Snodo, and Anna's coming!" Snodo's tail made firm 'whomping' sounds against the mattress. How could a fairly little tail make such a loud noise? "C'mon," said Digger. "Let's go out. Where's Bumper?" In the kitchen, the black cat was not sitting sedately before the glass-paneled door, as usual. Where was he?

Outside, snow was falling, but not much and gently. A New England postcard. White Christmases in the lower northeast were rarer than most Americans realized, but this one was setting up to be special. The fluffy snow looked to be no danger to Anna. When Digger cracked open the back door, late December rushed in as Snodo rushed out, and beneath the soft snowfall, Snodo danced around for a bit before squatting. The sky reminded Digger of a warm comforter, something that his mother might have wrapped around him as a child. He would have to call her today, maybe before Anna arrived. She had said 'elevenish.'

"Let's go in," Digger said to Snodo, sitting on the porch and staring at his face, and the white unicorn wagged in response, scattering a feathery layer of snow.

Inside again, Digger clicked on the coffee maker, enjoyed the snuffling sounds of the brewing, and looked around for Bumper, who usually joined Snodo on the first backyard jaunt of the day. "Bumper!" he called, and then the stately black Tom came around the corner, from the living room probably. "There you are," he said, and the black cat blinked at him, twice, with those wild golden eyes. The cat went right out when offered an open door, and Snodo, of course, went out again, too. The chickadees and sparows complained about Bumper's presence even though Digger had never seen the cat so much as bat at a bird. Digger enjoyed his first half cup of black coffee and the sight of his two companions out back. Snodo was following Bumper around the yard, nosing at everything, and by the time Digger had finished the cup, the two animals were ready to come in. Snodo leaped through the cracked door first, and then Bumper entered, calmly, properly. *As calm as a cat*, thought Digger, creating another cliché.

He decided to call his mother, partly so that the rest of the day would be open with Anna, with space in time.

"Merry Christmas!" he said into the phone.

"Oh, yes, Merry Christmas to you, too. It's snowing here. Carol and Mary probably won't want to drive in this, and they shouldn't be driving anyway!"

"It's snowing here, too, but very gently. I don't think it will build up. Carol and Mary will be fine. When are they coming?"

"Around noon, but those two are always late. They're supposed to bring stewed oysters. You never liked those, did you, Matthew?"

"Not especially, not anything 'stewed,' really."

"You never liked to try new things, Matthew. Even as a boy. All you ever wanted was hot dogs and potato chips."

"Not anymore," said Digger, wondering if he should tell his mother about no longer eating meat and deciding instead to change the subject. "Anna's coming in an hour or so. We're having scallops for dinner, sea scallops, the big ones."

"Good, those *little* scallops are hardly worth the effort of getting one on a fork. I'm surprised you aren't cooking salmon."

His mother seemed a little ornery, but Digger plowed on. He knew that he could smooth her out after a bit, that Jean Diggerson just had to unleash her complaints, her anxiety. Perhaps doing so made his mother feel as though she were doing something about the problems themselves, or the imagined concerns. "How does Rachel like the snow?" he asked, adding, "Snodo loves to race around in it, but Bumper doesn't seem to care, one way or the other."

But his mother didn't answer. "Oh, God! Who is this? Someone's at the door, Matthew. It's Jan Green, what does she want! She seems to have a package. I had better go, Matthew. You enjoy your day with Anna, and try to remember who shot you in the head!" She hung up then, not waiting for her son's response, and Digger giggled. Jean Diggerson was one of a kind. She would be beaming at her neighbor now, inviting her in, offering her coffee, being the perfect host, and despite her *intruder* anxiety, her joy would be real. His mother wore no mask.

Around eleven, Digger heard tires crunching in the driveway, a sound that he had never forgotten, one that made his heart dance, and then Anna was at the back door, smiling through the glass. Digger was smiling, too, *like an idiot,* he thought, but he just kept grinning.

After letting her in, Digger motioned by hand to his pets, Anna's greeting party. "Look at them! They *adore* you! Snodo and Bumper have never seen anyone quite so beautiful."

"Oh, right! They probably just aren't used to any other people being in here, right? Have you two never seen another human?" she asked the pair. Snodo's tail wagged, and Bumper blinked slightly. "Look, Matt! She blinked at me!"

"A kiss," said Digger, adding, "And I think she's a he, remember?"

"Have you checked?" laughed Anna.

As he took her coat and they took seats at the kitchen table, Digger giggled in answer.

"There's that giggle of yours, Matt. I don't remember those giggles back then, in our past, not that you were overly serious, of course."

"It took a bullet to my head to make me laugh!"

"That's not very funny, Matt. Have you remembered anything about, uh, that night, about who shot you?"

"Now you sound like my mother, Anna," he said, smiling to show that he was not criticizing her. "I still can't remember a thing, and I'm fine with that. I seem to have forgotten all sorts of bad things, from shootings, to Simba's dementia. My vet said that Simba had gone bonkers, didn't even know me anymore. I can't even fathom that happening, but if it did, I'm glad that I don't remember it. And my colleagues, apparently, didn't bother to read my book, or books, or talk to me about them, so I'm glad not to remember that, too. You see, I'm just better off. I'm grateful for this bullet, strange as it sounds."

"Who amongst your colleagues seems like the main suspect? Which one seems most unhappy with your literary success?"

"That's easy, Eliot Gladstone."

"Professor Happy Rock?"

"The one and only," said Digger, adding, "Or I should say the two and only since Eliot, who's now the chair, has hired his older brother as a writing adjunct."

"Now there are *two*!"

"Two happy rocks, yup, and it's hard to tell which is the happiest."

"I suppose the real question is which was the unhappiest, and I guess that his brother's not really a suspect, that it would have to be Eliot."

"At Diana Pell's party, the one you couldn't go to—and thanks a lot, by the way!—I talked to the Gladstones. Glen, the older brother, was sort of mean to Eliot, and Eliot told me about his book, *Into the Fire*, from the mind of a *serial killer*. Now why would he tell me that if he had shot me? It makes too obvious of a connection."

"Unless he couldn't help himself," said Anna. "Isn't that a textbook definition of a serial killer, a man who can't help himself?"

Digger didn't answer. Because, of course, Anna was right. Yet he still just did not care. Even if Eliot had shot him, he hardly cared at all. Could not care less, as the saying went. "Into the Fire," he said, instead. "That's a great song by Bruce Springsteen, in reaction to 9/11, the burning towers. Have you heard it, Anna? It's powerful stuff!"

"You're hopeless, Matthew Diggerson! What about Snodo's safety, and what about me? A killer could be out there right now! And you don't even plug in your motion detector!" Ah, she had found him out, but how? She was probably just fishing. Had he remembered to plug that damn thing back in?

"I don't know what you mean about the motion detector, but I do know that you're right, Anna. But I also know they're not out there, the killer, Eliot, anybody, whoever! And nothing seems quite real to me anymore. It's like I'm living in a fantasy world. I don't have to work, at least not yet. I wrote a second book without even trying. I got you back, into my life, without even trying. Snodo, too, and I don't even remember losing her. Simba's gone, but I don't remember losing her either. In my mind half the time, she's just in the other room, taking one of her deep naps. I can even hear her snoring sometimes, Anna. Simba's still here. You see? Nothing's real, so why would I worry about some shooter?"

"From what you told me about Simba, I half expect to see her myself."

"It's so strange not to remember her death, not to have an image of burying her, but I did. I talked to my vet and saw the churned up spot in the backyard, her grave. But I do remember her growing old and losing some faculties."

"You loved her."

"I read something once about love, about how a child sees love. Something about your name being *safe* in someone else's mouth."

"That's beautiful, and true." Anna looked down to see two animals looking up at her, one on either side of her kitchen chair. "I think love is also when your *face* is safe in another's eyes."

Digger motioned to the two staring creatures beneath the table. "They love you then. Snodo and Bumper must see your colorful aura. They're entranced!"

"They probably want me to feed them!"

Christmas passed slowly, the best day Digger could remember in decades, for the conversation was both light and serious, back and forth, never difficult. Anna told him again how she had contacted Digger's mother after he had been shot and left for dead and how her telephone number was still the same ("Old people are like that," he had laughed. "Their numbers never change."), and Digger told her about his Grammar Jam songs ("I remember them," she said). Anna said that she had dated ("just a bit") and that one man had even proposed, getting angry and leaving when she said that she still felt married already ("The old Catholic weight, just not the daily habits," she said), and Digger replied that he had not dated at all, that he had added dogs instead, Simba. He told her about the dog pound, about how some dogs were so excited to see someone that they banged their tails against the bars and wall until blood flew, but that Simba had not been like that, that the Lion Dog had done nothing to plead for freedom but look him in the eyes.

And, of course, they talked about teaching, about Digger's coma revelation to create dual assignments, two with the same purpose, the first paper counting less so that students who actually learned from his comments could raise their papers' effectiveness (and grades) the second time. Anna mentioned the role of the computer in teaching, even for Art, the most hands-on of subjects, and Digger bemoaned the creation of cell phones, of their addictive qualities, their effects on the 'uncoachables,' a term that made

Anna laugh and say, "Some horses just won't drink the water," a reply that made Digger laugh.

The conversational thread returned to Snodo and Bumper often, and the two animals also enjoyed their day by sleeping through most of it. Later, though, Bumper's eyes expanded humorously when Anna passed the cat a piece of her sea scallop, and Snodo woke up at the transaction and quickly trotted over to investigate. Digger enjoyed the scallops, too, but didn't really care about the food, hardly remembered it the next day. His nourishment was deeper, more sustaining, a desert downpour after many seasons of drought. All Christmas day and evening, his head felt light yet expanded, as though he could float away on the breeze and glide toward the sun or maybe the stars. If he had died right then, right on his couch, right at home, with Anna's voice dissolving into peaceful silence, then *that* would have been fine with him. In the starlight. With Anna.

Like his mother, Anna enjoyed talking about Digger's books, and the writing teacher luxuriated under her questions and comments. She had cried when Yusef was forced into the Whirlpool (*Composition Murder*), and she also felt bad for Ned Dunlap, the murderer, a disgruntled adjunct with a bitchy wife (*Murderous Mistakes*). Digger told her about his less-than-enjoyable Facebook experiences, adding posts to various group sites to beg strangers to purchase his book, an action that made him feel "unclean."

"You just need to see the fun side of social media," said Anna.

"You mean when I'm not on it?" laughed Digger.

After dinner, Anna used Digger's laptop to show him her website and then gave him some tips on how to create one himself. You could add your Grammar Jam songs to your site," she said, and Digger realized that he could maybe even create videos around the songs.

"That would be perfect! Then you wouldn't have to beg. You could offer a song on Facebook and put the video on your site. When you post, you would give your site's link, which leads to your website, where you have lots of info about your books. And links to Amazon and Kindle, of course."

"That's a plan I can follow, Anna. I think that you've saved me again, saved me from Facebook."

"We can get your website set up tomorrow, through Wix, like mine. It's really easy to navigate."

"Looks great," said Digger, seeing Anna's site and some of her artwork. "Your pictures are very soothing. Can I buy one?"

"Well, why don't you open your presents first!"

Digger laughed. "I gave you copies of my books! I signed them!"

They both laughed at that, and Snodo raised her head, wondering what she was missing. When they let the pets out back, they noticed that the snow was still falling gently, but not building up much. They drank white wine (good with scallops) and watched the dog and cat in the snowfall, the birds—more chickadees, a pair of cardinals, sparrows, sea gulls off in the muffled distance—the daylight seeping away, the lacy bay, the snowflakes, and Digger knew that no moment in life would ever be better than this one and that it would never go away again, this moment, this feeling, that this little speck of the present would forever light his future.

Later that night, on the couch, the wine bottle having been emptied, Anna told Digger that she had left two decades past to see if she could do it, survive without an 'adult,' that he was just *so responsible*, that she had begun to doubt herself, and that art had begun calling to her, representing a path not taken, that needed to be taken. And Digger responded that he would not have stopped her from reaching for her dreams, that he would have supported her. And since she had brought up the sad past, Digger wanted to ask about those divorce papers, about that strange phrasing: "irreconcilable differences involving present and future." But he decided to let it go, to let it stay buried. That future was now *past*, same as always, sooner or later.

Even later, Digger told Anna that she could have the bedroom, that he would take the couch, that he slept there often anyway, simply nodding off before the TV, and she said, "That would be fine, Matt." Digger saw a 'V' form just above her eyes, her frowning face, and then she returned to a theme almost as common as the animal thread: the shooter.

"Have you ever thought that somebody's out to kill Diggersons? Don't laugh, don't give me that giggle of yours! Look at the facts. Your father died in a single-car accident. Nobody knows how or why. He wasn't a drinker. And then your sister dies in a similar way. And then somebody tries to kill you, or somebodies, twice now. Isn't that incredibly unlikely? Maybe we should tell Jean to keep her eyes open and her doors locked."

"Oh, my mother's eyes have never been shut! And her door's always locked now. And those car accidents were just that, accidents. The cops didn't even suspect suicide, which never could have been the case anyway, at least not with my father. With Emma, I don't know, maybe, but I don't think so. Out of all us Diggerson's, I'm probably the one most prone to suicide, and I survived, too. No worries."

"I could have caused it," said Anna. "I took our love away."

"No, Anna. You never took our love away. I've always kept it inside, tucked away, safe."

That night, Digger slept alone on the couch, Snodo's having decided to slip into the bedroom to spend the night with Anna. Where Bumper had gone, Digger could not guess. Probably in there with Anna, too, but he himself could wait.

The next day, after Anna had driven off, Digger realized that he had forgotten to tell her about his *Silence of the Lambs* revelation, his decree to never again eat an animal that screamed. Ah, well, another time, for many more awaited him. That afternoon, he drove north to the Home Depot and bought a big concrete German shepherd statue to mark Simba's grave, and forever after, sparrows would land on the stone dog's pointy ears to survey his backyard for all of its riches.

Even though she was looking forward to her Christmas night

out with friends, Diana Pell was frowning because she could not find the spare house key. It had disappeared from its little hook, although the others remained, the extra car key and the one never used, the shed key. Where could a key go? Nobody ever used it, and yet it was gone. It had not fallen to the counter, it was not on any other kitchen counter, or the floor, or the table, or even in the living room. Why would it have gone there anyway? Could Alfred have batted it off its hook? Cats loved to take whacks at things, but her calico 'Prufrock' had never done anything like that. Alfred had outgrown such playful nonsense. What about her son, though? Michael seemed to be reverting, traveling in a big downward circle.

"Michael!" she yelled up the stairs, and she didn't like yelling, hardly ever yelled.

"What!" came her son's irritated reply. She had hoped that he would appear at the top of the long stairway, but the hall above remained empty. He wasn't in the bathroom, anyway, for she could see right into it. He must be in his room, as usual. What could a forty-year-old man do all day in his room?

"Michael!" she cried again, and when he still failed to appear, Diana Pell all but bellowed, "The spare house key, do you have it? Did you lend it to a friend?" She expected his answer, especially since he had no friends.

"No!"

The boy treated words like they were days ripped from his life! Diana turned from the stairway and glanced around the living room again. Alfred was curled up in his usual spot, where he had mainly stayed during her party a couple weeks ago. Could one of her colleagues have taken the key? *Silly!* Michael no doubt had it right in his dirty pants' pocket. And why worry anyway about something so small, about a little golden key?

As Eliot Gladstone passed through the young night, the old year's last, he thought of the key, which he had washed and then placed in his pocket. He could squeeze on her fingerprint later, *after*. Like most homeowners, Diana the Queen of the Poets kept spare keys visible in her kitchen, on little hooks connected to a cabinet, and the one he sought even offered one of those little gold chains with the little white tab for labels. "House," it had told Eliot after he had wandered away from banal conversations during the great Pell party. House! Sometimes people could be so helpful. Eliot smiled as he drove and thought back on all his little adventures. Women were always so helpful, so open to conversation, so needy. If each *adventure* had not been so easy, then the acts would not have been so acceptable, right? It stood to reason, an expression that Glen would enjoy. "It stands to reason," he could even hear his brother announce, so he said it aloud to himself and to the little cone of light as he drove through the dark back roads to Diana's house.

He had taken this trip twice before, both times on Saturday nights, thinking that the son would be out at some bar, but both times discovering Michael's silver sedan parallel to Diana's own little Japanese car, and that would not do. *Staying home with Mommy!* But Eliot had a good feeling about this night, for it was New Year's Eve. What middle-aged man would stay home with his mother on New Year's Eve? Who would want to begin a new year in such a sad manner? No, the son would be out, at last. "It stands to reason," he said again and then laughed, sort of, the sound a clam might make choking. The mirth reminded him of Diggerson, of the only time his own actions had not stood to reason.

"I shot the silly sonofabitch and he came out giggling," Eliot said aloud, and then he declared, "The Giggler!" That word made him laugh again, louder this time, for *that* would be the new nickname for Matthew Diggerson. Eliot could even spread it around the office, fertilize the department into seeing his colleague as the goof-off he had become. Eliot would just have to sell the idea to Gloria, the big-haired secretary, and she would do the work. And then one day, one day soon, the Giggler and he would have another little adventure, take a giggle-ending path.

"Bang, bang!" Eliot began to sing, smiling, nodding his head to the Beatles' tune about a "silver hammer," wondering who "Maxwell" was, inserting "Gladstone" instead, and as Professor Happy Rock passed beneath each streetlight, the round lenses of his glasses blazed white, revealing nothing, emptiness.

He had arrived, and as Eliot drove by the Pell residence, he noted three promising signs: a single car in the driveway (his colleague's), the front light gleaming (to welcome Michael home at some point), and a dark interior (she had gone to bed). *So helpful! Stands to reason!* A light snow once again began to fall, and Eliot Gladstone welcomed it because it soothed him by waltzing so sweetly in his headlights. He thought about where to park, worrying momentarily about surveillance cameras, the new eye witnesses, the ones that lawyers could not argue away since *seeing is believing*. However, actual eyes were guided by actual brains, and who would drive by a parked dark SUV and memorize the plate number? They would have to be insane since every third vehicle in America was a dark SUV. *Global warming be damned!* Maybe the snowfall would muddy up the lenses a bit, too. Another sign of helpfulness!

Eliot realized that he had driven too far. Like most, this neighborhood comprised a checkerboard of lots, each divided by parallel roads and little wooded parcels, giving the illusion of living in nature. *Squirrels and skunks!* The key would be to park behind Diana's lot but not in front of any house, to find a dark patch where no camera could reach. After turning at the next four-way intersection, Eliot drove somewhat slowly by the target one more time and counted the houses to the corner, took a left, then another, and counted the backs of those same houses. *One, two, three, four.* Four! And the street behind Diana's was virtually deserted, mainly empty lots for future happy homeowners. Maybe one more opening soon, too! That depended on Michael. Would a son choose to live in a house with a ghost?

Eliot reached up and switched off the interior light. "Details," he whispered happily as he exited his SUV and slid his *silver hammer* up a sleeve, backwards so that he could let it slide right down and catch it at the base, ready for action. *Sweet!* He closed the door carefully with two hands. The quiet night was beautiful, and Eliot raised his head to the muffled darkness and let a few snowflakes melt on his face. One landed on a lens, so he wiped it away with his gloved hand, nice thin leather gloves, good for gripping.

Previous snowfalls, which had provided the region with a picturesque white Christmas, now showed Eliot where to walk within the civilized forest behind Diana's house, utterly dark and inviting. Her "back" door was on the side, so he headed that way, almost banging his head on a bird feeder hanging from an old, grossly contorted tree, a crab apple, no doubt. The near collision stole his peace momentarily, so Eliot Gladstone stood still just beyond the feeder, feet from the corner of the side porch, and just breathed, listening to the rush of blood and the low howl of spent oxygen. Gradually, his fear and then anger attenuated, along with his desire to take a home-run swing at that bird feeder. That would create noise, too soon, and soon he would find another outlet anyway. He pictured the calico cat.

The little key worked, as Eliot knew it would, and he replaced it on its little hook on the kitchen cabinet. Why squeeze her fingerprint on later? Too *complicated*, too easy to forget a little key in your pocket. Slowly, he moved deeper into the shadowed house, wondering where the Hell cat lay, and within a dozen steps found himself in Diana's dark living room at the base of the stairway up, up, where Diana slept the dream of poets, of imagery and eternity. He would have to interrupt those dreams for just a bit. Up, up, he went, thanking Diana for adding carpet to the steps and thus muffling the creaking. In the second-floor hallway, he stood immobile and studied Diana's bedroom door, which he had noted at her party after using the upstairs bathroom. The cat must be in there with her. Dreaming of mice and easy meals. Well, he could understand that.

In the small square hallway, with doors on three sides, he settled into the silence, searched it, his spectacles finding a flick of light and rotating, back and forth, like something electronic. He felt his own heart beat, he heard it! Eliot Gladstone thought of ecstasy and despair, how both forces erupted from a heaviness in the heart. He could hear his breathing. When Eliot closed his eyes, he pictured being back in Diana's woods, peaceful and alone, vitally alive, like a deer within the wooded glen. *No*, not a deer. Like a *predator*, a seeker of warmth and nourishment, for was not *that* the point of all this? Was there a point? Did life offer any meaning at all? *Bah!* Eliot vowed to think such thoughts later, afterwards, after the feast! He had *work* to do now. He opened his eyes and began to see within the darkness.

This time, it would have to look like an accident. How easy it would be to slip through her bedroom door and throttle her where she lay, feeling her heart bang and bang, quicker and quicker and then slower and slower. "That's right, Little Bird," he would coo to her. "You can rest now, in imagery and eternity. Become a poem, Diana." *Sweet dreams!* But that satisfaction would not last, for sooner or later he would get caught. Some camera or some fiber, something unseen and impossible to control. *Stands to reason.* Blood spatter, that was a worry, too, but he had an answer for that.

The intruder slipped into the upstairs bathroom, reached into his pocket, and scattered some of his opioids (care of the prior cat attack and a gullible doctor!) on the floor, behind the toilet and under the sink. That should make the cops think a bit, think of Michael. Who else would be the beneficiary? Unless the great poet had bequeathed her fortune to some literary society, but that was unlikely. *Michael Pell*, that was where the will would lead, so Eliot would simply point more clearly to that path. He put a towel in the sink, got it a little wet, and hung it on the shower rack after squeezing some out in the hallway on the top step, uncarpeted in one section. Eliot ran a path of water from the top step into the bathroom, as though someone had been negligent, someone named Michael, and then he moved into the corner parallel with Diana's bedroom door and flattened himself against the wall, like a big spider.

*Into the Fire*, he thought, and he imagined phrases he could use in his book, images to catch and immortalize. The feel of a corner, the sound of a shadow. The thrill of the right word, the power, the control! Yet words were sticky things, obstinate, and they had begun to slow down for him, to run out, as always. Why did the words always run out? Diggerson had said that he just had to find the right genre, that the story would write itself, and he had, he had found the right genre. His psychological thriller, with experience fueling the plot, acceptance, understanding. He would be understood and accepted. If only the words would not run out. Visualize! Eliot took stock of the small hallway, felt the closed doors, pictured the sleeping woman and a curled up cat, its eyes open and gleaming green.

"Mom," Eliot said to the closed door, whispered, and then he said it again, louder, and again. He could feel his silver hammer snuggled inside his left sleeve and wondered if he would need it. He would love to use it right here, right in the hallway, but worried about blood spatter, about forensic cops and their bright ideas. "Mom," he said, this time with some urgency, and finally he heard movement, a creaking bed, then "Michael?"

"Mom," Eliot Gladstone whispered, and perhaps he was pleading to two women, to the one who was dead and the one who soon would be, to Mom, to mothers everywhere, to all those scared, stupid, useless mothers. "Mom!"

"Michael?" He could hear her get out of bed, the creaking and then the footsteps. She had turned on the light, he saw, and as it reached thinly out from beneath the closed door, he nestled further into the wall, became the shadow. When the door opened, the light spilled out, but Diana Pell was still groggy and thinking only of her son, who seemed to need her or perhaps it was all just a dream. She took a step out into the hallway, not yet noticing the shape to her right, pushed into the corner. "Michael?" she said again, and she took one more step, her last.

Eliot Gladstone moved forward, grabbed the sleepy woman by the arm and back, and flung her into the open air of the stairwell, where she disappeared in a flash. He had expected her to fall more dramatically, picturing slow motion even, but Diana Pell just left the second floor like a light going out. A bang, a thud, a slithering sound, and that was that, not exactly satisfying.

From the fallen bedroom light, he could see her at the base of the stairs, her robe crumpled up in an undignified manner, her legs still stretched up the stairs, as though they had not wanted to leave the steps behind. Diana Pell certainly looked dead, both arms hanging above her head, the only part of her that had actually reached the living room. Eliot almost laughed aloud, for her hands seemed to be trying to cup the sides of her head, her ears, as though attempting to drown out some unpleasant sound. On second look, she appeared to be reaching for something, a gift or maybe a face. She looked dead, yet he had made that mistake before.

Eliot moved down the stairs, careful not to step on blood spatter, but he couldn't see any anyway. And with any luck Michael would use the stairs before the cops came. Maybe Eliot should drag the body off the stairs so that the son would not see it, would just stagger up the stairs and go to sleep. The thought amused the gloved man, but then he dismissed it. *Forensics!* Right now, who could argue that Diana had not simply fallen down the stairs, slipping in the water obviously dripped by a drug-addled son? If Eliot started dragging the corpse about, then suspicions would follow. Suspicions would follow anyway since OVC writing teachers appeared to attract murder, but this death would be too obvious for prying minds. *Accidental.*

Stooping over the body, Eliot heard nothing but his own heart and breath, yet he felt for a pulse anyway, pushing wrinkles from the old bat's waddle. The gloves didn't help, but Eliot feared to take them off. He pushed a finger into her neck, and it seemed to go pretty far, felt good. The old lady was all skin, and from up close, he could see that her eyes were half open, glassy. No light in and no light out. *Stands to reason*, thought the murderer, and he straightened up, looked around to see if he had forgotten anything. *That cat!* Where was it? Would it leap out at him, steal some of his blood in its claws, gather forensic evidence against him?

Eliot Gladstone let the little wooden club slide down until he had its handle firmly in his left hand, and then he switched it to the right. "Here, puss, puss," he cooed to the darkness, but the shadows did not answer him. What was he doing anyway? *Forensics!* A dead woman at the base of the stairs was one thing, but a bludgeoned cat elsewhere told a more complex tale.

"Anyway," thought the killer as he made his way out the side door, through the porch, and back across the Pell's backyard, "I *have* taken care of that cat, too, for I have dispatched with its feeder. It will no doubt end up at the pound, in a little cage, with no more petting and no more recited poems." *The last poem*, Eliot Gladstone thought as he passed through the little wood to his SUV. *What a nice thought.*

# Chapter Eleven:  Red Herring Fallacies

Yeah, this one's named after a fish, an especially smelly fellow, a scent that can cover a person's tracks—such as a sketchy point in his or her argument—and make the audience look elsewhere. Arguers often act as magicians. Don't be fooled.

The church was white and wooden, tall and thin, the usual angled roof on either side, a three-story or more steeple up front, leading to a bell, motionless at present. The building looked like one of those 1800's one-room school houses found occasionally along back roads of rural highways, just pumped up in size several times. Inside, in the space between the modest dark altar and the first row of dark pews, Diana Pell's coffin rested perpendicular to the stage, parallel with the wooden benches, and Matthew Diggerson wondered if that were by design, if the placement had some spiritual meaning, some "thee could be thou" warning. Diana's everlasting box, gleaming brown as they always seemed to be, either light or dark (light, in this case), looked far too big for the short poet, but eternity was, of course, very large, indeed.

Outside the Congregational church's two-story unadorned windows, no stained glass to reflect the wonders of worship, the bare branches of trees swayed silently, a dance for the dead, and Digger remembered this same view from his childhood when his parents had tried to get their son and daughter interested in religion. The windows looked just the same, framing brittle branches, never blossomed with green or yellow or red leaves either, always just bony fingers. Had he never gone to church from May to September? Who really knew about memory, about its selection of details, especially now? Digger wondered if he had gone to the adjunct's funeral, Johna Adams, or to the grocery store lady's, Valerie Something. Probably he had gone to the first, but that time was more than clouded. It was blacker than a moonlit night, surgically removed, gone.

Anna had promised to accompany him, and Digger had not dissuaded her even though he wasn't sure why she wanted to go to a funeral for someone she had never met or at least could not remember ever meeting. Maybe at some faculty function long ago. She was driving directly to the church from the Cape, but obviously she was a little late since he could see no blond heads in the small crowd, which sparsely filled up the first four rows of pews, both right and left. Although he recognized few of the brown-haired heads, he probably would know many faces when the people turned to see who else had come, as funeral-goers everywhere always did. Suddenly Eliot Gladstone appeared at his side, and startled, Digger admitted to himself that being snuck up on was fairly easy. In his dark suit, Eliot looked business-like and somewhat pleased, gazing at the gathering congregation, his eyes or maybe just the lenses of his round glasses twinkling. Digger thought that his colleague looked very much in place at a funeral, and he remembered what Lou had said about the two Gladstones.

"Not much of a crowd," said Eliot, a jolly beginning to a conversation.

"It's early," said Digger.

"Poets have a limited audience." Eliot was breathing heavily, as though the air in the church offered little oxygen.

"This is a funeral, Eliot, not a book signing. And Diana's family was small now, just like all families tend to get as members die and move away."

"True, and you should know about that, Digger. But so do I. When your parents go, it is all just air above you. Empty. But your mother still lives, yes? You have told me about your mother."

Digger always felt compelled to argue against negative people and their opinions, which pessimists always seemed to take as gospel, as facts. "What about memories, Eliot? They're always there, stars in the night sky, shining memories."

Eliot made a noise, something that sounded like a flatulent smirk. "Shining memories, how poetic, Digger. Diana would have liked that, probably would have used it in a poem."

"Immature poets borrow, mature poets steal."

"What is that? Some sort of poetry?"

"T.S. Eliot, Eliot. I never thought of that, that you two share a name. You and Prufrock, you and Diana's cat. Doesn't that make you like cats a little more?"

"Detestable creatures! But you will find out about the emptiness, when your mother's gone. Then you will feel the emptiness of the sky. Stars, clouds, the moon. All those objects provide meaning, interpretations, symbols, even hope, but not empty air. You will see."

Digger thought that Eliot was probably right, had even felt some of that emptiness with each of his great losses: his father, his sister, Anna. *Anna!* She was coming soon. Soon her light would come toward him down this darkened aisle.

"Maybe you're right, Eliot. Maybe that's why most people have children. You and I wouldn't know about that."

"Children!" replied the tall man, in the same tone that he had summed up felines.

Digger giggled. "Children and cats," he said.

"Diggerson, Diana's accident is a damn shame, but it is also an inconvenience. I now have four new sections to staff. Nobody else is an expert on poetry, so I might just cancel that class, but that still leaves me with two 102's and Creative Writing. What do you think? Are you up to more work now? You seem, well, healed."

"I feel, well, healed," smiled Digger, "but that's a lot of extra work. My doctors would argue against the added responsibilities, and I could not teach creative writing anyway. I just don't know enough teaching tactics for that."

"But you are a published author, Diggerson, a creative writer. Surely you could draw from your writing experiences, or at least fool the fools into thinking that you know what you're talking about."

Digger glanced up and saw that Eliot was smirking. The thin smile did nothing for his appearance, and Digger thought of Diana Pell's smile, how it would blossom slowly on her face and light up the room. If Eliot's smile ever opened that wide, the room would run screaming.

"You're smiling, Digger. Does that mean 'yes'?"

"No, I was just thinking of Diana, of her smile. Remember how sweet it was?"

"Quit stalling, Diggerson. Yea or nay?"

"I could take one of the 102's, Eliot, but no more than that. I need to take things slowly, and I wouldn't teach Creative Writing, not yet anyway. You need someone like Diana for that, or maybe Jolie. She writes lots of songs, so she probably writes other things, too. Has she added any stories to the Dream Board?"

"I have not looked." Eliot then swiveled his rather big, round head to peruse the cavernous church again, searching for Jolie's stories, it seemed, or perhaps for the fiery woman herself. Digger stifled a giggle.

"Little ditties," Eliot suddenly said. "No, those students want an actual published author, and that is you, Diggerson. Twice, right? An actual author as a teacher. Would add some clout, and include a lot more money for you. Of course, you get paid per course until next fall, when your usual full-time compensation will begin again. Good of OVC to reinstate you with no fuss."

Hadn't Diana said something about his being reinstated this spring? No matter. *Good of Diana to fight for me*, thought Digger, who said instead, "Yes, or should I say 'yea'? But just one course." His mind had shifted to the 102 class, for which he could once again apply his dual-assignments approach, maybe two assignments for imagery, one for Robinson's "Richard Cory," which always startled students, and perhaps another for some other genre, a short story or narrative essay. Selzer's "Abortion" worked for most assignments, and it was more a creative than non-fictional piece. After imagery, Digger could move up to a harder element of fiction, perhaps symbolism, one paper on Carver's "Cathedral," the most positive short story he had ever read. As he stood quietly in the word-muffling church, ideas danced in Matthew Diggerson's mind, imagery fueling enthusiasm, the reason why he loved his vocation.

"When do her two 102's meet?" Digger asked.

"One section runs at one o'clock on Monday, Wednesday, Friday, so that is the section you would want, correct? Your current single class would follow." Digger nodded.

"Well," continued the Humanities Chair, "that is one less worry then, one less *inconvenience*. Perhaps the little ditty *can* take Creative Writing, and the other 102 should be easy to fill. I will just dangle it in front of the adjuncts and choose whoever jumps high enough."

"Why, Eliot, you sound sort of like Tobias, don't you? He often talked about part-timers that way. He once called them 'pigeons.'"

"Pestilent birds!" said Eliot, and then the happy fellow moved up the hallway toward the outer door. Maybe he was leaving already. Digger hoped that he was and that maybe some pigeons were waiting, poised to be *pestilent*.

Turning back, Digger saw that Diana's son was standing before her coffin, alone, and Digger tried to remember if the Reluctant Smiler had had other offspring. He thought that he remembered Diana Pell's talking over the years about a son, one who was out of the picture, though, far away, one who turned out to be Michael, obviously. But no other son, no daughter? Did Michael have a wife? Digger could remember no middle-aged woman accompanying him at the party, and certainly he stood by himself today or nearly so. The Pells seemed to be attenuating, just like the Diggersons.

He imagined Diana Pell's own parents, pictured one of those stern couples who posed smile-less for Time in old black-and-white photos, starched collars, dark hair pushed back, rich and educated and privileged. Did educated people have smaller funerals? Fewer kids, of course, so less of a chance to branch out. Smaller family trees. *The Diggerson Tree*, its limbs broken, a stunted old crabapple. No green twigs, no hope of more blossoms. Digger realized that he would be lucky to have this many people at his own funeral. He thought of Anna and wanted to ask her why other people's funerals always made a person think of his own. "Proximity to death," she would probably say and then smile. *Where was she?*

Digger noticed that Michael Pell was running his hand across the coffin's smooth surface, and the poignant image made him think of a nature show from PBS, an hour about an elephant herd. When one old member had died, of old age for a change, not due to humanity, the other elephants had gathered around the body and touched it with their trunks, softly, reverently. Then later on, after time had passed and the elephants had returned to the same area, the herd had gathered around the deceased member's bones, reaching out with their trunks again to fondle the pale remains and push them about a bit, remembering through touch, honoring the individual. Digger imagined that Diana's coffin would be cool and smooth, like those old elephant bones, and the thought was almost too much to bear alone. So he took a dozen steps up the aisle and joined Diana's son at her coffin.

"She was a great teacher and poet," he told the son (the last Pell?), "and a good friend." Digger put one hand on Michael Pell's shoulder and reached out to the coffin with the other, and together the two men stood in a huddle with the dead, quietly, a little less alone. Yet none of the other elephants joined the pair. Forgotten bones already.

When Digger released the son and the coffin and turned to the crowd, he immediately felt and then saw Anna's approach. In the dim church, her aura stood out obviously, like a glorious golden mane about her head, and for a moment Digger could only gasp at the air, as Eliot had seemed to, but for opposing reasons, no doubt. When Digger saw Anna's striding through the church toward the altar, *toward him*, he knew then that they were once again betrothed, that it was now only a matter of time. Not of *if*, but of *when*. The congregation must have wondered why Matthew Diggerson was beaming above the deceased's earthly remains, so pleasantly boxed.

She walked right up to him, smiling, and held out her hand, nodding to Michael Pell but looking quickly back at Digger, who laughed inside thinking about the strange scene, the couple standing near the altar, the coffin, the main mourner. What must it look like? Digger giggled, Anna's hand in his own.

"Maybe Diana will marry us," he said into his ex-wife's bottomless eyes.

"Married by a poet," replied the shining woman, who had stolen all of the church's thin light, who wore it now like a robe. "Wouldn't that be a magical life!"

It would. Digger found once again that he could not speak, so he turned back to the coffin and touched it once more. *Elephant bones*. Loyalty, remembrance, faith. After the funeral, he would tell Anna about those elephants and why he had joined Michael Pell to caress the smooth coolness of memory, to touch eternity.

After the service—during which Michael told the crowd about his mother's passion and quiet humor, while a young relative, a cousin, recited one of the deceased's more optimistic poems, a recent one—the minister invited the congregation to proceed to the cemetery for the burial and reminded the mourners to return back to the church's recreation center for refreshments and camaraderie. Around them, the congregation was stirring, and Digger soon recognized many faculty faces and even a couple administrators, such as Omar Johns, whom Digger forever connected to Danny Jones due to the round-headed man's eulogy for the sad-student's memorial outside the OVC library. Gwena Schmidt had been there, too, back when she had led the Humanities Department. Was the Grammar Nazi here, as well? Digger saw some gray and silver heads rising around him, but none belonged to Gwena, whom he would have enjoyed seeing again. She probably spent most of her time visiting her poor husband, and Digger wondered if the old fellow even recognized his wife of a half century.

"Are you looking for someone?" said Anna as they, too, rose.

"Yeah, the Grammar Nazi," said Digger. "Remember Gwena?"

"Vaguely. That's a hard nickname to forget. Is she here?"

"I don't see her," he said, nodding and smiling to several other faculty members, full-timers most, but Patricia Pauley did pass by, accompanied by a big man, her husband apparently.

"Matt," said Anna. "That was a long ride from the Cape, and I, well, need to use a bathroom."

"Do churches have bathrooms?"

"You'd better hope so! All public places have bathrooms, I would think."

"Is a church a 'public place'? I guess so, but I didn't see any doors up front, you know, off to the side, so if there is one, it's probably in back. Maybe a unisex bathroom."

"I hope so and hope not," said Anna, slipping off against the scattered groups of retreating mourners, all trailing after the coffin itself, following the dead. Digger tried to untangle her last comment. Men are messy, he concluded. He watched her turn left at the altar and speak to a young fellow in a black robe. He pointed toward the corner, and Anna headed that way. Digger watched the young man watch Anna, couldn't blame him. Then Eliot appeared again at his side.

"Are you sure you don't want both 102's?" he said.

"Just that Monday, Wednesday, Friday one, Eliot, and good luck staffing the others."

"An inconvenience," the man repeated, as though their prior

conversation had never ended. Eliot seemed to be looking at the empty space that had held Diana's coffin, no doubt chastising the fallen woman for causing him so much trouble, and from this angle, his glasses caught the altar's candlelight and held the flame, obscuring Eliot's eyes. Digger was reminded of a comic strip from his youth. One character had worn glasses, and the artist had not sketched in eyes behind them. Digger had never liked that comic. He had been loyal to Peanuts, to Linus and his blanket, to Snoopy and his dreams. Eliot just stood there, gazing at nothing, his eyes hidden beneath pale fire.

"Was that your ex-wife, Digger?" Eliot said. "Attractive woman."

"It's nice to have a person who loves you," said Digger, somewhat reluctantly, for he wasn't sure how the unmarried man would react. Usually best just to go with the truth. But Eliot Gladstone didn't react at all, so Digger prompted him. "As you said, your parents are both gone, aren't they, Eliot?"

The other man seemed far away, not standing right next to Digger, as close as bones, and couldn't that be another cliché? *As close as bones.*

"My mother died like Diana, ironically," said Eliot Gladstone. "Fell down the stairs. Of course, she was drunk at the time, and I do not know about Diana. She certainly seemed to be tossing them back at her party."

Now Digger was not sure what to say. *Diana drunk?* Digger wondered about Eliot's upbringing, about his parents, who had left his peer with only *empty air.* "And your father? I don't remember you talking about him much, Eliot. You said something at the party, that he liked scotch."

"Do we talk *much*, Digger? We colleagues." Eliot paused, glancing about the empty church, right and then left, his glasses catching fire and then dying. Maybe he was looking for his father.

"Yes, my father loved Glenlivet scotch, named my brother after the brand. Maybe me, too—'livet' and 'Eliot'—when he was too drunk to hear the difference. Of course, Glenlivet was very expensive, just for the important occasions, like my mother's funeral. Usually, my father bought the cheap stuff, the clear bottles. Then he would transfer the cheap scotch to the dark green Glenlivet bottle. He even had a funnel for the job, one of those oil-changing funnels. I once asked him why he did it, and he said that he liked the green bottle. *That* was the understatement of all time."

Digger had never heard Eliot Gladstone spiel so many words, so many secrets. "I'm sorry," he said, but Eliot didn't seem to hear him.

"My father died of somewhat natural causes," continued the bespectacled man. "*Natural* if having a liver like a flattened football is natural."

Digger felt bad for the man, the bitter fellow whom he had apparently once ratted out to the cops, considering him a possible murderer. That's what the cop had told him—that dark haired woman—that Digger had named Eliot and even Lou as possible killers, and that thought took him back to Bill Jacobs, whom Digger had also once suspected of murder. Maybe Bill *was* a suspect, or should be, just a ten-years-later one. The thought startled him, but then he remembered what Eliot had just said.

"Alcohol's never the answer, is it, Eliot, never the solution? But you don't seem to have a problem with it, with addiction."

Eliot laughed at that, the Gladstone scoff. "Oh, no, not with alcohol." He paused then, letting the utterance sink in. *With what then?*

"You want to hear an odd fact, Diggerson? My mother, after her accident with the stairs, she still seemed to be present in the house. Just in another room. The kitchen, for instance. Sometimes my father, after an hour on his big brown leather chair, would yell to the kitchen for another drink, as though my mother would pop out with it. 'Diana, get me another!' Then he would just forget and get one himself, or make me do it."

"Your mother's name was Diana?"

"Diana? What? No, it was Judith." He paused again, and Digger realized that Eliot had not noticed his own mistake. "My mother was still in that house, still present, until he died, my father. After his funeral, I stood in that living room alone and felt the silence and emptiness of that house. No presence at all. She had waited for my father. For some reason. Why, I will never know."

"That's sort of sweet, Eliot. That one would wait for another, and I know what you mean about a deceased person's still seeming to be present."

Eliot failed to respond. He had that faraway look again. All of the mourners except them and Anna had passed through the church's double doors, which had closed. Void of a congregation, the church seemed even larger. "Your father died in an accident, too, if I remember correctly, Diggerson."

"He did, a car accident. My sister, too."

Eliot seemed not to hear, and Digger was reminded of students who spent all class doodling on notebooks, although those were becoming rare, replaced by laptops. Oftentimes, those doodling students were actually listening, their minds on both the fantasy of the sketch and the reality of the room. Eliot was apparently inhabiting two worlds now.

"You and I had better watch out for accidents, Digger. They seem to run in our families." Then he made that noise again, like a sick goose, a sort of strangled honk.

"I don't think accidents are my problem, Eliot. More like knives and bullets."

Eliot honked again. "And fingers, don't forget those. That adjunct was strangled."

Digger wondered how the conversation had gotten to the *adjunct* he could not remember, a place he did not wish to go, could not go. He looked at Eliot's sickly grin and noticed again the thin white lines on his forehead, not the typical horizontal wrinkles of age, but perpendicular slashes, pale with just a hint of pink running on each side. *Eliot's cat.*

Digger nodded to the scars. "And watch out for cat claws, too, right? Your scratches have finally healed, I can just barely see them."

For Eliot, the word 'cat' was obviously a hot-button issue, for the spit started to fly. "Cats, vile creatures, Digger, vile! Something evil and watchful about them. Diana Pell had one, you know. I hope they put it down!"

Digger frowned. Where had 'Prufrock,' aka Alfred, gone? Probably Michael took over his care, and probably the cat helped him to bear the loss, to remember his mother's presence, she who had loved that cat. And why did Digger keep getting stuck with Eliot? Where was that carbon copy brother of his? Why did this man always make Digger want to argue? Bill Jacobs had been that way, too.

"I have a great cat, named Bumper. He's sweet and smart, acts sort of like a dog. Snodo and he are friends. You know, Eliot, cats are as different as people. They're not all the same."

"It will turn on you, Diggerson." Eliot touched his cheek for some reason, as though he felt the scar there, lower on his face.

*Not like people do,* thought Digger, but he kept that conclusion to himself. It felt strange standing in an empty church, like the ultimate of endings. *Where was Anna?*

"Here comes your ex-wife," said Eliot, adding "I hope she's no cat." *Words as weapons,* thought Digger. Negative, smelly, distracting. The younger Gladstone stalked off up the aisle toward the front doors, never even waiting to meet Anna. That was fine with Matthew Diggerson, who felt a little worn out after the negative conversation. He pictured Simba's shaking off rain drops, usually in the kitchen, and imitated her beneath the church's vaulted ceiling. Shaking off Eliot.

Anna laughed as she reached him. "Are you shaking off fleas? Who was that?"

"One big flea, Professor Happy Rock himself, being especially 'happy,' too."

"Oh, I would have liked to meet him, to tell him our name for him."

"I'm not sure *he* would have *liked* it. Eliot's a bit touchy, and he was even touchier today. He told me that his parents were alcoholics and that his mother had died after a fall down the stairs."

"That's weird, just like your teacher friend, like Diana."

"Detective Doyle from way back, the cop I talked to about Tobias' murder, he would not have liked hearing about that coincidence. But I just can't see Eliot Gladstone hurling Diana down the stairs. He's not strong enough."

"He moved pretty quickly right now, when I was coming."

*True*, he had. "You know, I call Eliot the Breather because he always seems out of breath, but he told me a couple long stories, long for him. One was about his mother's presence still being in their house after she died. In short, it wasn't until his father died that his mother's 'ghost' left, too, and then the house was completely empty."

Anna replied, "My father's presence was never in our house, but Deena's was big enough for both of them. Her presence was more than enough!"

"Your mother's a nut, to say the least, but I can understand Eliot. When I visit my mom, I always think of my father around, usually just upstairs, taking a nap. Even after twenty years, more than that."

"That sounds symbolic, upstairs, napping."

"Well, Anna, I guess we writing and art teachers have something in common, a leaning toward symbolism. Where were you, by the way? If you haven't noticed, everybody's gone." He smiled to show that he was not criticizing her.

"The bathrooms are way in back, near the rec center, which is all decked out with tables and plates and even food, covered up in wrap. I stole a cookie."

"Did you steal two?"

"Sorry," laughed Anna, the sound echoing in the lofty church, like doves flapping to the rafters. "But I was hungry. If I had stolen two, I would have eaten them both."

"Well," said Digger, leading Anna up the aisle, "unless there's more like you about, there should be plenty of cookies left for later."

Outside, the procession was still unraveling, disappearing into automobiles, forming a line with a hearse for a head. Digger suggested that Anna ride with him, of course, and he pulled his black Yaris into place, the tail of the snake. The two smiled at each other for a bit, saying nothing much. The sky was blue and clear for a change, for it had been a snowy winter so far, not any big shoveling storms, but many little poignant ones, storms without winds, New England postcards.

In the quiet car on the slow ride, Digger and Anna each pondered separate thoughts. Digger thought of Eliot and his past suspicions and considered calling a department meeting to ask peers outright who had shot him, explaining that the cops theorized that a colleague had done so because of his books, out of jealousy. He imagined asking who had read *Composition Murder*. Wouldn't only Lou answer *yes*? But why would a book (*books*, he had to keep reminding himself), a murder mystery, not great literature full of insights, but a novelty book, almost, why would that push a person over the edge? But then Digger would imagine holding his creation, feel the warmth and solidity of the text (*texts!*) and know that they were his 'niche,' a unique place all his own, for all time. What would others say to that? Was a niche worth killing over?

He thought of Eliot, his lack of niches—no publications, no wife or kids, not even a dog. Definitely no cats! And a job he didn't seem to like, a position full of 'inconveniences.' Eliot had no niches, but he was too old to kill. *Too breathless.* How could he have throttled two healthy women? *No way!* Then he thought of the female cop with the strange name, Zorn, of her point about the victims having been struck and rendered immobile. Even an old guy, or a woman for that matter, could strangle a person knocked unconscious, right?

"What are you thinking about, Matt? You look sort of serious."

"Oh, I guess I'm just doing what you and my mother think I should be doing, thinking about who shot me."

"Do you think that it was someone at the funeral, someone we'll see again in just a few minutes, at the cemetery?"

"Honestly, no. I think the killer's long gone, some freak, nobody I know at all."

"You mean a stranger? But what about those two women who were strangled?" Anna reached over and pinched his cheek. "You know, the ones who were sweet on you."

Digger giggled. "No other woman has ever had a chance, Anna. But I don't remember either one of them, so I don't know about that theory, even if I'm the one who gave it to the cops. *If* I did! I don't even remember that."

"I thought the cops might be at the funeral. You know, the way they sometimes show up on TV shows, looking for the killer in the crowd."

"But this wasn't a murder, Anna. Diana just sleep walked or tripped or something and then fell down the stairs. Why would the police think twice about her death?"

Like Eliot before, though, Anna didn't seem to be listening. "Maybe they *were* there," she said. "Incognito."

At the cemetery, the minister finished Diana Pell's last rights and then invited everyone back to the church for food and memories. These Congregationalists do things *quickly*, thought Digger. He liked the peace and quiet of this graveyard, and soon he and Anna were alone, once again, except for two workers who were waiting for everyone to vanish so that they could start filling in Diana's grave, which was the main presence itself, the great hole beneath the heavens. Each worker was eating an earthly apple, though, and didn't seem too concerned about having to wait to do his job.

"Do you want to skip the, uh, reception, Anna? We could just go back to the cottage."

"No, we should go, and don't forget those cookies!"

"Cookies!" said Digger. "What a wonderful word!"

Back at the church, Digger noticed that the crowd had thinned again since not everyone at the funeral had gone to the cemetery either. Still, Diana Pell must have had thirty or so mourners, having outlived some who would have been in attendance. Digger was surprised that Gwena Schmidt had not come, for she and Diana had been friends or at least friendly. Colleagues weren't really friends, were they? Digger had discovered that fact when nobody read his book or asked him about it (about *them*!). Maybe some would do so today, as they sat and reminisced. But who really cared anyway? Anna was at his side, and her aura protected them both.

The good cookies were all gone, the chocolate chips, so Digger put a sugar cookie and an oatmeal one on a napkin and brought the meager fare to Anna, sitting with Jolie and Lou and Todd, the OVC contingent still remaining. Anna took the oatmeal, as Digger had expected. "There's a lot of salads and cold cuts, too," he said, but Anna was happy nibbling on the cookie for now. Probably, she didn't want to be the only one eating since his colleagues had mostly empty paper plates before them, Styrofoam coffee cups half filled. Digger didn't want to sit down. "Do you all know Anna?" he said, and the three teachers nodded and smiled. "This is Jolie, and Lou, and Todd. He's from the mid-west, Denver, right?"

"You reckon right, pardner," mocked Todd. Lou laughed and then did his lip thing, one meaty passage. Jolie was already talking privately with Anna.

"I'm going to talk with Michael," said Digger to the two men. "Be right back. Could you tell Anna?"

Michael Pell was sitting with some relatives, probably, some nieces and nephews and their parents (his siblings?), the biggest table in the big, high-ceilinged room. "Michael," said Digger. "Can I talk with you?"

The two men moved to an empty table. Michael Pell, close up, looked older than Digger had imagined, but maybe it was just the gravity of the day rather than gravity itself. "That was a nice service," said Digger. "You did well, and so did your niece reading that poem. Your mother was a talented writer."

"Thank you," said Michael Pell, adding "The cops think that I killed her, that I left a watery mess on the stairs, that I'm responsible. The cops think that I killed my own mother."

Digger felt for the man. "Why do they think you were

responsible for the, uh, accident?"

The son's face was doing strange things, emotions pulling the skin in various directions, creating wrinkles that then smoothed themselves out only to reappear elsewhere. Digger had the image of a flower blooming and sleeping and then blooming again, and that made him think of the man's mother, of her reluctant smile. He almost giggled at the nice thought.

"Pills," said Michael Pell. "They found pills, opioids, in the bathroom. They must have been my mother's, they weren't mine. I've never taken opioids, or rather just once, but they made me so spaced out and dizzy that I threw the rest away. Pain is better than that!"

"Did Diana have to take opioids? I never noticed her in any physical pain, but, of course, I haven't seen much of her for quite some time. She did visit me at Breezy Seas, and then, of course, I saw her at the party a month back."

"She never told me about any opioids," said the boy-man, and his eyes looked wide and vacant, as though he were looking not at Digger or this large room, but instead far away, at scenes including his mother, in the kitchen probably.

"If the pills weren't yours or your mother's, where would they have come from?"

"That's just what the cops said. But they weren't mine, and I told the police that I didn't think they were my mother's pills either. Maybe somebody from the party, but we would have seen them at some point, right? My mother or I would have seen the pills. Do you think the cops could have planted them, you know, to get me to confess?"

"To what, Michael? Your mother wasn't murdered. She just had a terrible accident. Nobody's to blame."

"Somebody's always to blame."

Digger thought about that. Sounded like a Protestant New England guilt mantra, and he couldn't help but agree a bit. "How's Alfred doing?" he asked Diana's son.

"Alfred's fine."

"You're keeping him then?"

"Yes, yes, what else could I do? He's always at my feet, always meeeowing."

"He misses your mother."

Michael Pell nodded at that and then said, "And if I were to get rid of the cat, my mother would haunt me forever." Then he smiled, a bit reluctantly, and Digger responded in kind, with a giggle. Like his mother's, the son's smile stole a decade from his weary façade.

On the drive back to his cottage, Digger told Anna about Michael Pell's summation, and she surprised him, saying, "It is strange that so many writing teachers have died, been murdered, in the past decade. It makes me wonder about your poet friend's death, too. She died right after publishing a book, and the other murders occurred right after you published a book, right? There's a *book* connection. Do you think that another writing teacher could be so jealous and bitter that he would kill new authors?"

Digger had apparently had a similar question back before the bullet, for the policewoman had told him as much. Could one of his colleagues, a bitter non-writer, have killed Diana Pell? Was a composition instructor capable of murder, of strangling women, throwing one down a stairwell, shooting another in the head? He thought of the pressures of teaching, the frustration of having even one student in twenty who didn't seem to care, wouldn't listen, repeated the same silly mistakes, and about how that one bad pupil could occupy a teacher's mind, pushing the nineteen other good ones (or at least pretty good for most) out and just squat there. A Jaba the Hut worry, immovable and grinning. Digger called such students 'uncoachables,' and it took him three-quarters of a semester to shake them from his black river, where such students liked to cavort. After two-and-a-half months of such blahness, of skipped homework readings and short, broad, boring essays, of absences and cell-phone obsession in class, Digger could release responsibility with just a few weeks left in each semester. But before then, an uncoachable could torment.

Then there were the papers, the piles of essays and reports, and the advisees and the meetings and the pressure to publish something, to make some difference in the field. *Yes*, Digger could see how a writing teacher could snap. Paul Smith had, but that had been due more to his deceased wife than to the pressures of teaching writing. *Who else?* Eliot came to mind, but he was too old. Did he even have the breath to kill? Diana Pell would have thrown *him* down those steps, not the other way around.

"Matt?" said Anna, and he turned quickly to look at her, at the 'V' above her eyes. She looked so beautiful. Then he looked back at the road. They were almost home.

"I was thinking about your question, not ignoring you," he said. "And I would have to say 'no,' that the writing profession does not lead one to kill. Maybe to want to kill, but not to actually do it. Besides, we teachers can kill without doing a damn thing. Just look at my colleagues, who kill me every time they don't read my book, books, or even mention them. And am I any better? Am I any less uncaring? I never read Diana's book."

"But it just came out, Matt, and you would have. I know you. You would have wanted to discuss some of the poems with Diana."

"But I never talked with her about her other poems, the ones on the Dream Board. I can't remember mentioning even one to her."

"But you probably did, you just don't remember. Don't forget that you lost a year, and I'm sure that you talked with Diana about those board poems. It's just not like you not to reach out like that, to show interest."

"Thank you for saying that, but I'm just like them. I can see it now. They all no doubt think the same thoughts, that when they have time they'll read *Diggerson's book*, or books, and then time goes by and they think it again. Time, as usual, is the real obstacle here. I'm being too hard on people."

"From what I know, you're hardest on yourself, Matt. You always have been. Why is that? Is it because you lost your father when you yourself were just a young man? Why are you so different?"

"I'm not, Anna, but I'm glad that you think I am."

In response, his ex-wife leaned over and kissed him on the side of his head, on his right cheek and just a bit on the corner of his mouth. *So soft*. Digger wanted to pull over and dissolve right into Anna's aura, but instead he just kept driving, smiling and driving.

At home, Snodo was bouncing about at the back door, barking and laughing, and when Digger unlocked it, the white tufted beagle shot right past him and snuffled about Anna's legs.

"She's bored with me already," laughed Digger.

That night, they lay on the couch, watched TV, and leisurely finished off a bottle of white wine, but they did not yet sleep together, Digger once again giving up his bed and shivering under a quilt on the couch. Snodo again slept with Anna, but Digger was glad to see Bumper on the chair near the TV. His life was full once again. A black companion, a white one, and another full of light. Yin and yang, the full circle. And Simba, too, tucked away in her backyard nook, sheltered from the winds and cold, giving herself no longer to the sparrows but to the blue spruce instead, her energy traveling up the tree and making the branches ripple. A nice image.

In the deepest hours of the night, Digger listened to the turning earth, to Simba's whispering through the pine, to the stars' twinkling, and especially to the slight snoring sounds coming from his bedroom, probably Snodo's, and the composition professor vowed not to let his job *consume* him anymore, to devote more time to Anna—*this time*. He would no longer volunteer for committees or accept the department chairmanship again. Eliot could have that job forever. He would let younger colleagues worry about upward mobility. Lou, Jolie, Todd. He would get more papers graded *during* office hours, and maybe he would stop at two books, not allow himself to get obsessed with writing, as he had with the first and no doubt the second, which he could not remember. Maybe he would push away the third-book thoughts that had begun to surface, something to do with rhetoric chapter beginnings and a title like *Twisted Reasoning* or perhaps *The Point of Persuasion*, the latter cover showing a knife-wielding shadow, à la Paul Smith.

Digger would have to talk with Anna about a third book. She might even urge him to write it, and together they could write and paint, to take coffee breaks and animal ones, as outside the New England winter would blow and shake snowflakes and accent their little harbor amidst all of life's intensity. He couldn't sleep, not with such a future awaiting him, and he looked forward to coffee in the morning. Leonard Cohen's voice and one particular song, a rarer one that he had recently heard on the radio, "So Long, Maryanne," slipped into his mind, and the writing teacher began to substitute his own words into the melody:

> Now go along comma marks.
> It's time to show the parts
> That pause and guide and guide and pause
> Word group ends and starts.

*Grammar Jam!* Students would like this stanza, and Digger could add more verses with useful comma details. It would be fun to sing. Cohen would have laughed, too. Leonard Cohen, so bitter and so optimistic, crying at life but always laughing last. Digger mourned his fairly recent exit from the world. Cohen, Bowie, and Tom Petty. Diana Pell, too. All great creators gone, and Digger lay in the dark, listening to his loved ones' slumbers and hearing the winds, too, their almost decipherable language, for they continuously urged and echoed and danced, never stopping, forever scooping souls away, doing the bidding of Time.

# Chapter Twelve:  Straw Man Fallacies

This twist in logic operates as another distraction, a mirage, for if an arguer makes a point deemed too controversial and unlikely to take hold, he or she will often quickly add another point, a more palatable one, a pleasing shield, an empty shadow decorated favorably.

The Spring semester began with more falling snow, the kind that looked pretty but failed to amount to much, just a nuisance for Ocean View College's maintenance crew, who were out with brooms instead of shovels. On his way to the Faculty Offices Building, Digger repeatedly said hello to men he recognized but didn't know, and each time the sweeper mentioned the snow and smiled.

Digger passed the Administration Building and half expected Don Domberg to emerge from the basement, where Tutorial Services kept its hours, and where Digger had once tutored a sad black boy who later flew from a great height and stayed forever in the writing teacher's mind. Where was Doctor Joan Powers now? She had once told Digger about monkeys, chimps, and compared them to human societies. He almost wanted to say hello to her today, for the beginning of a semester always felt fresh and optimistic. Nobody appeared, though, not even students, who tended to use the middle sidewalk across Ocean View College's campus since that path led to not only the library, but the large cafeteria as well. Digger used this top walkway almost exclusively, and until this past November, he could not remember ever taking the low path past the Classrooms Building, the trail that led to the water, the bay, the Whirlpool, the scene of the fictional Danny's death.

Looking up, Digger saw a low ceiling of off-white clouds, a heavily painted canvas, which completely covered the sky and appeared thick and strong enough to keep even the winds away, allowing the flakes of snow to take their time, to fall at their own vertical pace. *Nice!* Where were the gulls? Usually, those big birds were slicing across the skies, screaming warnings, but not on this muffled winter day. Probably, they were all sleeping like buoys on the rooftops of every building.

Passing the Psychology Building, Digger thought of its fearless leader, the renowned Professor William Watkins, and even his appearance would be welcomed. Digger thought of that contact. He would say, "Beautiful snow," and the bearded nut would reply, "What snow?" suggesting a mind walking far from the mundane. Then he heard his name, "Digger," and wondered for just a second why William Watkins was being so informal.

"Gloria!" he responded to the Humanities Department's long-time secretary, who was approaching from their building.

"I have to go to Admin," she stopped and said, making it sound like a real chore.

"Called into Human Resources for trying to fix everyone up?" smiled Digger.

"I don't do that anymore, Professor. No need to with you, right? I saw you at Diana's funeral with Anna." She winked and smirked in a nice way.

"I am seeing Anna again," said Digger, smiling, too.

"Do you mean that you're dating her again or mainly just having visions of dating Anna?"

"All of it, Gloria! Seeing, dating, holding hands, walks on the beach. Actual visions and some fantasies, too. She once again fills up my senses, as John Denver would say."

"I love him, and that's 'Annie's Song,' right? Pretty appropriate." Then she looked up the sidewalk, perhaps wondering when the snow would stop or thinking about what to cook for dinner, and said that she had to get going, that the administrators couldn't wait, so Digger didn't hold her up with questions.

"I'll see you later," he said. For a second, he watched Gloria stride off and then felt a prickle in his neck, a sensation of being watched. *Watkins!* Turning toward the Psyche building, he saw instead a little sparrow head disappear into one of the towering arborvitae bushes that had long since grown into trees, almost hiding the building behind the widening, reaching dark green torches. "Hello," he said to the bird, but it disappeared. He saw twitches within the tree, more than one, so a whole family must be in there keeping track of a passing humanity. Suddenly, from the farthest tree on the southern edge of the building, a dozen small brown balls rose above the spiky green flames, like disturbed bees, and then settled down again and were swallowed by the thick fir tree, which vibrated and then became still. Arborvitaes always had two or three pointy branches in a race to the sky, and the one with the hidden colony showed two, a third a foot or so below, looking like either a sickly sibling or maybe a child. Digger could hear no peeping.

He smiled at the tucked-away sparrows, which always made him think of Simba, of the way the little birds used to fly off with tufts of the lion dog's thick hair. He thought of all those little hearts beating within the dark arborvitaes. Hidden yet pulsing in plain sight. Right outside the door. The image darkened, became unsettling, reaching fingers, but Matthew Diggerson shook it away with a snowflake that had landed on his forehead. Today was a new beginning, the possibilities of a young, innocent semester. Not even Eliot Gladstone could take the shine off of this day, or even Bill Jacobs, the retired adjunct. Digger would have been happy to see him again, at least until the pessimistic fellow voiced an opinion. Some people were just like that. Digger thought of a quotation made by a blind man, probably an author, something about how the blind man had never met an ugly person until he or she started talking. "Opened their mouth" was how he remembered the quote. *No,* not even negative Nellies would bother Digger today.

Without Gloria at her desk, the FOB was quiet and seemed empty. Then Digger met the newest adjunct writing teacher, the one whom Eliot had waxed poetic about to Lou Knightly, the astounding Beverly Douglas, who was sitting alone before a computer in the Adjunct Faculty Office. Although full-timers tended to stride right past that open door, Digger stopped and said hello. "You must be new," he said, introducing himself.

"Professor Beverly Douglas," she said in a voice with no inflection, no flight for any of the syllables, no dance in the words. She did not get up.

Digger giggled. What else was there to do? He asked the reticent woman if she had taught yet, discovered that she had, learned nothing more about the experience, though, and decided to exit before the Ice Queen sucked all of his warmth away. "Good luck," he said in departure, noticing that Beverly Douglas had already turned back to the computer.

As he unlocked his own office door, he said the word 'Beverly' in his mind, but that label didn't sound right, didn't fit the person he had just met. *Beverly Douglas.* Yes, some people simply failed to fit their first names alone, needed the whole designation, and she was one. Digger could easily picture the woman, apparently hovering somewhere along the autism spectrum, standing next to Eliot Gladstone, a big barn in the background, a pitchfork or shovel in their hands, or a gun! *No, no way.* Eliot might lean on the side of the macabre, but he was too old to be a killer. The bullet in his head just didn't feel like Eliot's. How could he find out if the Gladstones owned a gun?

He turned and looked across the hall to Diana Pell's old office. The door was closed. The permanence of death, a symbol, a closed door. But then Digger thought of his own father, how his mother's house still held him, just upstairs, taking a nap. Perhaps Diana's closed door could be like that, with the poet just inside, grading a paper, writing a poem. *No.* That room was dark and empty, that door shut tight.

His own office welcomed him with a peaceful silence and

continuity, his nook, his home away from home. *His hole.* All of the offices as holes, hiding places (*except Diana's*). He and his colleagues were really just sparrows. *Clinging to our arborvitaes.* Digger took the four steps into his hole and looked out the thin window to see the library and its clock towers, the left announcing that he had a dozen or so minutes before he had to head to his 102 class (Diana's) in the Classroom Building. The twin towers provided the usual racing shadows across the quad, pale but still just present on this cloudy, snowy afternoon, and Digger thought again of Beverly Douglas and Eliot, and then of Paul and Debra Smith, the Morbids. Maybe Eliot had a shot at love. *A shot!* Matthew Diggerson discovered that he had been rubbing his temple, feeling the scar tissue. He remembered Anna's saying something about shadows being crucial because they accented the light.

Then Lou Knightly (the Lip Licker) stuck his head around the corner and said, "Hello, Digger" before disappearing, and then Todd Thomas did the same. Todd was as short as Lou was tall, as round as the other man thin, and Digger realized that those two colleagues could create quite the vaudeville team. *Abbot and Costello.* One was even named 'Lou,' right? Neither comedian had mentioned Diana Pell, but both had been in a hurry, no doubt for class at one. *Class at one!* Digger grabbed his briefcase and left the building, saying hello again to Gloria Swanson, back from Admin. Outside, the slow snow continued to charm, and Digger looked repeatedly up to the heavens on the short walk to the Classroom Building. On his forehead, each flake landed cold but then blossomed warmly, felt nice.

Diana's 102 class seemed receptive, the usual mix of male/female, approximately ten each, and Digger concluded that they would be a good group. The next class, though, his scheduled professional writing one, WTNG 200, stood out for other reasons. The Registrar had been considerate in giving Digger the same room, so instead of packing up, wiping off the white board, and then adding more words to another room's board, he just had to change a few words on this one and wait. Soon a lanky student with a large smile strolled in, almost a young Lou Knightly, Digger thought at first, but this lad had some individual quirks, one being a grin that wouldn't thin, the other something deeper, more genetic, a strange twitching of the shoulders, almost a full-body hiccup.

"Hello, Professor!" the boy declared and then, "Remember me!"

"Yes," said Digger as the boy took a seat right before the teacher's desk. "Of course, how are you?" The composition teacher had no idea who this student was, not even a wisp of recognition. Yet Digger did not want to tell his tale to this class—that he had a bullet in his head, for instance—so he chatted with the amiable fellow and asked the boy to talk more with him after class.

By that time, the minute hand had reached the top again, so Matthew Diggerson began. He put his name and the course name on the board, introduced both, welcomed the twenty students, and then directed them to their course page on the Bridges software site, where he showed them how to check what was due (Calendar), submit their homework summaries (Drop Box), and send him their actual papers (Assignments). Then he directed them to seven Lesson's pages, one per assignment, and the class got going on Project One, checking the directions, which focused on logical fallacies used in a presidential speech. Digger used this reading-analysis assignment as a bridge between the 100- and 200-level courses, as well as a way to stress logos, an argument's logic—or in this case, with the dark side of logic, fallacies, twisted reasoning. For the dual assignments of Projects One and Two, Digger would focus on topics like generalizations, faulty emotional appeal, false analogies, and begging the question, common manipulative tactics that bypassed logical, sound reasoning.

When he read the definition for 'generalizations' from the directions sheet, the grinning student announced, "Like the killer, right?" Digger agreed and said that they could discuss that connection after class.

Besides twitching and grinning, nothing else strange occurred, and right before dismissing the students at ten of the hour, Digger took attendance, asking the students to let him know how they would like to be addressed. He made a map of their responses, too, since doing so would help him to memorize the names (students tended to take the same seat every class). None of the roster's first names led to the grinning fellow, none of the middle ones either, and just as Digger was thinking that the odd pupil was not even registered for the course, the professor read the last name, Michael Whitman, which resulted in a waved hand and an unexpected declaration: "Twitch!"

"Twitch?" said Digger, not understanding the student's reaction, yet almost remembering the strange word. Where had he heard it?

"My name," laughed the tall lad. "Like you said, how you would like to be addressed. Twitch! You remember."

"Yes, let's get caught up," said Digger, who then announced that he was glad to get the semester going and that students should definitely take advantage of his office hours, that fallacies in logic were tricky to spot and explain, but that they were very effective 'thinking and reading tools,' that armed with their knowledge, manipulators, such as politicians, had no chance to hoodwink them. Then he giggled at his choice of words, 'hoodwink.' "See you Friday," he concluded (the semesters always began mid-week).

Twitch stood and said, "Hoodwink, like the killer, right?" and Digger waited for the students to pass by the desk.

"Twitch," he said, "how do you know about the murders?"

"We talked about them a lot my freshmen year, and the killer even spoke to me, up near your office, told me about the second murder, before it was even announced by the press. I'm a Junior now, but I waited to take this professional writing class because I wanted you to be my teacher. I had faith that you'd wake up from that coma"

Digger's mind was spinning. This boy seemed to know more about his recent life than even he did. "You said that you talked to the killer? But that means that you know who it was. Who? Did you talk to the police?"

"You don't remember?" said Twitch, his face forming a frown for the first time.

"No, I don't remember anything that happened before I was shot, before my coma. I lost more than a year. I don't remember either woman who was killed. I don't even remember you, to be honest."

"You don't remember me!"

"I'm sorry, but no, Twitch."

The lad retrieved his laptop from the ever-present backpack, which every student in America seemed to have, and typed in some commands, then clicked a bit more, seemed to be scrolling. "Look," he said, turning the screen to Digger. "That's Johna Adams. She's still listed in the faculty. She was the first to die. I saw you two during the summer and then recognized you in my writing class. That's how we got talking about the murders."

"Yes, that's Johna Adams," said Digger, remembering that he had meant to talk to Eliot about getting her deleted from the list of faculty. "But I don't remember her at all. I don't remember talking with her that summer or seeing you, or talking with you about her, for that matter. My mind's a blank for that year."

"Wow!" said Twitch, who seemed to think that a forgotten year was amazing.

Digger redirected the boy. "Let's go through these other faculty pictures, now that you're on the page. Do you recognize the person who talked with you?"

"I won't remember, Professor. I did this with the cops and couldn't find him. He was a smiling older guy, but everybody looks old when you're my age."

Digger nodded, for that was true. To a young adult, any actual adult seemed ancient. Still, he scrolled past faculty bios until he got to the full-timers, stopped on Lou Knightly, the most 'smiley' of any faculty members. "Was the man this one?"

"No, I know that guy. He's tall and skinny like me."

Digger went to another picture, Eliot Gladstone's. Eliot had offered the camera no teeth, not even upturned lips. "This guy's not smiling, but could it have been this teacher?"

"No, I don't think so. That guy looks way too, uh, severe, frowning. The man I talked to, and it was just a quick talk, he was all smiles and happy. I didn't realize until later that he knew about a murder before anybody else did."

Digger showed Twitch more pictures, all of them, even back to one other part-timer, Jay Moore, whom apparently Digger had hired and then suspected. But Twitch just kept saying "No," "Nope," and "Not him." The boy said that he was sorry, that he was just *no good* at remembering faces. Yet he had remembered the murdered woman's face, Digger thought, wondering about this lanky lad.

"I'm sure that the police were very appreciative of your efforts," he concluded. "In fact, I know that they were, because they told me about their past investigations." That's where he had heard the strange name 'Twitch,' he had realized. That detective Zorn had mentioned a student.

At that, the young man's open face lit up even more, and then he announced, "Hey! I just remembered something, a song I wrote, you know, one of your Grammar Jam songs, I wrote one about combining sentences, you know, 'subordination.' I remembered you always talking about subordination and about using subordination to combine sentences, and you always added those blue #2b's on my papers, reminding me how to subordinate and what to look for, so I wrote a song. Want to hear it?"

Digger giggled again. This boy was all light, no shadows at all. "Definitely," he said. "Who's it to, the melody, I mean?"

"Some old band my father listened to when he was young, Metallica. Do you know their song 'Unforgiven'?"

"A great song, their best one. Let's hear it!"

Twitch clicked a tab and began scrolling through files, stopped and clicked again. "Here it is! 'Subordination.'" He opened the file, and pushed the laptop in front of Digger, who read it and smiled.

"Nice!" said the teacher. "Lots of great details, and you did a great job fitting in your words. Let's sing it." Then they did, laughing, and the song went like this:

Two sentences are short, and both begin with nouns.
So see if they relate, if logic can be found.
Then add a word like 'since,' or maybe 'if' or 'when.'
Try 'while,' 'because,' or 'as,' unlock the connection.
Choppiness, coherence less, combine to start a flow.
With 'whereas,' with 'although,' a contrast you will show.
So use 'because' and add 'when,' to show logic and then time.
Connect your thoughts, readers could get lost.
So use subordination.

"That's really good!" said Digger. "I'm serious. I couldn't write a better one than that. I love the 'unlock the connection,' 'a contrast you will show,' all of those specifics, plus the words themselves."

"You always said that they were your favorite words, especially 'because.'"

"You've got a good memory, Twitch. Did you write any other songs?"

"No, but the semester's just beginning. I'm sure that we'll sing a bit, right?"

"Maybe, but we won't work on grammar as much in this course. We have a lot of paragraphing control elements to cover, content needs, such as using visuals and research. But maybe I'll sneak in a song or two."

Twitch's slowly developing frown exploded. "Most excellent!" he declared, making Digger think of the 1980's. Twitch was sort of a boy out of time.

Ten minutes later, back at his office, the short January afternoon passed, and Digger felt good, having started once again, being a teacher. Then the solitude and silence settled in, like the cold. Stretching his arms and yawning, the composition instructor gazed out his office's narrow window and watched gulls launch themselves from the library's towers, like pouncing gargoyles. The snow had stopped, and a quickly descending sun actually cast shadow beams across the land, making Digger think of an octopus' tentacles, groping.

In the afternoons, the Humanities hallway was commonly deserted, and Digger liked that, usually, although he would have been happy for some company to dispel the creeping shadows, which leaked alongside the sun beams across the white quad outside and across his office within. Anna's shadow theory didn't always fit, for these shade fingers were eating the light, not illuminating it. Digger thought of Twitch's twitches, wondered where they originated and who had talked to the boy, *right out in this hallway.*

Diana Pell's closed door began to weigh heavily in his thoughts. The cops, reporters, his colleagues—nobody seemed to suspect that the long-time professor and poet had been murdered, but Digger couldn't keep the word 'coincidence' from his thoughts. He remembered the short detective's, Doyle's, mistrust of that word, and thinking of the past reminded him that Tobias Mann had been killed right where Matthew Diggerson was now sitting. Eight years ago, nine, or was it ten? *A decade past.* The aura cast by the infamous hallway set his thoughts tumbling, but then the solitary man giggled. *Anna*, he thought. Anna! This past Christmas still shone brightly.

Then he heard the rattle of a doorknob, steps. Digger swiveled his chair to face the empty corridor, Diana Pell's dead door, and the approaching human. Then Eliot appeared and stood in the doorway.

"Diggerson," he said. "You're back, and you have succeeded, no doubt."

"Hi, Eliot, yes, the classes were good. Diana's looks like a good group, and I even met a past student in my own professional writing class."

At that, Eliot's head cocked, making Digger think of Snodo and of Simba, who used to rotate her head in both directions, almost perpendicularly, to find answers in Digger's eyes. Digger giggled. "You look like my dogs, with your head cocking like that."

The tall man disregarded the dogs, cut the thought right out of the conversation, saying instead, "Did you remember him, the student?" Eliot's round glasses caught the dying light and flashed away the man's eyes, but then the shadows took hold again. The dark eyes were aimed right at Digger.

"No, I still don't remember that year, Eliot, and this guy would be hard to forget. He calls himself 'Twitch,' and that name fits because his shoulders do this spasmy thing, sort of hunch up uncontrollably. I'm not sure what his condition is, but it doesn't bother the young guy. And he's as tall and skinny as Lou, or you for that matter."

"I am not 'skinny,' Diggerson. Merely 'thin.'"

*And defensive.* Digger thought of Twitch's song, of subordination. Did this man feel subordinated by life? "How's your book going, Eliot? You mentioned that you were writing a psychological thriller."

Eliot stared at his peer, blankly, and then said, "The words dry up, run out. How do you keep the words from running out?" He seemed to ask the question not to Digger, but to himself or maybe to the empty office.

Digger felt sympathy slip in. "You need to keep at it, Eliot. With me, I used my experiences to create a sort of parallel universe, and then I had a character enter a scene, a place, and I just walked around with him, saw what he did, spoke to people who appeared. When you're in that parallel world scene, the ideas and words just bombard you. They won't dry up at all, just the opposite. If you do that, they won't run out, Eliot."

His colleague failed to respond, just stared across the office, so Digger continued. "Sometimes you take an experience and build it into a fuller one, or even a non-experience, something you just heard about, and build on it. Like I did with the Whirlpool. I had never even seen it, but I used what I had heard, from students. Have you seen the Whirlpool, Eliot?"

Eliot's gaze rose. "What?" The Whirlpool? Yes, I have seen it. I was unimpressed. A shabby place."

"But even a shabby place can be used, changed, embellished. You just need to create that world, Eliot. How far have you gotten?"

The tall man cocked his head again, as though Digger's question had come from a far place, as though Eliot were just hearing it now. Digger expected to see his peer's turning spectacles blaze again, but the coals seemed to have died out within the man.

"Maybe for *you* they do not dry up. Did you ever think of that, Diggerson? Maybe it's just not that easy, except for you and Diana and *David Reed Winslow*." The volume on those last three names rose with each, and the words were hissed as much as spoken. Eliot was clearly upset, incensed even, and Digger remembered how his colleague, or maybe it had been his brother, had called the famous author 'David Two Last Names.' That old envy, dark, still seemed to be burning.

"The words will come," said Digger, wanting to support his colleague. "But the semester's beginning is not a good time to write, just too much to do. And you're the Chair, lots of extra responsibilities. I'm glad that you have them and not me."

Eliot's head leveled. "You do not wish the throne, Digger? You do not feel dispossessed? Deposed, I mean. Lou Knightly wants my chair, did you know that?"

"No, Lou? Are you sure?"

"Oh, yes. He wants my chair. You hear all sorts of sordid gossip when you sit where I do, Diggerson. You should remember that. Oh, you don't remember, though, do you?"

Was Eliot now smiling? If so, it did not improve his countenance.

"I didn't forget everything, you know!" Digger replied, and when he recognized the prickle of defensiveness, he smiled it away. "I don't recall much departmental gossip, but as Chair, you do have to talk to everybody. And that reminds me. Johna Adams, her biography, it's still listed on our website's faculty bio. Shouldn't you talk to someone about having it deleted, updated? With her gone, it doesn't seem quite right to leave her smiling in the bios."

"Yes," said the current Chair. "Johna Adams should be deleted, and Beverly needs to be added. One out and one in. Does not life provide such perfect balance?"

Digger wasn't sure what Eliot Gladstone, now definitely smiling, albeit with crooked lips, meant by 'balance,' so he nodded his assent and agreed.

"Have you met Beverly Douglas? The best credentials. Went to Brown. Even took law classes, like my brother, but she wanted to teach. She is a *riser*, Diggerson. Soon, she will be one of *us*, perhaps very soon, with the sudden opening."

*One of us?* It took Digger a moment to realize that the other man meant a 'full-timer,' not an adjunct, but he didn't care for the judgmental implications or for the casual discarding of Diana Pell. "You mean a human, like us!" he responded, not expecting Eliot to laugh and not being disappointed in that assumption.

"I observed her class last fall," the tall man responded, "and Beverly had complete control over those students, complete control." He seemed to be visualizing that classroom, behind where Digger sat, but maybe his old colleague was actually somewhere else. Perhaps walking hand-in-hand with Miz Blah along the beach, neither talking but both wearing slight smirks. The world was their oyster. They had *control*.

"I will finish my observations this semester, Digger. When should I call on your class? Either one would do, but perhaps the second would be best."

"Are you supposed to observe full-timers' classes, Eliot? I thought that only adjuncts could be observed. But no matter. You can visit either of my classes, whenever you want. Just let me know so that I'm a little extra prepared."

"Of course," said the standing man, adding as he turned toward the silent hallway "Preparation is essential." Then the current OVC

Humanities Chair disappeared, but Matthew Diggerson could hear no footsteps diminishing, no sound at all. 'Merely thin' was definitely an understatement. Turning back to his desk, he saw that the shadows had overtaken his office, that he was now seated in the dark.

# Chapter Thirteen:  Generalizations

One of the more dangerous fallacies, a generalization often plays on people's fears and stereotypes, attempting to position the audience on the right side of "us," not the wrong side, with "them." While this fallacy is often attached to people, it also works on places and things, such as using a certain product (highbrow or low!), going to a Metallica concert (Motorheads!), or even just Tweeting (Idiots!). When you substitute "all" for "some," you tend to shed ethos.

February carried with it the burden of a long semester, the papers, the meetings, the advisees, the inter-office politics that plagued every workplace, white-collar or blue, but for Matthew Diggerson the spring semester was as advertised, a new beginning, new life. Partly, the attitude grew from his initial feelings every semester, the hope and expectation of student success, the enthusiasm of trying new tactics (such as his paired assignments this year), but mainly his mind's lightness had two roots:  one, the lessened workload, just two classes with no added responsibility of meetings (since he was officially not back to full-time employment until the summer, apparently) or advisees; two, the increased presence of Anna, via the phone or in person. She would visit now on every other weekend, and although they had not yet shared his bedroom, Digger knew that they would, that *that* closeness waited just ahead on the path. Never had he quite felt the way he did now, so sure, so peaceful. In the past, problems had always arisen, such as money and even prestige, as well as motherly responsibilities and all of the strange occurrences at Ocean View College, and then, of course, the decade of airy emptiness after Anna's departure, the slow crawl back to life, through Simba's eyes, through nature's canvas out his kitchen door and windows.

The view was full of life, his life, his little piece of a pie too large to envision, the blue earth spinning amongst the stars. With a cup of steaming coffee, the college professor surveyed his patch of lawn and pictured how it used to look, back when Anna had lit up the cottage, just as she would again, in time. Back then, no blue spruce swatted at the little birds that cheeped and landed for seeds and searched forever for the tufts of Simba's hair to soften their nests. No stone shepherd guarded the house, no curled-up memories slept beneath the soil. Back then, the yard had been a blank canvas with all of life waiting to supply texture and color.

As Digger sipped the hot coffee and gazed out at these contrasting images, Bumper appeared silently at his feet and looked up, golden eyes sending silent signals. Looking at the beautiful, mysterious animal, Digger could understand not only why so many people loved felines, but also why so many others seemed to dislike them. Fear. An inability to control. Bumper met his gaze as calmly as Buddha, as wild as the first tiger that stalked the undergrowth, and within the small animal Digger sensed magic. "You want to go out?" he asked, and when the black cat blinked, he opened the door a half foot for her to slip out without too much outside slipping in. Then he watched as Bumper casually sat on the top step and perused the world, the thin blanket of snow across the yard (and beneath his butt), the breezes that swept clear the sandy beach, the inevitable gulls slicing the sky beneath this winter's inevitable cloud cover, like an old mattress flipped over and covering the land, and all the little avian visitors, the single-note songs of the sparrows and cardinals, the happy chorus of the chick-a-dees, the disgruntled warning of the blue jays. And Digger wondered if Heaven had made all of this, igniting each little world, or if all these creatures, all the yearnings and dreams and beating hearts, if all of them had created Heaven instead. Was the life force created, or did each member build it up individually into a great whole?

It was too much for one mind to grasp, or was it? Maybe existence was as simple as its surface suggested. Eat to live. Breathe or die. Nourishment was all. But was nourishment just a simple noun, or did that hard nut crack to reveal entire galaxies? Matthew Diggerson decided that he didn't really care, for he was at peace. And the winter's continuous little storms helped, for they provided post-card views but no real road dangers or shoveling responsibilities. The thick cloud covers, too, kept the heavenly winds from washing across the land and the icy temperatures trapped far above. Digger smiled, for he noticed Bumper's ears twitching as they caught fat snowflakes. Where was Snodo? Usually, any opening of the back door would create a stampede of hairy legs and lolling tongue, but the white hyena must be fast asleep, perhaps on his bed waiting for Anna.

In the peace, the full silence, Billy D. Wilder began to whisper to the two-time author. Images and dialogue, plot, meanderings like the ones Digger had when gazing out this back door. Digger had begun to jot down these ideas, tentatively titling the new text *Perilous Persuasion*, for he had decided to use rhetoric-based chapter titles and to add a villain who talked himself into killing. Maybe Billy would have to talk the killer, as yet unidentified, out of his evil pursuits or to persuade him in more action-oriented ways. Digger had tentatively decided to include Billy D's father, perhaps even having the man perish in a car accident, or was it murder? Increasingly, the writer would get ideas and jot them in his notebook, where he knew that they would begin to take shape and to multiply on their own, the genesis of creativity. He vowed not to get too obsessed with this next book, at least when Anna was present, for Digger planned to devote the rest of his life to her, mainly, and to rest side-by-side in eternity with her golden aura beneath a stone that read "Listen, you can hear them sing."

At OVC, as the spring semester began to settle into routines and responsibilities, Digger discovered that the Dream Board had stagnated, perhaps because Diana Pell was no longer pinning up poems, and that few colleagues mentioned his books, most focusing on the weather (more snow) or on his memory and health. In his mid-western drawl, Todd asked, "How's the head?" Of course, Digger giggled in response, adding, "Still functions." Only Lou Knightly, the would-be Chair (according to Eliot), sought Digger out to discuss his writing.

One February afternoon, before Digger's two classes, Lou strolled into his office and said, "You know, Digger, I like your narrator, Billy D, but sometimes I don't. He's a little reckless, makes some bad decisions."

"I'm more ruled by logos, yeah, not so much pathos. But I didn't want Billy D to be me, not really, just enough so that I could add more truth to the fiction."

Lou nodded, cocked his head, and with that movement came the tongue, swiping horizontally across his face, making Digger think of reptiles. "Maybe I shouldn't tell you this, but Eliot, that creep, he calls you the 'Giggler.' He told it to me as a joke, repeated it, too, and I got the feeling that he wanted me to repeat it. But I didn't. Maybe I shouldn't have told you now."

"Eliot's sort of a sad old man, Lou, and what do sad people do but try to make others sad, too. That's the really *sad* part."

Lou surprised Digger by smiling. "You know, he would make a great killer in your next book. Are you planning the next?"

Digger didn't respond immediately. Hadn't his writing created problems before? Then he thought of the Dream Board. "Yeah, I am, but just in the note phase. I haven't told anyone, because, well, sometimes publishing a book is dangerous around here, seems to be, anyway."

"You and then Diana, but her death was accidental, right? The police didn't suspect foul play, did they?"

*Foul play.* The expression made Digger giggle. "Sorry," he said. "When you said 'foul play,' I thought of a TV show, one of those old detective movies maybe, Humphrey Bogart in a trench coat or that other guy, William something or maybe Robert, yeah, Robert Mitchum."

"Robert Mitchum? I don't know him. But you're right, Digger. You should probably keep your third book to yourself."

"It wouldn't make much difference around here anyway since you're about the only one to ever even mention my writing."

Lou Knightly deflected the compliment, saying, "You wrote a book, two of them, and got shot. Diana wrote another and fell down the stairs. My students would conclude that writing books is dangerous." Lou laughed at his own joke. Then he added, "Everybody's busy, Digger. Don't take it personally. And don't tell anyone, I won't. Your head probably can't take any more bullets! Have to run. We never talked about books."

"Mum's the word," said Digger to the retreating man. Once, as the female detective had told him, he had suspected Lou Knightly, the Lip Licker, of murder, of killing those two women Digger couldn't remember. Lou and Eliot, too. Digger wondered whether Eliot had taken steps finally to delete Johna Adams from the school's website. Eliot and Lou? Tall and thin, but definitely not bookends, more like those two opposing masks depicting plays, one frowning while the other smiled. The two sides of humanity.

He carried that thought with him into his two classes, but since both were just fifty minutes long, in no time Digger found himself back in his office chair. In the second class, Twitch had been absent, but he had probably emailed Digger an excuse. Twitch was a great one for emailing, not only questions but comments, even just greetings. Digger really liked the strange lad, who worked well in groups but had a tendency to blurt out odd comments, such as references to the murders that Digger could not remember. Would he *ever* remember that lost year? Did he even want to?

Out his narrow office window, Matthew Diggerson saw that one of the library's clock towers was still ahead of the other. Ironic to think that a clock never changed. Either way, ahead or behind, the time was just a little after three. He would be collecting papers this weekend in both classes, the second of his first paired assignments, and Digger wondered whether those second papers would be much stronger than the first ones. He hoped so. He wanted to go home, but office hours demanded that he stay until at least close to the bottom of the hour. If he left early, Eliot would probably reprimand him, treat him like an adjunct. Digger wondered how Eliot's classroom observations were going. Had he visited one of Jolie's classes? She would not acquiesce as Lou had. Yin and Yang, those two men, but could one mask hide a murderer? Digger thought of that poem about masks hiding "grins and lies." Lou's mask was the grinner, yet Eliot Gladstone made for a more convincing killer. The way his round glasses would catch the light and hide his eyes, the heavy breathing, his worry about words *running out*, his obsession with that famous fiction writer, David Reed Winslow. Eliot Gladstone? *Professor Happy Rock. Anna!* He would see her again soon.

For now, another empty office hour beckoned. Bored, Digger decided to skip it, to risk Happy Rock wrath! Deciding to check his email at home to discover Twitch's whereabouts, the composition teacher exited his door, checked that it was locked (a habit, the doors were self-locking), and moved down the long hall, closing the adjunct faculty office door as he passed it. Out in the foyer, near Gloria's desk and across from the elevator, a janitor was mopping the floor, his back to Digger, who noticed headphones, probably an essential piece of equipment for any job involving rote physical work. Something about the man seemed familiar, and then the janitor turned around and saw him.

"Hello, Professor," he said, pushing the headphones to rest around his neck.

"Hi," Digger responded, searching his memory for this face. "George North?" he said right after the man had started grinning into the silence.

"You remember me! After all these years, and you remember my name! I must have made quite an impression on you." Even though his ex-student (and Tobias Mann's) grinned broadly, his face seemed cold, closed, and Digger thought of the Gladstones and of that poem, the "grins and lies."

"That was a memorable time, George, wasn't it?"

"Two murders, and you were almost three," said the Grinner. "And I was grinding away as a student, right before my father yanked me out and made me stock his grocery shelves, and now here I am, still basically stocking shelves, but not *his*."

A whole lifetime floated in that small soliloquy, so Digger simply bypassed all the innuendoes, the angst. "I remember that class when we were putting topic sentences, I think, on the board, about Professor Mann's killer, and yours were good."

"That was fun," said George North. "But it was more than just topic sentences, all kinds. First sentences in the essay, final sentences. I liked that exercise."

*Positive Peer Review*. "I still use it."

"I heard that you lost your memory, Professor," said the one-time boy, who pantomimed getting shot in the head with his hand as a revolver. "Bang, bang!"

More and more, the writing teacher was remembering his old student, the irreverence, for one thing. "Well, I did get shot, and I did lose some memories, but just recent ones, not everything."

"Shot in the head!" said George. "I'm surprised you can even make sentences. Was it a bad shot or a little bullet? I shot a bird once with a bb gun, and after flopping around a bit, it just flew off."

Digger ignored the question and anecdote, both of which bothered him. He told his old student that it was *good* to see him and to enjoy Spring Break.

"Back at you," said the boy-man, pulling his headphones back into place and turning his back on Digger, who took the stairs and left the building.

On his way to faculty parking, the writing teacher pictured George North's mopping of the Faculty Office Building's hallways every night, back and forth. George North alone in the night swinging a big stick.

# Chapter Fourteen: Concessions

To win a debate, an arguer must usually concede at least a point or two, but concessions do not mean failure. That approach often reveals objectivity, one key to a credible arguer, an acknowledgement that the opposition possesses a modicum of logic—just a bit, anyway. Notice the word that follows most concessions: "But." That coordinating word offers the key to effective concessions.

It had been a strange winter, one little storm after another, none so big as to cancel classes, the type of season that would cause people leaning to the political 'right' to smirk, "What global warming!"

March but still snowy, with 'spring' vacation on the way. Days and days with Anna. Just last weekend, when he had invited her for Spring Break, they had talked about a future. When he had told Anna that he "always loved" Cape Cod, she had responded, "But how could you leave the cottage?" He had realized then that he *could* leave, but that he would have to dig up Simba's bones, that her earthly remains would have to travel with him.

"Would she be bones?" he had asked. "How long do you think it would take?"

Anna had had no idea about bones. "Faster in sandy soil, I would think," Digger had ruminated, and Anna had said something about "salt" and "preservation" and then, "But how could you leave your home?"

"You're my home, Anna," he had told her, feeling just the tingling of fear that perhaps he was going too fast, opening up too much. Yet when the words appeared, he knew that they were both right and safe.

"Maybe OVC needs another art teacher," she had said.

Digger had replayed that statement in his mind a hundred times a day since then. By the month's end, the maple trees would have red-tipped fingers, beckoning the change of seasons, warmer winds and gentle rains, the pathway to spring, to new life.

Down the Humanities corridor at Ocean View College, Eliot Gladstone was sitting in his office with the door closed, wondering why he so rarely thought of suicide anymore. Maybe it was Glen's return into his life. *Family!* Memories of pop and mama, the progenitors. *Pop!* An ironic title there. Glen seemed untroubled by the past, not like him. Who was it who turned the Past into such an antagonist, Faulkner? All of them really, all the great authors. *Into the Fire!* His book, his *legacy*. Yet the words came but reluctantly. Why? Diggerson had said that they would flow if only he were to walk around in his fictional world, but he lied. Probably, Diggerson didn't want to give away any secrets. *Who did?* He could hardly blame the man for that.

What else had Diggerson said, something about using experiences, as he had with that wacky adjunct? *Paul Smith.* Once, Eliot had talked to Smith and that bearded adjunct, the snickering bastard, Bill Jacobs (*and good riddance to you*), in the part-timers' office. Yes, they had all laughed at students and even at teachers, at Diggerson for losing his wife ("misplacing her," Paul Smith had said). A fond memory, but not repeated. Except to nod at his older brother, Eliot had never ventured into that adjunct office again, had hardly even thought of it as he strode by the always open door. Hard to break old habits, such as looking down on some colleagues, most of them. Paul Smith, where was he now? In some cell. He had cracked because his wife had died, eternally misplaced. She had moldered away right at home, if Eliot remembered correctly, a real-life Bates Motel, a real-life "Psycho." Smith had used a knife, too, and what had Diggerson said about it? That it was long, and serrated, like shark teeth, and that Smith had called it a *family heirloom*. What a loon! Oh, but that was good stuff, stuff to get the words flowing. Getting into a mind like that and thinking about that big beautiful pig sticker! How it must have felt going into Tobias Mann. *Into the fire!* Tobias and that mouthy janitor, the Holy Mopper, Eliot used to call him. How must that have felt? *Damn sweet*, that's how! It stands to reason.

Then Eliot had an epiphany. *A lawyer!* His killer did not have to be a professor, he could be a lawyer, like his brother. *Yes!* That way, his book would be less a confessional and more a piece of fiction, a real novel, not some trash genre like murder mysteries, but a novel, like David Reed Winslow's, yet even better, more readable, more sellable. Diggerson wrote only about his own life, turned himself into a super hero, into what's his name, Billy D Wilder. *What crap!* How could it be considered fiction when a person wrote about only their own experiences? *Use them*, certainly, but not just report them. Why, Diggerson was just a damn reporter, a journalist, not a writer at all. No David Reed Winslow horror to relive again. *Into the Fire!* Now that would be a story, an accomplishment, a lawyer. His protagonist could even defend killers, all the while learning from them and going way beyond them, too. Eliot could even make it so the reader would not know the killer's identity, think that it was a client or maybe the opposing council, a judge, a jury member, and Eliot would lead them oh so subtly to the truth, bring his readers into the fire, into the mind of power and logic. It was right there, his masterpiece! If only the words would not run out, *not this time*.

*Inspiration through experiences.* The younger Gladstone visualized two of those, both at night, beneath the stars, a pair of bonks and squeezes. Oh, how the squeezing seemed to last forever but then was over in a flash, sort of like a semester with those teenagers pretending to be adults, acting like they knew everything already. But the women's actual ends, their release of life, was not as satisfying (it's the journey, not the destination!), just an end, and he had known that each was dead, hadn't had to peep open an eyelid and click on a flashlight to see if the pupils had shrunk. No, those two women in the night, Diggerson's *loves*, their eyes had been broken for good, dull and empty, no light in and definitely none out, cracked bulbs, the ones you shook to hear a death rattle. Diana Pell, though, laid out with her arms hanging above her head, pointed down, diving into Hell, undignified, especially for a poet, who should have exited the mortal coil with hands clasped or better yet with fingers pointing, making a little church. The Undertaker had no doubt done that for her, restored her posture, her dignity, with staples and glue. Before he crammed her into that box. *Hands off, you fiend!* No black crow would ever be folding Eliot Gladstone's fingers or jamming him into a box!

*Fire.* The words would flow with fire.

*Flaming inspiration through experience.* All of his plans had run like Swiss clockwork, except for one, Diggerson. For close to a year, he had made the man's life miserable, killing his love interests, his adoration, and then for a coup de grace, he had killed him, a bullet to the head. But all that little bullet had done was to take away all of Eliot's prior work, sending it to the shadows of the man's mind, where all of those words were, popping out when called. *My God!* Diggerson had actually come out giggling, with the love of his life by his side, reunited with one of his mutts, protected now by some Hell cat. Eliot had outlasted David Reed Winslow, the Supreme Poetess, and almost Billy D Wilder. He had checked off all his demons, and each had been easy. He thought again of that blinding instant in the little hallway when Pell had frozen, her split second of recognition and fear, the heaviness of her body as he shoved it mightily, how her solidity had carried her to a crashing conclusion, the doom of gravity, how her eyes had reflected the shadowed empty living room, how her arms had flown up, reaching down the stairs, surrendering. Too late for any white flags. *No prisoners in the fire!* They were all moldering now, like Paul Smith's wife, and he had left no traces, suffered no defeats. It had all been easy. *Except for Diggerson.* Eliot had a vision then—the Whirlpool, Matthew Diggerson's head going round and round, down and down.

But life was *never fair*, never just, and suddenly Eliot Gladstone felt alone. Maybe he *should* end it all after all, take a long walk up the Bay Bridge or off that rickety pier at the Whirlpool, into those swirling waters. Better yet, he should have kept that little revolver, not tossed it into the bay where it now settled into the silt like a crusty oyster. Eliot felt alone.

The hallway sounded quiet, as usual, but people should be returning from eleven o'clock classes by now. Glen would be packed into that ugly little office, he thought, and the idea warmed him. A visit to the adjunct faculty office!

The warmth faded, though, when Eliot found his brother seated by himself in complete wellbeing amongst all those empty chairs and desks. "Glen," he said, his older brother replying in kind, with his name, and then grinning.

Eliot felt vulnerable, as he often did with his sibling, yet the lonely feeling spurred him to lower the usual shield, the mask. "Glen, do you ever wish, ur, want, ur?"

The fragmented question broke open a torrent of statements in the seated man. "Wish and want, Eliot? All the time, and at those times I take. Just like Pop taught us. Take what you want, my boys! Have you forgotten that, Eliot? Have you forgotten how to take? You need to remember, brother."

The intended guilt began to sizzle, firming up the meat, so to speak. Eliot was himself again, mask in place. "Mostly, what dear old Dad was good at taking was another drink. And Mom, she was good at taking, too, was she not? She took many another beating. You and I were quite good at taking those, as well, but you were also quite adept at taking a step out of Dad's way. I remember all of the taking, brother."

"Don't get yourself into a huff, Eliot. Maybe you should try *forgetting* since our memories don't sound as though they're doing you much good. You sound as though a heart attack's just around the bend. Take some deep breaths."

"First I should remember, then I should forget! What kind of teaching is that? Is that what you teach your students, contradictory advice? 'Never make a fragment, boys.' 'Try using a fragment, girls.' Maybe I should fire you, brother. Your classroom observation was not the best, Glen."

"Sarcasm does not suit you, Eliot. You're just too obvious. Our mother used to tell you that. Don't you remember?"

"Mother rarely said a damn thing, that is what I remember."

"And there's a lesson in that, too, brother, a lesson in silence. The lesson is this: Buckle up, shut up, and take what you want."

Eliot frowned, opened his lips, clamped them shut. Although he didn't want to concede, his brother had a point, undeniable. Glen was preaching to the choir.

"Excellent, little brother," said the grayer man, and in his dark eyes blazed a white light that might have been love but probably grew from a different source. Then it went out.

"Are we still getting together for Easter?" Eliot said, and his older brother just nodded twice and grinned. As he left the adjunct faculty office and headed back to his own, Eliot Gladstone vowed never to return to the part-timers' den. In actuality, only his toes had entered the office, for he had been standing in the doorway.

Alone again, he envisioned two faces for company, Digger's and his pretty wife's, each going round and round. Into the fire!

Spring Break began for Matthew Diggerson with two classes of Project Three papers submitted through his online sites, but he didn't mind the work. Behind all that grading, Anna awaited. Since her school, Cape Cod Technical Institute, also held vacation in mid-March, she would be spending multiple days at the cottage. *Perhaps the beginning of a lifetime*, thought Digger. Paper-grading days went quickly, too, all the focused work. His "Diana" class had submitted their literary elements paper, the first of two, and his professional writing students sent in their "problems/solutions" reports, which focused on a list of fictional employees (Mary Green, Paul Purple, Rachel Red, etc.) in a company Digger called Color My World. Since Digger tended to work his way down the roster on his course site, Twitch's paper (Michael Whitman) came last, and Digger had been pleasantly surprised by both of the lad's previous papers, both B+'s. Although the odd student seemed somewhat goofy, Twitch had a lot to say and did so in a mostly effective manner.

Of course, like everyone, Twitch used too many words in a sentence, relying on weak verbs far too often. Even professional writers used "is" and "are" too much, as evidenced by the best sentence Digger had ever found in a textbook, one he used to use in this very class (before he had simply written his own *Professional Writing Guide*). The professional author had given this warning: "Wordiness is often a sign of sloppy writing." Every semester since, Digger had put that sentence on the board to see if students could spot the irony, and somebody inevitably did. "What does what?" Digger would ask, and then a disjointed chorus would reply, "Wordiness often signals sloppy writing." He had already used that sentence in both classes, during the editing day for Project One, and each time he had giggled. His students often smiled at those little mirth eruptions, which Digger could control about as well as his memory of the recently shadowed year.

Thirteen or fourteen papers per day, Saturday, Sunday, and Monday, and his responsibilities were just about over, nearly one full free week ahead, what he and Anna had called "space in time." That space made him think of his mother, who perhaps would expect him to visit, but when he called her and told her of Anna's visit, she had been happy for him. "Give her a kiss for me, Matthew," she had said, repeating that Anna had been her "angel" this past summer and fall, urging her son to "take care" and not to worry about her, to find out who had shot him and to visit when he had the chance.

"When the semester's over," he had vowed, and after hanging up, he had juxtaposed his own mother with Anna's, with Deena Grimes, who had used guilt in an attempt to control her daughter, to get Anna to visit more often, to take her out to eat, to get little gifts, shirts, bracelets. When a person married, he accepted more than just a spouse. Digger would gladly accept Deena once again.

Perhaps not 'gladly.'

While all mothers seemed to understand pathos (how to evoke guilt, for instance), his own mother had not played that joker during their talk even once, and the son wondered about that held hand. *True love.* Being happy for another, no strings. Digger remembered Anna's mother, how Deena would ask about the *next* visit before the current one had even ended. In her defense, she had been deserted by Anna's absentee father, yet hadn't the same thing happened to his own mother? Instead of desire or weakness stealing away a father, death had taken Robert Diggerson. In both cases, Digger realized, a vacuum had arisen, an empty spot. *Holes.* The Diggersons had cultivated their share of those, so perhaps his mother now simply appreciated that her son still lived, that he had climbed out of the earth. Maybe she had made a conscious change in attitude. *His mother?* Why, she had not even mentioned her age during the entire call! *Eighty-three,* Digger thought, and he vowed to visit her more often. The three-plus hour car trip would be more manageable with Anna in the passenger seat. *And Bumper?* Graham and Donna, his neighbors, could feed the cat.

A couple hours later, late Tuesday morning, Digger heard a car's tires crunching the remaining little stones in his driveway and thought "Anna!" Like him, Anna had been dealing with her students' projects, clearing the decks. He wondered how she graded those art works. She must have criteria ("rubrics" was the pedagogical term in vogue), such as his organizing logically, focusing clearly, developing specifically, etc., but what could those be for art? Balance, technique, but how could a teacher objectively grade those? He would have to ask her later.

When she came through the unlocked back door, she was knocking the snow from her shoes. "Some spring!" she said and then "Hello, Snodo!" The white beagle was bouncing around her, making cooing noises and grinning ear to ear.

"Down, Snodo, C'mon!" said Digger, but Anna laughed and said that she didn't mind at all. She wondered where Bumper was, and at the sound of his name, the mysterious, stately black Tom cat strolled into the kitchen, walked right up to Anna, and rubbed his big head against her shin. Snodo stopped hopping, except for her tail, churning the air. "They don't see too many people," Digger said and then giggled.

"Do they want to go out?"

"Snodo always wants to go out, and then she wants to come in, and then she wants to go out. 'In and Out,' I should have named her."

"Do you want to go out, Snodo?" asked Anna, and the dog jumped straight up, two feet at least, in response. When she cracked open the door, a white streak shot past and then a black ripple followed. When Digger got up, kissed Anna hello, and looked out, he saw that Snodo had scattered the birds, which perched in the tree and on his neighbor's high fence and looked judgmentally down at the white and black animals. Against the snow, the dog almost disappeared, but her constant motion drew all eyes. She peed and dashed back inside, looked up at Anna, wagged and wagged.

"Does she want a treat?" asked Anna.

"You are the treat," said Digger.

"Are you going to offer a traveler some coffee? Oh, here comes Bumper, too."

"Help yourself," said Digger. "You know where everything is, I'm sure."

"Not much hospitality!" his ex-wife laughed, getting a cup from the cupboard and pouring some coffee from the pot near the sink. "This looks pretty strong, Matt! You never change."

"Not my coffee, anyway," he replied, and they settled in at the table, all four of them, with Snodo curling up at their feet and Bumper leaping onto the table itself, staring at Anna for a bit, and then nonchalantly cleaning himself.

"Are you sure he's a he?" Anna said, looking at Bumper.

"You tell me?" laughed Digger. "Have a look!" Anna declined the offer.

Before long, the conversation landed on the topic of 'mothers,' as children's thoughts inevitably do, and Anna offered this soliloquy: "Jean loves you, Matt, and we talk on the phone quite often. It's almost like I have a mother again! A real one. I'd forgotten how much I liked and respected your mother. She used to scare me a little, as you know. She's so smart and well read and has pretty strong opinions. I used to be intimidated by her. But now I'm not. She's very vulnerable, very appreciative of my seeing you and my calling her. She wants us to, well, I won't go into that, and you can probably guess what she wants. She wants you to be happy."

"I am happy," Digger had giggled. "She calls you an 'angel,' you know. She just did, earlier, on the phone."

"She calls you an angel, too."

Matthew Diggerson could not remember a nicer Spring Break, for although he forgot to ask Anna about her art grading criteria, they had discussed teaching techniques and sung some of his Grammar Jam songs. He had showed her Twitch's Metallica song about 'subordination,' having requested that his student email him those lyrics, and Anna had sung them perfectly, in a low and humorous voice. Then he had showed her his website, the Wix one that she had helped him to create and that his publisher had urged him to promote. Digger rarely did much promoting, but he planned to do so with his songs, the lyrics of which he had added to his site. Anna had been impressed with the website, had spent time going over the lyrics, especially the "Stuck Inside of Memphis" song breaking down how to use commas. "I can't use commas right," she had said, and then she had impersonated Bob Dylan pretty well.

"Nice," he had concluded after she finished the fourth stanza. "You sing Dylan even better than he does." They had laughed, and then Anna had repeated the chorus, slurring the words nicely.

"I'm going to steal this song," she had said, and Digger had invited the theft.

Anna extended her stay until Saturday, leaving reluctantly, and

Digger discovered something amazing. She had never changed her last name; she was still Anna Diggerson, not Anna Grimes, her maiden name, which she no longer wanted any part of since her father had deserted the 'family.'

Speechless, Digger had beamed inside, his long loyalty rewarded.

# Chapter Fifteen: Refutations

Concede when you must; refute when you can: the battle cry for all serious arguers. When you can spot just a few logical fallacies, you can defeat the most ardent of arguments. Just remember this (especially at family gatherings): People do not like to have their illogic illuminated, their beliefs labeled "fallacious." People often get mad.

A person never wakes up realizing that 'this day' will change his or her life. The first few fuzzy moments provide no clues, no epiphanies, rarely any foreshadowing. The sun looks the same, the clouds, the winds, the rains, all those gentle snowflakes tumbling this past winter. No morning stands out, no voice whispering "Take heed! Today will be different. Be warned!" So on this mid-April day, Matthew Diggerson ambled through his usual routine of switching on the coffee (set up the night before), opening the back door for the white and black blurs, listening to the choking gurgle of the java, smelling the brew, soon sipping it hot, watching his pets explore a yard that seemed new to them every day, reveling in their enthusiasm, gradually finding it himself as the cup's level lowered.

It took the writing instructor a moment to realize that winter had finally been swept away, not a patch of snow anywhere, not even in the shadows up against his neighbors' fence. Digger could see forsythia blooming bright yellow in Graham and Donna's backyard. When had they planted that? For Digger, those yellow bushes meant spring, for they seemed to be the first foliage to show life. On the news, just last night, he had seen that Washingtonians and tourists were now goggling beneath the cherry blossoms, which would be traveling northward within a week or two. Some New Englanders called that pink display "ten days of glory." Not yet, though, but looking past Graham's yard, Digger could see that the maple trees sported red tips, like handfuls of paint brushes. What a beautiful world. Skies of blue and trees of green, well, *almost*. Then Digger saw a pair of cardinals, one red, one green, each watching his pets from the safety of the blue spruce. *That's me and Anna again,* he thought. *Tonight!* She would be coming for the weekend tonight.

When he opened the door, both Snodo and Bumper turned and ran across the plot of grassy sand, Snodo with glee, Bumper with a casual trot, and as soon as the yard was empty, the cardinals zipped to the bird feeder, the red male first. *Chivalrous!* Then a robin landed and surveyed the scene in all directions, its vest more orange than red. Digger giggled, for Anna had always been a little creeped out by robins. "They stare at me!" she had said, and Digger could see why: that thin white ring around each dark eye, the way they looked about for danger, too, seeming more like bravado than fear. Digger thought about calling her to say that the robins were looking for her. She would be in class, though, for unlike him, Anna enjoyed morning classes. He pictured her in his left bicep since Cape Codders often used that image, a flexed arm, to point to where they lived. Provincetown at the tip of the fingers, Chatham at the elbow, Hyannis within the bicep. Cape Cod Tech and Anna Diggerson in the bicep, the summer hub of Hyannis.

Another robin crashed into the ground, apart from the first, not friends. Each patrolled a circle of yard out back, looking serious and accusatory with those white circles around the black eyes. *April showers bring robin scowls.* The orangey brown birds looked impatient, angry even, as territorial as sunfish. Whose favorite bird could be a robin red breast? *Eliot's maybe.* But perhaps Digger was being too hard on the hard-breathing fellow. Eliot seemed to be filling the Chair well enough, although the job required little extra work until fall scheduling. Just the occasional teacher problems, sudden absences to fill or wait out, student complaints. Eliot probably liked the latter, remembered details on colleagues. But what about Eliot's own students? Whom could they complain to?

Digger realized that Eliot was visiting his late class today, but that was fine with him. Full-timers were not required to be 'observed,' just adjuncts every so often, but if Gladstone wanted to analyze his class, he could have at it. What was Digger doing today? Oh, yeah, papers due, so positive peer review, in both classes. That would be a good lesson to show Eliot, who probably rarely let his students huddle together and share. In fact, Digger had trouble picturing what Eliot Gladstone did in class.

A third robin had appeared, and Digger's coffee needed reheating. What were microwaves for! The robins' landing like lobbed grenades in his yard, the image of Eliot Gladstone surfacing, Digger did not recognize the warnings, but who could under skies so blue?

Since Eliot had not emailed him a reminder of his class visit, Digger half expected not to see him during the second class, Professional Writing, but he did, sitting right in the back corner. *Joe won't like that*, thought Digger, for his students tended to keep to whatever seat they chose on the first day even though Digger moved them around fairly often. He nodded to Eliot, who perhaps nodded back, hard to tell. Digger said hello to a couple of students in the front row and then wrote "Positive Peer Review" on the board. Twitch bounded into class, said "Sorry," apparently for being late, which he wasn't anyway, and sat down up front, as usual. As expected, Twitch had emailed Digger about his past absence, a "family emergency" the young man had written, and Digger had giggled over that common refrain.

"Okay," he said to his WTNG 200 class, "since your first presidential report is due by tonight, we're going to share content elements again, and since we've done this before, I don't need to explain 'Positive Peer Review' [he motioned to the board] much. But since we have a visitor [he motioned toward Eliot], Professor Gladstone, who has heard what a great class you are [some twittering], let me just explain a bit after I get you in groups, or maybe I'll just let you make trios today, groups of three or four at the most, at least three. Remember body language. Show that you want to work with your peers by facing them, move those desks."

Joe strolled through the door, glanced at Digger with a sheepish grin of apology, and then noticed that a strange old guy had stolen his seat in back. "Trios or quartets, Joe, and access your papers. Share and compare."

Joe recovered and took a seat close to his usual one, just not too close. Twitch was staring at Eliot, too, and Digger saw the lad's shoulders spasm, which they did quite often, several times per class. Nobody laughed or seemed to mind the odd movement, and Digger realized that teenagers today were more accepting of diversity than his own peers had been. Perhaps today's young adults were all addicted to their phones, but at least fewer of them bullied a peer who was different. In fact, Digger had never noticed a racist or homophobic incident in any of his OVC classes.

"You ready, Twitch," he said, and the boy twisted his desk to face two peers in the second row, making a triangle. The student kept his eyes on Eliot, though, and Digger noticed that his colleague was staring back, somewhat rudely. Eliot had probably never seen spasms like that before, but why did he have to stare? "Okay," Digger continued, "open your report files, and we can start comparing elements and earning free minutes. You see, Professor Gladstone [Eliot finally looked away from Twitch], I'm going to ask students to share something specific from their reports, such as the sentence right before their table, and each group will choose the best one from their group and put it on the board for a chance at free minutes. Two if what they add is 'great,' one if it's 'good,' and just a great example for everyone if it's less than good, even just pretty good. That way, they compare once in their groups and then again when all the examples are on the board. And they take notes, right, people?"

A few heads nodded. "Okay, let's get going, as quickly as possible, too, so that we can get as many content elements on the board as possible."

"What are we sharing first?" said a girl on the right, and Digger giggled, a sound they were all used to by now.

"Oh, yeah, right. Well, I said it already, the sentence right before your table. Whose is best, right now? Maybe not later, but right at this moment. Share and compare. Then up, up!"

Despite this urging, it took each group a couple of minutes before emissaries approached the board. Twitch usually went up for his group, but he seemed preoccupied with Eliot, who looked at the board and at his notes and talked to nobody. After all six groups had added their sentences, Digger explained that what he was looking for was an effective introductory statement for the table. He then asked questions to get the class to see which board examples would earn minutes, and he used a red marker (the students had black, blue, or green) to mark minutes (slashes) on the board for the 'great' and 'good' sentences. Then he urged students to check their own reports—for the correct introductory mark, the colon, for instance—and then the class moved on to another content element to share and show on the board.

With that process, the class moved through several areas that Digger wanted to stress, such as table titles (students often neglected to add those), table subtitles (single nouns worked best usually), first headings (parallelism required between these), a topic sentence (short as possible), a structural point (transition showing shift), a quoted piece of research (citation matching its source's beginning), and the first sentence after a quotation (key-word reasoning to make the explanation more specific).

By that point, a couple of the trios and one quartet had left already, having earned more minutes than their peers. Twitch's trio had just left, the odd lanky student frowning as he packed away his laptop into the inevitable backpack, but at least his group mates were smiling as they slipped out the door. Maybe Twitch would email him to explain his lack of enthusiasm. That student loved to send emails. Picturing his computer, Digger thought of all the essays and reports coming in tonight, some of the compositions no doubt already submitted from his prior class. Anna was not due to arrive until after sundown, so maybe Digger would stay late today and get some of those papers graded and returned. More space in time that way.

"Okay, a little extra teaching for you groups," Digger said to the remaining three clusters, one of which included the late student, Joe. "Check everyone's final sentence, the very last one before the sources list. Whose is best?"

Digger had advised that students end most of their professional genre conclusions with a 'next-step' sentence, a suggestion to the reader about what to do with the document's contents and recommendations, such as when to start or whom to contact. Soon, all three groups having taken his advice and offered effective endings, Digger found himself alone with Eliot Gladstone, who rose from his back corner seat and said his first words of the hour. Just one.

"Interesting."

Digger waited and then giggled. "That's it?" he said.

"You will get my report within the week, Digger, and as I said, 'interesting.' Especially that odd boy with the shoulder lurches, spasms. What's his problem?"

"That's Twitch," said Digger. "He's the student I had during my forgotten year, and he's usually in a very good mood. He wasn't talkative today, but usually he's a group leader."

"Does he get laughed at by other students due to those ... movements?"

"I was just thinking about that, Eliot. You read my mind. I think that today's generation is more accepting of differences. I guess all that diversity training actually pays off."

"Society is going to pot," said Eliot, and he left the room. Digger was left standing alone, so he giggled again. Eliot was about as *diverse* as it gets, yet somehow he didn't think that the man had that self-realization. What was wrong with Twitch?

When he left the Classrooms Building, Digger saw no sign of Eliot, who must have hoofed it back to his office, no doubt to pen his 'observation.' Outside the FOB, a chickadee slung past almost at head level, cheeping at the passing human, exclaiming either surprise or joy, and Digger imagined the little birds in his backyard. Anna would be coming in a handful of hours to spend the entire weekend, and Snodo would be curled up right now on the couch, dreaming, perhaps emitting little hiccup noises, and out back beneath the chickadees, cardinals, and sparrows, beneath all the birds dipping down from the heavens, Simba, too, would lie curled up, nestled in the warm, cool ground. *Home!* Perhaps a place was not really a home until the bones of a loved one grew into its roots. Above him, the thickly clouded sky still spoke of winter, but the air itself was warmer, spring.

Inside the FOB, even Gloria Swanson was gone, her desk out in the third-floor vestibule looking deserted and a bit sad. As the campus emptied out, the roads would swell, Digger thought, visualizing the traffic jam he endured each late-afternoon at week's end. It seemed that the whole world waited until Fridays to leave their houses, and that conclusion settled it. Digger would avoid the congestion by staying late and doing a dozen papers or so, maybe more if his students had submitted them early (they had until midnight, but he didn't mind if they added their work to the course site late in the night or even early in the morning).

Walking down the Humanities corridor, Digger felt a bit like an intruder, a strange feeling brought about by the stillness and quiet, but then he heard a chair squeal. The adjunct faculty office door was open, as usual, but the small scream had not issued from there. *Unless it had been the ghost of Dan Pinsky,* thought Digger. No, the sound came from Eliot's office, and Digger stopped and knocked since the door was swung close to closing.

"How did you get back here so quickly?" said Digger.

"I walked."

Digger realized that what Eliot needed was a dog or two, a happy creature who could teach the man how to play, but then he thought of the poor animal, living with a Gladstone.

"You don't need to write up a report on our classroom

observation, you know? You can just talk to me about it? What did you think, Eliot? I like to get my students up at the board."

"I write a report for every observation, Diggerson, and your class is no exception. You will see my conclusions soon, but do not worry. You will still be rehired full-time for next fall, probably for the summer even. The paperwork just takes time to go through the machine."

Paperwork. The argument of administrators everywhere. Digger recognized another straw man, but instead of pinning it to the light of day, he giggled. "Okay, Eliot. I'll look forward to your critique. How late are you staying, by the way? I'm going to stay late and grade papers. Anna's coming tonight, and I'd like to clear the decks as much as possible."

"I have work to finish, too," said Eliot without looking up, but then he did. "Did you see that strange student? Was he waiting for you?"

"Do you mean Twitch? No, why would he be waiting?"

Eliot didn't answer, just turned his face back to the desk, to a scattering of papers. Digger felt a need to stand up for his *strange* student. "Twitch can be a little needy, but if all my students were like him, I would be very happy. He cares about his papers and about learning. He actually comes to my office to discuss his graded papers, wants to understand. He doesn't come to *argue* his grades, but to understand them. I love that, Eliot. Do you have students like that?"

"My students would never second guess my grading."

*Okay, Eliot.* Digger said nothing and just stared at the narrow-minded man. *Skinny*, like Lou, and like Paul Smith, too. Digger was surrounded by tall, thin colleagues, both in reality and in his memories. But Anna was coming tonight!

"I'm going to get to my papers, Eliot, get a bunch of them out of the way. And if Twitch emails me, I'll let you know why he wasn't himself today. Since you seem interested in him."

"*Strange* things are interesting."

"True. Enjoy your weekend." *Get a dog!* Then Digger realized that a person like Eliot Gladstone should never get a dog, that the poor animal would be neglected, left tied up out back, probably. People like that should be imprisoned.

Digger pushed open his office door after glancing at the Dream Board, seeing no new additions, and wishing that Diana Pell were still here. To feel less confined, he left the door open and tapped the keyboard to make his computer screen come to life. He tapped in 'bridges.ovc.edu,' but then decided to check his email instead, remembering how clean the house would get and how empty the sink would be whenever he had a stack of papers to do. Now those stacks were all online, less burdensome that way and far better for students, who no longer had to read his poor handwriting. Nobody had emailed him, not even Twitch, but Digger thought of his publisher, Pat Covington, and sent him an email about plans for a third book. Pat would no doubt respond quickly, so Digger left his email open and switched screens to access his 102 class, Diana's literature students (he always thought of that class as *Diana's*, even now, with less than a month to go in the semester).

Twelve papers already submitted! Two-thirds of the class, and those early entries meant either that the students knew what they were doing or perhaps wanted to clear the decks themselves before the weekend. *Well, time to find out!*

The first paper was very good, especially the content. The student had even chosen irony as one of his body-paragraph topics, using key-word reasoning after quoted illustrations—*impressive!* The next paper was broader but not bad, and then another good one, really good, and then another. Strong papers buoyed Matthew Diggerson, who preached that students should *not* expect 'easy B's' and *not* to worry about grades so much. "Worry about learning," he always told them, and sometimes his advice actually seemed to stick. After the fourth paper, Digger stretched his neck and looked out his narrow window to the library towers, seeing that an hour had passed, that the afternoon was winding down. He saw just one person out in the quad, a lonely image. At least the towers' shadows were not reaching toward the solitary figure, due to the cloud cover, but then Digger realized that they were, that the shadows were still there, just hidden, pale lines. Something golden glowed above the distant western horizon, and the writing teacher thought of Anna.

After he graded two more papers, one pretty good, the other just okay, Digger gazed out the window again and noticed that the gold glow had ignited into a unique orange lava line, which had expanded a bit, so that the sun and clouds appeared to be arguing over who would rule the sky. In just a couple of hours, both would lose to the night. Not a soul walked the quad, but Digger knew that many students, even most, stayed on campus each weekend. They were no doubt eating in the cafeteria or maybe pretending to work at the library. *Silence*. Apparently Eliot had gone home even though Digger hadn't heard him leave. *Some* colleagues might have yelled, "Have a good weekend," but most wouldn't. Eliot was really no different in that way. *Back to work!*

Two more papers and then the quad, then one paper and then the quad. Digger was running out of steam, and only Anna's visit spurred him to keep grading. He had finished all thirteen 102 papers, one more arriving before he could switch sections. The clouds appeared to have ceded the battle for sky supremacy, donning their adversary's orange cloak. Digger couldn't remember such a beautiful New England sunset or what the weather was supposed to be like for Saturday, either. He heard the computer ding, announcing the arrival of an email, and the noise sounded loud in the otherwise empty surroundings. *Probably Pat*, congratulating him on the plans for a third Billy D Wilder book, perhaps urging him to push his work on Facebook, too. That made Digger frown and kept him from checking the email. Instead, he switched to his professional writing class, noticing that just seven papers had been submitted so far. *Seven*. Did he have the energy to do seven more papers before leaving? The clock towers said that the six-o'clock hour was halfway gone, so seven papers would be too much. *Maybe just two more*, and he clicked on one student's file, set to grade again.

"Did you get an email, Digger?"

Digger jumped in his chair, and his arms stayed hunched into his shoulders. "Jesus, Eliot! You shouldn't sneak up like that!" Then his body began to settle, and he giggled.

Eliot grinned, but then his mouth closed again. "You got an email. Maybe it's from that odd student. Was it?"

"I haven't checked, Eliot." Why was this *odd* man so interested in Twitch? "I think it's from my publisher, anyway." Eliot frowned even more, if that were possible.

"Why don't you check now?"

A bell rang in Digger's mind, and then he saw Anna, smiling. She strolled into his thoughts easily and often, and he realized suddenly that he had forgotten to tell her about his non-meat-eating ways. Anna would be astounded and pleased. He would tell her tonight. *Tonight!* Tonight would be a new turning point for them, a turn back and a turn forward. *Tonight!*

"Why are you smiling, Diggerson?"

"No real reason. I guess I'm just happy. Look at the sky, Eliot! Have you ever seen a more orange sunset around here? Maybe out west, but not in New England."

The bell again, and Digger thought of email. Had another arrived? A little voice had whispered not to mention the great southwest, to stay clear of Eliot's past. *David Reed Winslow*, it whispered, but Digger wasn't listening clearly enough.

"I saw the orange from my office window," said Eliot. "It reminds me of New Mexico, how the big horizons would make you feel so small."

"Tucson, too," said Digger. "That big beautiful sky, and when the color leaked back into the horizon, the stars would appear. Thousands and thousands, all the way to the black line of the turning earth."

"A pretty image, Diggerson. I remember the colors, the stars, the emptiness. I remember David Reed Winslow."

At the name, Digger saw a green gleam in the standing man's eyes, or perhaps he had just imagined it. Eliot turned to the narrow window, and the dying day's light caught his round glasses and turned them to ice. Digger heard the bell again, and this time he understood. Words could be weapons, even unintentionally. Who had said that? Harold Pinter, the dramatist? Digger thought of David Two Last Names. "Don't think of him, Eliot."

But Eliot was lost in thought. "The sky is never orange here, Digger, not like this, not often anyway. Purple at times, pink. Cirrus clouds on the horizon. Is it a sign, these orange skies? You should read your email."

Digger didn't want to read his email. He thought of signs, of the orange fingers in the sky. They seemed to be coming this way, pointing toward the Bay Bridge or at least the bay. Perhaps Danny Jones had seen such a finger, like the Ghost of Christmas Yet to Come, and had followed its command.

"Maybe it *is* a sign, Eliot," he said. "Live and let live." He thought of cirrus clouds. Eliot knew things that he didn't.

"Into the fire," whispered Eliot Gladstone, gazing out the narrow window from the doorway.

"Your book?" said Digger, but he saw that the other man was far away. He wondered where. Had this man killed two women with his hands and then held a gun to Digger's head, fired it? Although Eliot was troubled, he could *not* be a killer. No way! Maybe his brother, though.

"Someone once said something about age, an old man, Digger, and he said that he did not feel like an old man, but like a young one with something wrong with him."

"I've heard that, too. It was Dick Cavett, you know, Johnny Carson before Johnny. I saw an interview with Cavett on PBS." Matthew Diggerson talked but thought about rising, saying so long to Eliot, getting out. Instead he sat motionless in his chair.

"Yes, I remember now. I once watched Dick Cavett late at night. He was erudite and witty. My parents did not care for him, nor my brother."

"Just a bit too early for me, Eliot, but I liked him in that interview. Very understated humor." Digger stared at the other man's forehead, saw three little scars.

"I am an old man now, Digger, with not much time left to leave a legacy. Every morning I see less hair on my head and more on my ears. Why is that, Diggerson? Why does hair stop growing in one spot and start in another? Is God playing some joke? That is what it all feels like, and I can accept that, the unfairness, the boredom, life's *grayness*, I can accept it all because I see that it is the same for everyone." Eliot Gladstone paused and then added, "But then you published that book, Digger, and suddenly I just could *not* accept that, not *that* on top of everything else."

Eliot was addressing him but talking to the window, above Digger's head. *Could not accept that?* Another beep rang out, another email, a virtual bombardment of suddenly sinister missives.

"Are you not going to answer that email, Professor Diggerson?"

Eliot was looking at him now, almost through him, and his eyes looked magnified behind those round glasses. For the first time, Digger realized that Eliot had on a spring jacket, black and hooded (*Eliot Gladstone in a hood?*), and that his right hand rested within the coat's front pocket pouch. He noticed a point.

"Email, Diggerson."

The point in the pouch expanded. More than just a fist in there. *A gun? Impossible!* Digger turned to the computer and minimized his course site, showing the other screen, his list of emails, three new ones: one from OVC, one from his publisher, one from Michael Whitman. *Twitch.*

Eliot had stepped closer, was looking over Digger's shoulder, the pouch in reach of Digger's lunge. The seated man stayed still. *Anna,* he thought.

"Who is 'M. Whitman'?"

Digger still had no idea why Eliot cared so much about Twitch, could not remember the two ever having come in contact, but clearly his colleague was interested, beyond interested, paranoid. "Just a student," answered Digger, "and that one's from my publisher, and that one's to us all, from Human Resources apparently."

"Stop saying the word 'publisher,' Digger. Let us hear what young Whitman has to say."

"Probably just some excuse as to why his paper is late," said Digger, though at this point no paper was late, not for many hours yet. The office seemed dark suddenly. Night was coming. After a sky so pretty, so strangely orange, rest was required, regeneration.

"I am curious," said the looming, leaning man. "Click, click, Diggerson."

Digger clicked and read this:  "Professor Diggerson, it's Twitch, I wasn't quite myself in class, it was because of that other Professor, the one in back with the big head. That's what reminded me, the head, I had to delete the glasses and the little beard and to add a smile to that big head. He was smiling when he talked about the woman's murder, you know, way back when I was a freshmen. That's what stood out to me, it didn't fit. The professors were all smiling in their pictures on the website but none of them stood out, and then he wasn't smiling in that picture so he didn't stand out. I'm sorry it took me so long. Are you going to call the police?"

"Well," said Eliot from above, "Do I really have a 'big head,' Digger?"

"I don't follow any of this, Eliot. Honestly, I don't know what Twitch is talking about. I forgot that whole year. I don't remember Twitch or Johna Adams or that other woman, or even who shot me." It was true. Matthew Diggerson was not scrambling to save his life, he was simply confused. Could this man have shot him? Was it really Eliot Gladstone? *Professor Happy Rock.*

"Even a forgetful man is not a fool! Are you a fool, Diggerson!"

*Was he?* In some ways, *yes*. Had he been foolish to pine and wait for Anna, to hope for decades that she would return, to live a cold life for so long? *No*, not cold, not with Simba, with Snodo, with feral cats and singing birds. And Anna had *not* changed her name, she was *still* Diggerson! She had come back, and Snodo had come back. Simba had never really left, either.

Eliot stepped back again. The point in his pocket stood out even more. *The gun?*

"I thought you were dead, Digger. I shot you right in the head. I could see the bullet hole right above your left eye. Blood, lots of blood, Digger. How did you survive it? I must say, killing you was not like the others. They were, well, invigorating, but you, you, I just felt cold. It was no fun, Digger. And I would have shot you again or maybe throttled you, but the joy had gone out of it. It was not the same."

Reality had vacated the scene, gone! Digger heard a seagull scream and thought of dinosaurs, flying pterodactyls, with reality dripping from their mouths, limp prey, dead. Eliot had *shot* him! Eliot Gladstone had *put* a bullet in his head, just like Richard Cory in that poem, and yet listening to the tall man made Digger feel sad for him. He just looked so sad. "I'm sure you did your best, Eliot."

The tall, slumping man laughed then, Gladstone, a pair of choked guffaws that sent water to his eyes, those great big magnified orbs. "Yes, oh yes, Diggerson, I did my best. And then, of course, I had to take care of your dog, that white beagle. You asked me to, so what could I do? When a dead man asks one favor, you have to grant it, do you not?"

"What did I ask?"

"You wanted me to spare your mutt, to feed him and then let him out. So that he would not starve alone, I suppose, or maybe *eat* you instead." The standing man's grin expanded, wobbled, and then popped. Apparently, mirth dried up quickly in Eliot's mind.

"Snodo's a 'she,'" said Matthew Diggerson to the mad, sad man, and he heard, or rather felt, an echo. *Paul Smith and Simba.* Smith had called Simba 'he' and threatened to kill her, long ago, a decade. Compared to Paul Smith, Eliot seemed almost innocuous. "And thank you for taking care of her," he said. Then he giggled, at himself, *thanking* the man who had shot him, discovering his identity at last.

"You think I'm *ridiculous*!"

"No, what you did for Snodo, Eliot, not killing her, that was great. I just giggle more now. The doctors say that the bullet, *your* bullet, affected my, uh, limbic system, or something like that, the part of the brain that affects emotions. I don't mind. The laughing seems natural to me, maybe just a little surprising at times."

"You see, Diggerson! You see what I must endure? I shoot my *enemy*, who instead of dying like a good victim finds existence even more enjoyable."

"It's nothing personal, Eliot, it happened before, too, with Paul Smith. Everyone who tries to kill me just makes my life better."

"Maybe I should shoot you again then, Digger, right here. Right where Tobias Mann floated from this mortal coil. The last time, you were so calm, but I can see anxiety in you now. I'm pleased to see it."

"I was calm before? I guess I had nothing really to lose. I've been told that my dog Simba had passed, so maybe I was thinking of her."

"And now you are thinking of *Anna*, or your *publisher*, your third *book*! You have much to lose now, do you not, Professor?"

Digger nodded, yet he still felt calm. Eliot was making up that point about anxiety or perhaps seeing what he wanted to see. Maybe being startled earlier by Eliot's sudden words and appearance in his doorway had resulted in a deep settling of peace. No, it was Anna again, her golden aura. It surrounded him, too, now. He realized that he had already gained everything, that he could lose nothing now, not really, not ever again. Matthew Diggerson kept this realization to himself.

"What are you going to do, Eliot?" he asked his opposition.

"I had nothing like this planned, you know, Digger. I had not awoken this morning and decided to kill you, not this morning anyway. If not for your odd student, you would not be in this predicament. What am I going to do? We shall see."

"When?"

"When I am ready, Diggerson, do not rush me now. You are not in a rush, are you?"

Anna? Digger thought of time and looked out at the clock towers. A little after seven, closing in on twilight, but perhaps not yet, not in May. All day, the clouds had dimmed the light, and now with the approach of night, the sun seemed defiant, unwilling to give way yet again. Digger glanced above the library, saw that the orange fingers had become a fat hand, even two. He thought of Tolkien then, of Sauron.

"One ring to rule them all," he said to himself as much as to Eliot, who didn't seem to hear. Fantasy and reality, what was the difference? Everything in life, both plot and attitude, was imagery and symbolism. How else could one view existence?

"Nobody's here, Eliot. Just you and me. What is it that you want?"

"An argument, I suppose, Diggerson. One last debate. To live or to die."

"To live, I should think."

"Both of us?"

"Yes, *both* of us. We both have much to live for. You want to finish your book, right, Eliot?"

"Get up, Diggerson, and do not talk about my book. Time we took a little walk, all by ourselves, where no one will see us, so that we can talk freely and honestly. Up, up, Professor, as you so like to say." Eliot was motioning with his hidden hand, with the gun, and backing out of the room. "Do not think of jumping me, either, Digger. I could shoot you, I could shoot some innocent victim, so if we come across someone, a colleague or student or just a damn janitor, then keep those words in mind. You do not want innocent people to die for you, do you, not more of them?"

Johna Adams and that Valarie woman, and maybe Diana even. *Who else?* Digger didn't ask, didn't want to know. Eliot made him go first, down the Humanities hallway (Digger had forgotten to take a last look at the Dream Board), down the three flights of stairs, out into the dying day, its colorful decomposition. *The time of the cardinal,* thought Digger, of their single cheeps against the arrival of night, but no red bird appeared.

Being outside made the situation seem suddenly even more unreal, perhaps because the looming sky mocked a human's tiny contribution to it all. Digger could see the ever fattening fingers of orange reaching out from the falling sun and could never remember such an image in New England. The fuzzy lines reminded him again of lava flows and that led to a volcano and then, of course, to Eliot Gladstone, behind him with a gun in his pocket, the same gun that had coughed a little bullet into his head once upon a time. The chickadee had gone, too.

"Where to?" asked Digger, and Eliot motioned with his pocketed gun to head up the sidewalk that led directly to the faculty parking lot. Along this stretch, shadowed by a killer, Digger could almost picture Tobias Mann, the way the silly fellow would nod instead of talking, and then the loquacious janitor, Dan Pinsky, if only he had nodded more and talked less, and Digger could almost see two wispy shapes, two women, Johna Adams and the Valerie victim, ghostly images who had once been filled out, detailed, but robbed of substance by this man, by Eliot Gladstone. Then he envisioned Diana Pell, her reluctant smile spreading. *Why her?* Of course, Eliot had probably done that, too, killed the poetry.

"Let us pick up the pace," said Professor Happy Rock, a step behind Digger, his hands within his coat pockets. *He was the robber, this bozo, not Time.* Digger saw that Time was just an allusion, not some Grand Thief, not some personified force lording over a pitiful humanity, but just a single gray paving stone from a billion eternal paths, several billion, more even throughout history, old stones. Time was nothing to fear. It was just a simple fact, just blue skies, clouds, the arc of a sea gull, a smile, tears, a nice sandwich. Time was simply an inevitability to recognize so as to appreciate each step, each paving stone, each path leading to a vertical rock. Where did the trail go after that? What did it really matter to each person on his or her own journey?

In silence, Digger thought about this current path, this walk with a madman, a trail taken so often and decorated with so many faces. Why, he had once had a fine talk with Gwena almost in this very spot, and up ahead he had seen Danny Jones for the last time almost. And what about the conversations with Professor William

Watkins, who apparently was correct about Digger's not being well liked, at least by his current companion. What was it that Doctor Joan Powers had said, something about chimpanzees killing each other? All these past paving stones, many holding earthworms, too, storm tossed and pathetic, needing a lift for survival. "Watch out for the worms!" Gwena had advised, and Digger realized that he had never really taken that advice, had never really been careful enough. Was this to be Matthew Diggerson's final path? Where was Eliot leading? The image surfaced again, the tombstone, its rough gray back with the words "Listen, you can hear them sing." *His and Anna's stone!* It would exist, but would she remember? *Of course!*

"Left at the parking lot, Digger. We are going to take the scenic route, I have decided. The water view."

Digger could see his little black Toyota Yaris a dozen cars away, dwarfed by an SUV, and again he thought of Anna, who would be coming to the cottage soon. She said that she would bring supper, too. *Supper*, thought Digger, and a light blossomed in his mind, a calming presence almost, as though Matthew Diggerson were not alone. Anna's aura. It covered him now, protected him.

He had never told her that he no longer ate mammals, she would never know. And what about the cottage? He had made no will, told nobody that he wanted Anna to have it all now, to live in *their* cottage, but now she would not get all of his earthly wares. Who would? His mother, supposedly, but maybe she would give Anna the cottage. That was silly, it would be sold, and other people would live there and not realize that Simba rested out back. Would Simba know? Would her bones get restless?

"Eliot," he said. "If you're planning to kill me, could you do me a favor again?"

"Yes, Diggerson, I will feed your dog, or rather, not this time. Your dog will not be with us."

"I know, Eliot, but what I'd like is for Anna to get the cottage, but I haven't made out a will. Could you tell, uh, the authorities, or someone, I don't know? Just tell someone that we had talked once about death and that I had said I wanted Anna to inherit my house. Could you do that?"

Digger could hear Eliot's cold chuckling.

"Maybe you could ask your brother," Digger continued. "Or maybe we could write a little note right now, and you could give it to the cops. You could say that you found it or that I had given it to you at some point."

"You are not making much of a case for this favor," chuckled Eliot Gladstone.

They had just passed behind the cafeteria, which had high windows still alight, people and plot, all that chewing, all that ignorance as to what was happening just beyond the wall. *Good fences make bad neighbors*, thought Digger, who decided to stop, turn, and face his foe. Midway through the turn, his gaze landed on the tip of the Bay Bridge, and he thought of the sad, scared boy, of Danny Jones' flight, and then all the images rolled out— Simba's look of woe and then hope in the kennel; Omar Johns' round head, his purple words about the Boy that Flew; the swastikas stuck to Digger's house, one rolling the wrong way; two little cats, one blinking; Tobias' little beard and Don Domberg's big one; Anna's Christmas cards; the Dream Board, all those colorful pins; the Spanish aide Ana at Breezy Seas, the way she launched the exclamation "Oh" into the sky, like a beautiful balloon; the Indian Doctor Sam and his missing th's; Nurse Addie, telling him not to *overdo* it, her chins jiggling like bracelets; his mother, telling him her age, cradling his book, saying, "I love this book!"; Simba and Snodo, frolicking brown and white within and between each image, their ears flopping, tails motoring; and Anna, *Anna*, the golden thread connecting it all—and Digger saw life as a great loop, that it was *all* coming round, and then he knew for sure, even more so than before, that he and Anna would be together again, that again the sun was rising, and that Eliot's gun hardly mattered, not now, not now that it all had come full circle.

"You don't want to kill me, do you, Eliot? What you really want is to die yourself."

"You sound like the esteemed Professor William Watkins now, Diggerson. How do you know what I want? How do you know what I will do? Turn around and walk. You enjoy water, do you not? Surely, you know how to swim."

*The Whirlpool*, that rickety jetty, the water mouth, the scene of his fictional student's death, Yusef, the Danny Jones character. Eliot was taking Digger *past* reality into fiction. Ah, but that is where Matthew Diggerson lived, where he felt right at home. *Full circle*. Digger looked up at the mass of orange clouds, an attempt at conquering the skies, and he could almost feel the spreading color. He was content, even happy!

When they reached the lower path, they turned left, per Eliot's instructions, and Digger said, "Are you planning to kill me, Eliot? I don't think you are. For one thing, I don't feel very afraid."

"You are a fool then, but I have not yet decided what to do. Pros and cons, Diggerson. We will see when we get to the end of the Whirlpool."

"You don't really have a gun in your pocket, Eliot, do you? You just have an eraser or something in there."

"You, of all people, Digger, should know that I *do* have a gun. It took a bite out of you already! Maybe you are planning to make a dash to safety. I would suggest that you *not* do that, Digger. I might have to start blasting away with my little 22 here, and who knows where those bees might bite, or whom?"

"No, Eliot. I'm not going to run off. We'll go where you want, out to the Whirlpool."

They took a dozen steps in silence. Digger noticed a sea gull, soaring just above the treetops, but it too made no noise. Then Eliot spoke. "You know what my nickname for you is, Digger?"

"The Giggler."

"Well, aren't you well informed, Professor Diggerson! Who told you that? Was it the busybody Gloria Swanson? No, it was that skinny bastard Knightly, right? Lou Lou. Well, no matter. It is just a term of endearment, of course. You probably have a name for me as well."

"The Breather."

"The Breather? What, because of my asthma? That's not very nice, Digger, to label a fellow human by his vulnerability."

"I didn't know you had asthma, Eliot. I've never seen you with an inhaler."

"Well, I have conquered that youthful infirmity, that and others."

"Youthful infirmity? Eliot, are you planning to shoot me again or to shoot yourself this time?"

The Breather didn't answer, yet Digger thought that he knew anyway. Even though he was being forced to a murder scene (albeit a fictional one of his own creation) by a killer (two times, three, more?) with a gun (maybe, probably), Matthew Diggerson felt strangely at peace still, calm again. *Anna, of course.* If only Eliot Gladstone had ever had an Anna, then Digger would be driving home now, and Diana Pell's smile would still blossom on her face, and other women would still be living their lives, not to mention neighborhood cats since Eliot *detested* them so oddly. Digger thought of Bumper, of the scar on Eliot's forehead, but he decided to keep that suspicion to himself. *Don't open the subject of cats*, he told himself.

The asphalt path looped off to the south, but another, made rustic by trodden grass and dirt, led toward the thin forest that lined the bay, and the two men, *walking strangely*, an onlooker would say, not side by side, but one before the other, like an old married couple, took to the grass. As he walked through the tunnel of trees, Digger felt night descend, the darkness of the wood. It was colorless but beautiful still, and suddenly the foliage ended and all that existed in the world was *water*. That's how it felt, like the horizon had run off to chase the earth's curve, but it was just a momentary illusion. Digger's eyes soon took in the other side of the bay, the town of Bayside, as well as the jetty that led out to the Whirlpool. The wooden pier went out about three times as far as his own backyard and then seemed to end ignominiously. Digger felt the water's whisper and looked up to find its breath. The sky was mostly still gray to the east and undulating, moving slowly, sleeping but not deeply, muscles twitching, and it mirrored the bay's water, sandwiching life in impenetrable gloom. But the orange western glow was still spreading, tinting the shoreline water with a reddish hue, racing the blackness of night, keeping it at bay above the bay.

Water, water, everywhere! Digger had heard that students frequented the Whirlpool, but the wooden jetty was vacant now. The students were still eating, maybe, or talking at the library, and Digger was glad that none were here.

"One step at a time," said Eliot Gladstone. "Perhaps we will see what it feels like to walk on water." Digger said nothing, but he did step onto the wooden jetty, which showed the sea between gaps in the planks. The little waves were jumping, lapping. *Crazy!* Why did the OVC administrators allow this death trap on campus? Yet no students had ever disappeared here, only his fictional Yusef. Still?

Digger could hear the water now, too, the little swooshes and splats, and he could smell the salt. Then he heard Eliot. "Do you know how it feels to live your entire life and suddenly realize that it has all been for *nothing*, that you have done *nothing*? No, of course, you don't, Diggerson. You have books!"

Eliot just did not *understand*. Digger stopped looking at the planks at his feet and turned halfway around. "Do you think that *that* matters, Eliot? Everybody feels the way that you do. Everybody, including me! It's not enough, life, for anyone! We all have basements that are cold and dark, and we *all* go there, Eliot. For me, I call it my Black River, my dark place, and believe me I know the path there. It's easy to get to the Black River!"

"Yes, the Black River, an apt symbol. And because of mine I will be labeled 'evil.' I will be despised. Dissected and scrutinized."

"Who cares about that, Eliot? Will that scrutiny be any worse than your own self-hatred? That's the hate, Eliot, that you need to conquer. The hate you have for yourself. And you still could beat it, you could! You will go to jail, of course, but what are little rooms to men like us, to readers and writers? You could write in jail, Eliot. You could write about all this! You have the story. You could still find that meaning. In that book you're writing."

Eliot said nothing to that, so Digger continued to walk the planks. The journey out took forever but was over in an instant, and Digger looked at all the water and thought, "Just like life!" Long and then gone. No more planks, the next stepping stone a fuzzy one indeed. Digger looked left into the water, to a spot where it slithered and gurgled.

"That water looks hungry," he said. "That must be why they call this 'the Whirlpool.'"

"Just currents, Diggerson, nothing more. Do not personify it. Do you need to fictionalize everything, just to show that you can?" Eliot had sounded angry, but then he didn't. "I cannot, I'm stuck, Digger. The words have run out. I need to generate more words, more experiences. I am stuck."

"You can get unstuck, Eliot, and without adding any, uh, experiences. You just need to step into that world and look around. The writing actually gets easier, you know, the fictionalizing, it comes faster and faster, once you've created your world. I've been working on another book, and it's been easier than the first time around. The second time was probably easier, too, but I have no memory of that book. But I found my notes for the second one, I had made a lot of notes."

"Creating worlds? Yes, that is *it*, Digger, the answer. I have been trying and trying to figure out why I killed those women. Diana Pell, for god's sake! Why? And you just solved it. I was creating my own world. Thank you, Professor Diggerson."

"Diana, too?" said Digger.

"Of course! Did you think it was just an accident?"

"She had the nicest smile, Eliot, did you ever really see it? How it would form and go through this long process and then suddenly bloom."

Eliot failed to answer, so Digger turned to look at his opponent.

Eliot had a little red worm nosing out from one nostril, and Digger realized suddenly that it was blood, that his peer had a nosebleed.

"You have a nosebleed," he said, and Eliot used his left hand to swipe at the worm, which disappeared, leaving just its raw skin on the man's face. Digger thought of "monster" movies, how the beast tended to get more and more monstrous as the movie played out, until it was barely human at all, and how sometimes the monster became so bulbous and freaky that the intent was for the audience to laugh. But Eliot elicited no giggles now—not yet, anyway. More sadness than anything. Digger even thought that he could now simply walk away from this sad man, back up the jetty to the tree line and through it to safety, to humanity, that Eliot would not shoot him in the back or even try to stop him. But Digger couldn't leave. Eliot was way too unstable, and he had a gun, probably, and he was on campus, and students were all about, beyond the tree line anyway, and no way could Digger just walk away and say, "C'est la vie." Eliot now had a little moisture snailing from one nostril, like a child. It didn't help matters.

To the west, the low, cloudy sky blossomed orange with moving petals that formed distinctly and merged effortlessly and just kept moving, above and beyond them now, like a kaleidoscope, seeming to reflect the Whirlpool's currents, sky and sea providing tangible proof of the great forces lurking behind all of man's trivial pursuits. And how odd it was that OVC built the jetty out so far, right out to where the water circled and swirled like a mass of mating snakes, the perfect spot for mobsters to flush away victims. Digger heard noises, laughter. A pair of students had exited the tree line and stopped, seeing Digger and Eliot out on the jetty. Their presence solidified the growing resolve within Matthew Diggerson. This scene had to end.

"Eliot, you have no gun in your pocket, do you?"

The tall man didn't answer; he was looking at the swirling, belching mouth of water ten yards off the jetty's end. Again, Digger thought that OVC needed to secure this jetty, that fencing was required out here and maybe even a sign warning about currents.

"I am a rich man, Diggerson. I have over a quarter-million dollars in the bank. *Rich!* Do you have money like that, you with your books?"

Digger said that he did not, that he had done no investing, didn't even know how to invest.

"You are really just a child, my literary friend, are you not? Imagine not making investments!"

Digger said nothing. Despite the obvious taunting, he did feel the prickles of guilt. He pushed them back by broadening the definition of 'rich' and 'investing,' but he kept these arguments to himself.

"I can see that I have hit a nerve with Professor Matthew Diggerson, a soft spot. He does not see himself as an adult, but as a child. Is that why you wallow in those fantasy worlds so much, Digger, in Tolkien and Harry Potter? Where children wallow, in fantasy. Imagine, Matthew Diggerson with an Achilles' heel!"

He looked into Digger's eyes then, a show of fortitude, of bravado, but then his stare disengaged, fell on objects unseen. The man seemed to slump. Eliot's eyes were huge and lost, making Digger think of George Bailey outside his mother's house after Clarence had erased his past existence. Eliot was lost, too. Not a 'wonderful life' for him. Behind the man, Digger saw the orange fingers of the sky expanding, branching out, reaching, and again he thought of Sauron, he couldn't help himself. He had proven Eliot's argument, he *was* a child. But so was Eliot Gladstone, just a little boy all alone on the edge of the world, over it, in fact. Eliot had gone over it at least three times. He was broken.

"Eliot, you don't want to kill me, I can tell, and you don't even have a gun in your pocket. What's in there, an eraser, your car keys, what?"

Eliot pulled his right hand from the pouch and showed Digger a stapler. The tall man turned it and studied the metal object as though it were a bone from the dawn of Time, or as though he had thought it *was* a gun and had just realized his mistake. "A stapler," he said and tossed it out into the water, toward the hungry ripples, where it splashed and instantly disappeared. Just one *plop*.

"Nobody else needs to die," said Digger, but he was no longer worried about himself or about Anna's not receiving the cottage. She would, years from now, and he would pledge funds to Ocean View's animal shelter, too, in memory of Simba. The circle of his life was not over, it just kept going round. Shades of orange now covered the sky.

"Professor Diggerson, the words have stopped."

Eliot hopped off the pier then, took a stumbling little leap between two posts, and Digger had to admit to himself that he never even contemplated jumping in to save his colleague, or try to. The man had not wanted such heroics. Eliot had won his argument at last, conceded what was required, refuted all other opposing points. Perhaps the unhappy fellow had been having this debate for years.

Digger heard a shout from somewhere, frenzied but indecipherable words that came not from Eliot, drifting away. Something had taken the Breather and was making off with him, some force without heart or conscience, and it pulled the man's bobbing body further out, right to the Whirlpool's greedy mouth, its toothless gums. Then Eliot's head and shoulders started going around and around in a tightening circle, his round glasses catching the orange rays from the falling sun and flashing white, over and over, round and round. Eliot put up no protest, kept his mouth shut, his lips neutral, his arms locked to his sides, rotating like a cork until he gradually disappeared, shoulders, head, last lock of hair. Gurgle and burp. Behind him, Digger heard other noises, disembodied words, shouting, but he kept his eyes on the little dark hole filling up with slate gray. He wondered if Eliot's head would pop out of the ripples or maybe appear elsewhere in the bay, like a seal. The Whirlpool suddenly looked calmer, *satiated* perhaps. It reminded Digger of a flushed toilet eased into rest.

*Goodbye, Eliot.* Professor Happy Rock.

"What happened?" A man Digger almost recognized was

standing by him suddenly, scanning the water, looking concerned and somewhat ready for action, as though he would fling himself into those thick, churning waters for a stranger, for any human, maybe even for a dog. Digger admired that. Then he noticed a handful of students, clustered at the tree line, having sent this *adult* emissary to do their work.

"He jumped in," said Digger, and when he felt the giggle emerging, ready to jingle, he suppressed it, so that only the first note slipped out and up, venturing indecipherably toward the orange heavens.

"Who?" declared the man, and Digger tried to place him. *Architecture?*

"Professor Happy Rock," said Digger, and then he giggled. He couldn't help himself. He began to walk away down the wooden jetty, away from the scene.

The architecture fellow called out to him once more. "Did you say 'Happy Rock'? Hello! Diggerson! Excuse me! Shouldn't you stay and talk to the police or to security?"

*Pittman*, Digger thought. Professor Pittman. He turned his head partway back. "Tell them that Diggerson sends his regards," adding "They know where I live." Then he started walking away again. The other professor watched his retreating colleague for a few seconds and then conjured up a flat cell phone from somewhere, like a magician. People, mostly students, were appearing and moving cautiously up the jetty's planks to be part of the sea-side excitement, no doubt to take pictures and entire videos to post on Facebook. Digger passed through the ever-darkening tunnel of woods and out to the dying light of an OVC twilight. The night had won, but only on the surface. Now more students appeared, and they were moving down the hill, some on the path, some off. Rushing to be part of something. *Social media*, thought Digger. The students swarmed by him on their way down, but he didn't glance to either side or turn back to the crowd, to the dark mouth of the tree tunnel, to all that gray water.

Matthew Diggerson was going home.

# About the Author

 After graduating from the University of Connecticut and then the University of Arizona, Dave Gillespie returned to New England to teach college composition and continues to do so. In Providence, Rhode Island, he lives happily with his wife (Elena) and two dogs (Belle and Holly). His "Simba" passed away peacefully in 2013 at the age of 16.

*The Dart of Persuasion* is the fourth in his Matthew Diggerson mysteries. The first three were *Rules to Die By, Planning to Die,* and *Marked For Murder.*